Never Underestimate a Lummox

"Tell me about this beast." He just couldn't believe the stories he'd heard.

"It's something like a rhinoceros, something like a triceratops. It's so big and powerful that it is likely to hurt people through clumsiness and stupidity."

"I note that its master claims that it is bright."

Greenberg smiled. "He is prejudiced. I talked with it, boss. It's stupid. Maximum intelligence lower than monkeys. Maybe as high as a dog."

Sergei Greenberg of the Department of Spatial Affairs was a bright man, adamant about his findings. Why, the chance of Lummox being anything more than a big lovable beast was ridiculous.

But Sergei Greenberg and a whole lot of others were in for the surprise of their lives . . .

THE
Star Beast

Robert A. Heinlein

A Del Rey Book

BALLANTINE BOOKS • NEW YORK

FOR DIANE AND CLARK

A Del Rey Book
Published by Ballantine Books

ISBN 0-345-26066-X-150

Manufactured in the United States of America

First Ballantine Books Edition: April 1977

Cover art by Darrell Sweet

CONTENTS

I

L-Day

LUMMOX was bored and hungry. The latter was a normal state; creatures of Lummox's breed were always ready for a little snack, even after a full meal. Being bored was less usual and derived directly from the fact that Lummox's chum and closest associate, John Thomas Stuart, had not been around all day, having chosen to go off somewhere with his friend Betty.

One afternoon was a mere nothing; Lummox could hold his breath that long. But he knew the signs and understood the situation; John Thomas had reached the size and age when he would spend more and more time with Betty, or others like her, and less and less time with Lummox. Then there would come a fairly long period during which John Thomas would spend practically no time with Lummox but at the end of which there would arrive a new John Thomas which would presently grow large enough to make an interesting playmate.

From experience Lummox recognized this cycle as necessary and inevitable; nevertheless the immediate prospect was excruciatingly boring. He lumbered listlessly around the back yard of the Stuart home, looking for anything—a grasshopper, a robin, anything at all that might be worth looking at. He watched a hill of ants for a while. They seemed to be moving house; an endless chain was dragging little white grubs in one

7

direction while a countermarching line returned for more grubs. This killed a half hour.

Growing tired of ants, he moved away toward his own house. His number-seven foot came down on the ant hill and crushed it, but the fact did not come to his attention. His own house was just big enough for him to back into it and was the end building of a row of decreasing size; the one at the far end would have made a suitable doghouse for a chihuahua.

Piled outside his shed were six bales of hay. Lummox pulled a small amount off one bale and chewed it lazily. He did not take a second bite because he had taken as much as he thought he could steal and not have it noticed. There was nothing to stop him from eating the entire pile—except the knowledge that John Thomas would bawl him out bitterly and might even refuse for a week or more to scratch him with the garden rake. The household rules required Lummox not to touch food other than natural forage until it was placed in his manager; Lummox usually obeyed as he hated dissension and was humiliated by disapproval.

Besides, he did not want hay. He had had hay for supper last night, he would have it again tonight, and again tomorrow night. Lummox wanted something with more body and a more interesting flavor. He ambled over to the low fence which separated the several acres of back yard from Mrs. Stuart's formal garden, stuck his head over and looked longingly at Mrs. Stuart's roses. The fence was merely a symbol marking the line he must not cross. Lummox had crossed it once, a few years earlier, and had sampled the rose bushes ... just a sample, a mere appetizer, but Mrs. Stuart had made such a fuss that he hated to think about it even now. Shuddering at the recollection, he backed hastily away from the fence.

But he recalled some rose bushes that did not belong to Mrs. Stuart, and therefore in Lummox's opinion, did not belong to anybody. They were in the garden of the Donahues, next door west. There was a possible way, which Lummox had been thinking about lately, to reach these "ownerless" rose bushes.

The Stuart place was surrounded by a ten-foot concrete wall. Lummox had never tried to climb over it, although he had nibbled the top of it in places. In the rear there was one break in it, where the gully draining the land crossed the property line. The gap in the wall was filled by a massive grating of eight-by-eight timbers, bolted together with extremely heavy bolts. The vertical timbers were set in the stream bed and the contractor who had erected it had assured Mrs. Stuart that it would stop Lummox, or a herd of elephants, or anything else too big-hipped to crawl between the timbers.

Lummox knew that the contractor was mistaken, but his opinion had not been asked and he had not offered it. John Thomas had not expressed an opinion either, but he had seemed to suspect the truth; he had emphatically ordered Lummox not to tear the grating down.

Lummox had obeyed. He had sampled it for flavor, but the wooden timbers had been soaked in something which gave them a really unbearable taste; he let them be.

But Lummox felt no responsibility for natural forces. He had noticed, about three months back, that spring rains had eroded the gully so that two of the vertical timbers were no longer imbedded but were merely resting on the dry stream bed. Lummox had been thinking about this for several weeks and had found that a gentle nudge tended to spread the timbers at the bottom. A slightly heavier nudge might open up a space wide enough without actually tearing down the grating . . .

Lummox lumbered down to check up. Still more of

the stream bed had washed away in the last rain; one of the vertical timbers hung a few inches free of the sand. The one next to it was barely resting on the ground. Lummox smiled like a simple-minded golliwog and carefully, delicately insinuated his head between the two big posts. He pushed gently.

Above his head came a sound of rending wood and the pressure suddenly relieved. Startled, Lummox pulled his head out and looked up. The upper end of one eight-by-eight had torn free of its bolts; it pivoted now on a lower horizontal girder. Lummox clucked to himself. Too bad . . . but it couldn't be helped. Lummox was not one to weep over past events; what has been, must be. No doubt John Thomas would be vexed . . . but in the meantime here was an opening through the grating. He lowered his head like a football linesman, set himself in low gear, and pushed on through. There followed several sounds of protesting and rending wood and sharper ones of broken bolts, but Lummox ignored it all; he was on the far side now, a free agent.

He paused and raised up like a caterpillar, lifting legs one and three, two and four, off the ground, and looked around. It was certainly nice to be outside; he wondered why he had not done it sooner. It had been a long time since John Thomas had taken him out, even for a short walk.

He was still looking around, sniffing free air, when an unfriendly character charged at him, yapping and barking furiously. Lummox recognized him, an oversized and heavily muscled mastiff that ran ownerless and free in the neighborhood; they had often exchanged insults through the grating. Lummox had nothing against dogs; in the course of his long career with the Stuart family he had known several socially and had found them pretty fair company in the absence of John Thomas. But this mastiff was another matter. He fancied himself boss of the neighborhood, bullied other

10

dogs, terrorized cats, and repeatedly challenged Lummox to come out and fight like a dog.

Nevertheless Lummox smiled at him, opened his mouth wide and, in a lisping, baby-girl voice from somewhere far back inside him, called the mastiff a very bad name. The dog gasped. It is likely 'that he did not comprehend what Lummox had said, but he did know that he had been insulted. He recovered himself and renewed the attack, barking louder than ever and raising an unholy ruckus while dashing around Lummox and making swift sorties at his flanks to nip at Lummox's legs.

Lummox remained reared up, watching the dog but making no move. He did add to his earlier remark a truthful statement about the dog's ancestry and an untruthful one about his habits; they helped to keep the mastiff berserk. But on the dog's seventh round trip he cut fairly close to where Lummox's first pair of legs would have been had Lummox had all eight feet on the ground; Lummox ducked his head the way a frog strikes at a fly. His mouth opened like a wardrobe trunk and gobbled the mastiff.

Not bad, Lummox decided as he chewed and swallowed. Not bad at all . . . and the collar made a crunchy tidbit. He considered whether or not to go back through the grating, now that he had had a little snack, and pretend that he had never been outside at all. However, there were still those ownerless rose bushes . . . and no doubt John Thomas would make it inconvenient for him to get out again soon. He ambled away parallel to the Stuart's rear wall, then swung around the end onto the Donahue land.

John Thomas Stuart xi got home shortly before dinner time, having already dropped Betty Sorensen at her home. He noticed, as he landed, that Lummox was not in sight, but he assumed that his pet was in his shed. His mind was not on Lummox, but on the age-old fact that females do not operate by logic, at least as logic is understood by males.

He was planning to enter Western Tech; Betty wanted them both to attend the state university. He had pointed out that he could not get the courses he wanted at State U.; Betty had insisted that he could and had looked up references to prove her point. He had rebutted by saying that it was not the name of a course that mattered, but who taught it. The discussion had fallen to pieces when she had refused to concede that he was an authority.

He had absent-mindedly unstrapped his harness copter, while dwelling on the illogic of the feminine mind, and was racking it in the hallway, when his mother burst into his presence. "John Thomas! *Where* have you been?"

He tried to think what he could have slipped on now. It was a bad sign when she called him "John Thomas" . . . "John" or "Johnnie" was okay, or even "Johnnie Boy." But "John Thomas" usually meant that he had been accused, tried, and convicted in absentia. "Huh? Why, I told you at lunch, Mum. Out hopping with Betty. We flew over to . . ."

"Never mind that! Do you know what *that beast* has done?"

Now he had it. Lummox. He hoped it wasn't Mum's garden. Maybe Lum had just knocked over his own house again. If so, Mum would level off presently. Maybe he had better build a new one, bigger. "What's the trouble?" he asked cautiously.

" 'What's the trouble?' What isn't the trouble? John Thomas, this time you simply will have to get rid of it. This is the last straw."

"Take it easy, Mum," he said hastily. "We can't get rid of Lum. You promised Dad."

She made no direct answer. "With the police calling every ten minutes and that great dangerous beast rampaging around and . . ."

"Huh? Wait a minute, Mum, Lum isn't dangerous; he's gentle as a kitten. What happened?"

"Everything!"

He gradually drew out of her some of the details. Lummox had gone for a stroll; that much was clear. John Thomas hoped without conviction that Lummox had not got any iron or steel while he was out; iron had such an explosive effect on his metabolism. There was the time Lummox had eaten that second-hand Buick . . .

His thoughts were interrupted by his mother's words. ". . . and Mrs. Donahue is simply furious! And well she might be . . . her prize roses."

Oh oh, that was bad. He tried to recall the exact amount in his savings account. He would have to apologize, too, and think of ways to butter up the old biddy. In the meantime he would beat Lummox's ears with an ax; Lummox knew about roses, there was no excuse.

"Look, Mum, I'm awfully sorry. I'll go right out and pound some sense into his thick head. When I get through with him, he won't dare sneeze without permission." John Thomas started edging around her.

"Where are you going?" she demanded.

"Huh? Out to talk with Lum, of course. When I get through with him . . ."

"Don't be silly. He isn't here."

"Huh? Where is he?" John Thomas swiftly rearranged his prayers to hope that Lummox hadn't found very much iron. The Buick hadn't really been Lummox's fault and anyhow it had belonged to John Thomas, but . . .

"No telling where he is now. Chief Dreiser said . . ."

"The *police* are after Lummox?"

"You can just bet they are, young man! The entire

safety patrol is after him. Mr. Dreiser wanted me to come downtown and take him home, but I told him we would have to get you to handle that beast."

"But Mother, Lummox would have obeyed you. He always does. Why did Mr. Dreiser take him downtown? He knows Lum belongs here. Being taken downtown would frighten Lum. The poor baby is timid; he wouldn't like . . ."

"Poor baby indeed! He wasn't taken downtown."

"But you said he was."

"I said no such thing. If you'll be quiet, I'll tell you what happened."

It appeared that Mrs. Donahue had surprised Lummox when he had eaten only four or five of her rose bushes. With much courage and little sense she had run at him with a broom, to scream and belabor him about the head. She had not followed the mastiff, though he could have managed her with one gulp; Lummox had a sense of property as nice as that of any house cat. People were not food; in fact, people were almost invariably friendly.

So his feelings were hurt. He had lumbered away from there, pouting.

The next action report on Lummox was for a point two miles away and about thirty minutes later. The Stuarts lived in a suburban area of Westville; open country separated it from the main part of town. Mr. Ito had a small farm in this interval, where he hand-raised vegetables for the tables of gourmets. Mr. Ito apparently had not known what it was that he had found pulling up his cabbages and gulping them down. Lummox's long residence in the vicinity was certainly no secret, but Mr. Ito had no interest in other people's business and had never seen Lummox before.

But he showed no more hesitation than had Mrs. Donahue. He dashed into his house and came out with a gun that had been handed down to him from his grandfather—a relic of the Fourth World War of the sort known affectionately as a "tank killer."

Mr. Ito steadied the gun on a potting bench and let Lummox have it where he would have sat down had Lummox been constructed for such. The noise scared Mr. Ito (he had never heard the weapon fired) and the flash momentarily blinded him. When he blinked his eyes and recovered, the thing had gone.

But it was easy to tell the direction in which it had gone. This encounter had not humiliated Lummox as had the brush with Mrs. Donahue; this frightened him almost out of his wits. While busy with his fresh green salad he had been faced toward a triplet of Mr. Ito's greenhouses. When the explosion ticked him and the blast assailed his hearing, Lummox shifted into high gear and got underway in the direction he was heading. Ordinarily he used a leg firing order of 1,4,5,8,2,3,6,7 and repeat, good for speeds from a slow crawl to fast as a trotting horse; he now broke from a standing start into a double-ended gallop, moving legs 1 & 2 & 5 & 6 together, alternated with 3 & 4 & 7 & 8.

Lummox was through the three greenhouses before he had time to notice them, leaving a tunnel suitable for a medium truck. Straight ahead, three miles away, lay downtown Westville. It might have been better if he had been headed in the opposite direction toward the mountains.

John Thomas Stuart listened to his mother's confused account with growing apprehension. When he heard about Mr. Ito's greenhouses, he stopped thinking about his savings account and started wondering what assets he could convert into cash. His jump harness was almost new . . . but shucks! it wouldn't pay the damage. He wondered if there was any kind of a dicker he could work with the bank? One sure thing: Mum wouldn't help him out, not the state she was in.

Later reports were spotty. Lummox seemed to have

gone across country until he hit the highway leading into town. A transcontinental trucker had complained to a traffic officer, over a cup of coffee, that he had just seen a robot pedatruck with no license plates and that the durned thing had been paying no attention to traffic lanes. But the trucker had used it as an excuse to launch a diatribe about the danger of robot drivers and how there was no substitute for a human driver, sitting in the cab and keeping his eyes open for emergencies. The traffic patrolman had not seen Lummox, being already at his coffee when Lummox passed, and had not been impressed since the trucker was obviously prejudiced. Nevertheless he had phoned in.

Traffic control center in Westville paid no attention to the report; control was fully occupied with a reign of terror.

John Thomas interrupted his mother. "Has anybody been hurt?"

"Hurt? I don't know. Probably. John Thomas, you've got to get rid of that beast at once."

He ignored that statement; it seemed the wrong time to argue it. "What else happened?"

Mrs. Stuart did not know in detail. Near the middle of town Lummox came down a local chute from the overhead freeway. He was moving slowly now and with hesitation; traffic and large numbers of people confused him. He stepped off the street onto a slidewalk. The walk ground to a stop, not being designed for six tons of concentrated load; fuses had blown, circuit breakers had opened, and pedestrian traffic at the busiest time of day was thrown into confusion for twenty blocks of the shopping district.

Women had screamed, children and dogs had added to the excitement, safety officers had tried to restore order, and poor Lummox, who had not meant any harm and had not intended to visit the shopping district anyway, made a perfectly natural mistake . . . the big display windows of the Bon Marché looked like a refuge where he could get away from it all. The duraglass of the windows was supposed to be unbreakable, but the architect had not counted on Lummox mistaking it for empty air. Lummox went in and tried to hide in a model bedroom display. He was not very successful.

John Thomas's next question was cut short by a thump on the roof; someone had landed. He looked up. "You expecting anyone, Mum?"

"It's probably the police. They said they would . . ."

"The police? Oh, my!"

"Don't go away . . . you've got to see them."

"I wasn't going anywhere," he answered miserably and punched a button to unlock the roof entrance.

Moments later the lazy lift from the roof creaked to a stop and the door opened; a safety sergeant and a patrolman stepped out. "Mrs. Stuart?" the sergeant began formally. " 'In your service, ma'am.' We . . ." He caught sight of John Thomas, who was trying not to be noticed. "Are you John T. Stuart?"

John gulped. "Yessir."

"Then come along, right away. 'Scuse us, ma'am. Or do you want to come too?"

"Me? Oh, no, I'd just be in the way."

The sergeant nodded relieved agreement. "Yes, ma'am. Come along, youngster. Minutes count." He took John by the arm.

John tried to shrug away. "Hey, what is this? You got a warrant or something?"

The police officer stopped, seemed to count ten, then said slowly, "Son, I do not have a warrant. But if you are the John T. Stuart I'm looking for . . . and I know you are . . . then unless you want something drastic and final to happen to that deep-space what-is-it you've been harboring, you'd better snap to and come with us."

"Oh, I'll come," John said hastily.

"Okay. Don't give me any more trouble."

John Thomas Stuart kept quiet and went with him.

In the three minutes it took the patrol car to fly downtown John Thomas tried to find out the worst. "Uh, Mister Patrol Officer? There hasn't been anybody hurt? Has there?"

"Sergeant Mendoza," the sergeant answered. "I hope not. I don't know."

John considered this bleak answer. "Well . . . Lummox is still in the Bon Marché?"

"Is that what you call it?—Lummox? It doesn't seem strong enough. No, we got it out of there. It's under the West Arroyo viaduct . . . I hope."

The answer sounded ominous. "What do you mean: 'you hope'?"

"Well, first we blocked off Main and Hamilton, then we chivvied it out of the store with fire extinguishers. Nothing else seemed to bother it; solid slugs just bounced off. Say, what's that beast's hide made of? Ten-point steel?"

"Uh, not exactly." Sergeant Mendoza's satire was closer to fact than John Thomas cared to discuss; he still was wondering if Lummox had eaten any iron. After the mishap of the digested Buick Lummox's growth had taken an enormous spurt; in two weeks he had jumped from the size of a misshapen hippopotamus to his present unlikely dimensions, more growth than he had shown in the preceding generation. It had made him extremely gaunt, like a canvas tarpaulin draped over a scaffolding, his quite unearthly skeleton pushing through his skin; it had taken three years of a high-caloric diet to make him chubby again. Since that time John Thomas had tried to keep metal away from Lummox, most especially iron, even though his father and his grandfather had always fed him tidbits of scrap metal.

"Um. Anyhow the fire extinguishers dug him out—

only he sneezed and knocked two men down. After that we used more fire extinguishers to turn him down Hamilton, meaning to herd him into open country where he couldn't do so much damage . . . seeing as how we couldn't find you. We were making out pretty well, with only an occasional lamp post knocked down, or ground car stepped on, or such, when we came to where we meant to turn him off on Hillcrest and head him back to your place. But he got away from us and headed out onto the viaduct, ran into the guard rail and went off, and . . . well, you'll see, right now. Here we are."

Half a dozen police cars were hovering over the end of the viaduct. Surrounding the area were many private air cars and an air bus or two; the patrol cars were keeping them back from the scene. There were several hundred harness flyers as well, darting like bats in and out among the vehicles and making the police problem more difficult. On the ground a few regular police, supplemented by emergency safety officers wearing arm bands, were trying to hold the crowd back and were diverting traffic away from the viaduct and from the freight road that ran under it down the arroyo. Sergeant Mendoza's driver threaded his way through the cars in the air, while speaking into a hush-ophone on his chest. Chief Dreiser's bright red command car detached itself from the knot over the end of the viaduct and approached them.

Both cars stopped, a few yards apart and a hundred feet above the viaduct. John Thomas could see the big gap in the railing where Lummox had gone over, but could not see Lummox himself; the viaduct blocked his view. The door of the command car opened and Chief Dreiser leaned out; he looked harassed and his bald head was covered with sweat. "Tell the Stuart boy to stick his head out."

John Thomas ran a window down and did so. "Here, sir."

"Lad, can you control that monster?"

"Certainly, sir."

"I hope you're right. Mendoza! Land him. Let him try it."

"Yes, Chief." Mendoza spoke to the driver, who moved the car past the viaduct and started letting down beyond it. Lummox could be seen then; he had taken refuge under the end of the bridge, making himself small . . . for him. John Thomas leaned out and called to him.

"Lum! Lummie boy! Come to papa."

The creature stirred and the end of the viaduct stirred with him. About twelve feet of his front end emerged from under the structure and he looked around wildly.

"Here, Lum! Up here!"

Lummox caught sight of his friend and split his head in an idiot grin. Sergeant Mendoza snapped, "Put her down, Slats. Let's get this over."

The driver lowered a bit, then said anxiously, "That's enough, Sergeant. I saw that critter rear up earlier."

"All right, all right." Mendoza opened the door and kicked out a rope ladder used in rescue work. "Can you go down that, son?"

"Sure." With Mendoza to give him a hand John Thomas shinnied out of the door and got a grip on the ladder. He felt his way down and came to the point where there was no more ladder; he was still six feet above Lummox's head. He looked down. "Heads up, baby. Take me down."

Lummox lifted another pair of legs from the ground and carefully placed his broad skull under John Thomas, who stepped onto it, staggering a little and grabbing for a hand hold. Lummox lowered him gently to the ground.

John Thomas jumped off and turned to face him. Well, the fall apparently had not hurt Lum any; that was a relief. He would get him home first and then go over him inch by inch.

In the meantime Lummox was nuzzling his legs and making a sound remarkably like a purr. John looked stern. "*Bad* Lummie! Bad, bad Lummie . . . you're a mess, aren't you?"

Lummox looked embarrassed. He lowered his head to the ground, looked up at his friend, and opened his mouth wide. "I didn't *mean* to," he protested in his baby-girl voice.

"You didn't mean to. You didn't *mean* to! Oh, no, you never do. I'm going to take your front feet and stuff them down your throat. You know that, don't you? I'm going to beat you to a pulp and then use you for a rug. No supper for you. You didn't mean to, indeed!"

The bright red car came close and hovered. "Okay?" demanded Chief Dreiser.

"Sure."

"All right. Here's the plan. I'm going to move that barrier up ahead. You get him back up on Hillcrest, going out the upper end of the draw. There will be an escort waiting; you fall in behind and stay with it all the way home. Get me?"

"Okay." John Thomas saw that in both directions the arroyo road had been blocked with riot shields, tractors with heavy armor mounted on their fronts, so that a temporary barrier could be thrown across a street or square. Such equipment was standard for any city safety force since the Riots of '91, but he could not recall that Westville had ever used them; he began to realize that the day that Lummox went to town would not soon be forgotten.

But he was happy that Lummox had been too timid to munch on those steel shields. He was beginning to hope that his pet had been too busy all afternoon to eat any ferrous metal. He turned back to him. "All right, get your ugly carcass out of that hole. We're going home."

Lummox complied eagerly; the viaduct again trembled as he brushed against it. "Make me a saddle."

Lummox's midsection slumped down a couple of feet. He thought about it very hard and his upper surface shaped itself into contours resembling a chair. "Hold still," John Thomas ordered. "I don't want any mashed fingers." Lummox did so, quivering a little, and the young man scrambled up, grabbing at slip folds in Lummox's durable hide. He sat himself like a rajah ready for a tiger hunt.

"All right. Slow march now, up the road. No, no! Gee around, you numskull. Uphill, not down."

Docilely, Lummox turned and ambled away.

Two patrol ground cars led the way, two others brought up the rear. Chief Dreiser's tomato-red runabout hung over them at a safe distance. John Thomas lounged back and spent the time composing first, what he was going to say to Lummox, and second, what he was going to say to his mother. The first speech was much easier; he kept going back and embellishing it with fresh adjectives whenever he found himself running into snags on the second.

They were halfway home when a single flier, hopping free in a copter harness, approached the little parade. The flier ignored the red warning light stabbing out from the police chief's car and slanted straight down at the huge star beast. John Thomas thought that he recognized Betty's slapdash style even before he could make out features; he was not mistaken. He caught her as she cut power.

Chief Dreiser slammed a window open and stuck his head out. He was in full flow when Betty interrupted him. "Why, Chief Dreiser! What a terrible way to talk!"

He stopped and took another look. "Is that Betty Sorenson?"

"Of course it is. And I must say, Chief, that after all the years you've taught Sunday School I never thought I would live to hear you use such language. If that is setting a good example, I think I'll . . ."

"Young lady, hold your tongue."

"Me? But you were the one who was using . . ."

"Quiet! I've had all I can take today. You get that suit to buzzing and hop out of here. This is official business. Now get out."

She glanced at John Thomas and winked, then set her face in cherubic innocence. "But, Chief, I can't."

"Huh? Why not?"

"I'm out of juice. This was an emergency landing."

"Betty, you quit fibbing to me."

"Me? Fibbing? Why, Deacon Dreiser!"

"I'll deacon you. If your tanks are dry, get down off that beast and walk home. He's dangerous."

"Lummie dangerous? Lummie wouldn't hurt a fly. And besides, do you want me to walk home alone? On a country road? When it's almost dark? I'm surprised at you."

Dreiser sputtered and closed the window. Betty wiggled out of her harness and settled back in the wider seat that Lummox had provided without being told. John Thomas looked at her. "Hi, Slugger."

"Hi, Knothead."

"I didn't know you knew the Chief."

"I know everybody. Now shut up. I've gotten here, with all speed and much inconvenience, as soon as I heard the newscast. You and Lummox between you could not manage to think your way out of this, even with Lummox doing most of the work—so I rallied around. Now give me the grisly details. Don't hold anything back from mama."

"Smart Alec."

"Don't waste time on compliments. This will probably be our only chance for a private word before they start worrying you, so you had better talk fast."

"Huh? What do you think you are? A lawyer?"

"I'm better than a lawyer, my mind is not cluttered with stale precedents. I can be creative about it."

"Well . . ." Actually he felt better now that Betty was present. It was no longer just Lummox and himself against an unfriendly world. He poured out the story while she listened soberly.

"Anybody hurt?" she asked at last.

"I don't think so. At least they didn't mention it."

"They would have." She sat up straight. "Then we've got nothing to worry about."

"What? With hundreds, maybe thousands, in damage? I'd like to know what you call trouble?"

"People getting hurt," she answered. "Anything else can be managed. Maybe we'll have Lummox go through bankruptcy."

"Huh? That's silly!"

"If you think that is silly, you've never been in a law court."

"Have you?"

"Don't change the subject. After all, Lummox was attacked with a deadly weapon."

"It didn't hurt him; it just singed him a little."

"Beside the point. It undoubtedly caused him great mental anguish. I'm not sure he was responsible for anything that happened afterwards. Be quiet and let me think."

"Do you mind if I think, too?"

"Not as long as I don't hear the gears grind. Pipe down."

The parade continued to the Stuart home in silence. Betty gave him one piece of advice as they stopped. "Admit nothing. *Nothing*. And don't sign anything. Holler if you need me."

Mrs. Stuart did not come out to meet them. Chief Dreiser inspected the gap in the grating with John Thomas, with Lummox hanging over their shoulders. The Chief watched in silence as John Thomas took a string and tied it across the opening.

"There! No he can't get out again."

Dreiser pulled at his lip. "Son, are you all right in the head?"

"You don't understand, sir. The grating wouldn't stop him even if we did repair it . . . not if he wanted to get out. I don't know anything that would. But that string will. Lummox!"

"Yes, Johnnie?"

"See that string?"

"Yes, Johnnie."

"You bust that string and I'll bust your silly head. Understand me?"

"Yes, Johnnie."

"You won't go out of the yard again, not ever, unless I take you."

"All right, Johnnie."

"Promise? Cross your heart?"

"Cross my heart."

"He hasn't really got a heart," Johnnie went on. "He has an uncentralized circulatory system. It's like . . ."

"I don't care if he has rotary pumps, as long as he stays home."

"He will. He's never broken 'Cross my heart,' even if he hasn't got one."

Dreiser chewed his thumb. "All right. I'll leave a man out here with a portophone tonight. And tomorrow we'll put some steel I-beams in there in place of that wood."

John started to say, "Oh, not steel," but he thought better of it. Dreiser said, "What's the matter?"

"Uh, nothing."

"You keep an eye on him, too."

"He won't get out."

"He had better not. You realize that you are both under arrest, don't you? But I've got no way to lock that monstrosity up."

John Thomas did not answer. He had not realized it; now he saw that it was inevitable. Dreiser went on in a kindly voice, "Try not to worry about it. You seem like a good boy and everybody thought well of your father. Now I've got to go in and have a word with your mother. You had better stay here until my man arrives . . . and then maybe sort of introduce him to, uh, this thing." He passed a doubtful eye over Lummox.

John Thomas stayed while the police chief went back to the house. Now was the time to give Lummox what-for, but he did not have the heart for it. Not just then.

II

The Department of Spatial Affairs

TO John Thomas Stuart XI the troubles of himself and Lummox seemed unique and unbearable, yet he was not alone, even around Westville. Little Mr. Ito was suffering from an always fatal disease—old age. It would kill him soon. Behind uncounted closed doors in Westville other persons suffered silently the countless forms of quiet desperation which can close in on a man, or woman, for reasons of money, family, health, or face.

Farther away, in the state capital, the Governor stared hopelessly at a stack of papers—evidence that would certainly send to prison his oldest and most trusted friend. Much farther away, on Mars, a prospector abandoned his wrecked sandmobile and got ready to attempt the long trek back to Outpost. He would never make it.

Incredibly farther away, twenty-seven light years, the Starship *Bolivar* was entering an interspatial transition. A flaw in a tiny relay would cause that relay to operate a tenth of a second later than it should. The S.S. *Bolivar* would wander between the stars for many years ... but she would never find her way home.

Inconceiveably farther from Earth, half way across the local star cloud, a race of arboreal crustaceans was slowly losing to a younger, more aggressive race of amphibians. It would be several thousands Earth years before the crustaceans were extinct, but the issue was not in doubt. This was regrettable (by human standards) for the crustacean race had mental and spiritual abilities which complemented human traits in a fashion which could have permitted a wealth of civilized co-operation with them. But when the first Earth-humans landed there, some eleven thousand years in the future, the crustaceans would be long dead.

Back on Earth at Federation Capital His Excellency the Right Honorable Henry Gladstone Kiku, M. A. (Oxon,) Litt. D. *honoris causa* (Capetown), O.B.E., Permanent Under Secretary for Spatial Affairs, was not worried about the doomed crustaceans because he would never know of them. He was not yet worried about S.S. *Bolivar* but he would be. Aside from the ship, the loss of one passenger in that ship would cause a chain reaction of headaches for Mr. Kiku and all his associates for years to come.

Anything and everything outside Earth's ionosphere was Mr. Kiku's responsibility and worry. Anything which concerned the relationships between Earth and any part of the explored universe was also his responsibility. Even affairs which were superficially strictly Earthside were also his concern, if they affected or were in any way affected by anything which was extra-terrestrial, interplanetary, or interstellar in nature—a very wide range indeed.

His problems included such things as the importation of Martian sand grass, suitably mutated, for the Tibetan plateau. Mr. Kiku's office had not approved that until after a careful mathematical examination of the possible effect on the Australian sheep industry—and a dozen other factors. Such things were done cautiously, with the gruesome example of Madagascar and the Martian berryroot always before them. Economic decisions did not upset Mr. Kiku, no matter how many toes he stepped on; other sorts kept him awake nights—such as his decision not to give police escorts to Goddard exchange students from Procyon VII despite the very real danger to them from provincial Earthmen with prejudices against beings having unearthly arrangements of limbs or eyes or such—the cephalopods of that planet were a touchy people and something very like a police escort was their own usual punishment for criminals.

Mr. Kiku had an extremely large staff to help him, of course, and, also of course, the help of the Secretary himself. The Secretary made speeches, greeted Very Important Visitors, gave out interviews, and in many other ways eased for Mr. Kiku an otherwise unbearable load—Mr. Kiku would be first to admit this. As long as the current Secretary behaved himself, minded his business, took care of public appearances, and let the Under Secretary get on with the department's work, he had Mr. Kiku's approval. Of course, if he failed to pull his load or threw his weight around, Mr. Kiku was capable of finding ways to get rid of him. But it had been fifteen years since he had found it necessary to be so drastic; even the rawest political appointee could usually be broken to harness.

Mr. Kiku had not made up his mind about the current Secretary, but was not now thinking about him. Instead he was looking over the top-sheet synopsis for Project Cerberus, a power proposal for the research station on

Pluto. A reminder light on his desk flashed and he looked up to see the door between his office and that of the Secretary dilate The Secretary walked in, whistling *Take Me Out to the Ball Game;* Mr. Kiku did not recognize the tune.

He broke off. "Greetings, Henry. No, don't get up."

Mr. Kiku had not started to get up. "How do you do, Mr. Secretary? What can I do for you?"

"Nothing much, nothing much." He paused by Mr. Kiku's desk and picked up the project folder. "What are you swotting now? Cerberus, eh? Henry, that's an engineering matter. Why should we worry about it?"

"There are aspects," Mr. Kiku answered carefully, "that concern us."

"I suppose so. Budget and so forth." His eye sought the bold-faced line reading: ESTIMATED COST: 3.5 megabucks and 7.4 lives. "What's this? I can't go before the Council and ask them to approve this. It's fantastic."

"The first estimate," Mr. Kiku said evenly, "was over eight megabucks and more than a hundred lives."

"I don't mind the money, but this other . . . You are in effect asking the Council to sign death warrants for seven and four-tenths men. You can't do that, it isn't human. Say, what the deuce is four-tenths of a man anyway? How can you kill a fraction of a man?"

"Mr. Secretary," his subordinate answered patiently, "any project bigger than a schoolyard swing involves probable loss of life. But that hazard factor is low; it means that working on Project Cerberus will be safer, on the average, than staying Earthside. That's my rule of thumb."

"Eh?" The Secretary looked again at the synopsis. "Then why not say so? Put the thing in the best light and so forth?"

"This report is for my eyes . . . for our eyes, only. The report to the Council will emphasize safety pre-

cautions and will not include an estimate of deaths—
which, after all, is a guess."

"Mmm, 'a guess.' Yes, of course." The Secretary put
the report down, seemed to lose interest.

"Anything else, sir?"

"Oh, yes! Henry, old man, you know that Rargyllian
dignitary I am supposed to receive today? Dr. What's-
his-name?"

"Dr. Ftaeml." Mr. Kiku glanced at his desk control
panel. "Your appointment is, uh, an hour and seven
minutes from now."

"That's just it. I'm afraid I'll have to ask you to substitute. Apologies to him and so forth. Tell him I'm tied
up with affairs of state."

"Sir? I wouldn't advise that. He will expect to be received by an official of your rank . . . and the Rargyllians are extremely meticulous about protocol."

"Oh, come now, this native won't know the difference."

"But he will, sir."

"Well, let him think that you're me . . . I don't care.
But I won't be here and that's that. The Secretary General has invited me to go to the ball game with him—and
an invitation from the S. G. is a 'must,' y'know."

Mr. Kiku knew that it was nothing of the sort, had
the commitment been expained. But he shut up. "Very
well, sir."

"Thanks, old chap." The Secretary left, again whistling.

When the door closed, Mr. Kiku with an angry gesture slapped a row of switches on the desk panel. He
was locked in now and could not be reached by phone,
video, tube, autowriter, or any other means, save by
an alarm button which his own secretary had used only
once in twelve years. He leaned elbows on his desk,
covered his head with his hands and rubbed his fingers through his woolly pate.

This trouble, that trouble, the other trouble . . . and

always some moron to jiggle his elbow! Why had he ever left Africa? Where came this itch for public service? An itch that had long since turned into mere habit . . .

He sat up and opened his middle drawer. It was bulging with real estate prospectuses from Kenya; he took out a handful and soon was comparing relative merits of farms. Now here was a little honey, if a man had the price—better than eight hundred acres, half of it in cultivation, and seven proved wells on the property. He looked at map and photographs and presently felt better. After a while he put them away and closed the drawer.

He was forced to admit that, while what he had told the chief was true, his own nervous reaction came mostly from his life-long fear of snakes. If Dr. Ftaeml were anything but a Rargyllian . . . or if the Rargyllians had not been medusa humanoids, he wouldn't have minded. Of course, he knew that those tentacles growing out of a Rargyllian's head were *not* snakes—but his stomach didn't know it. He would have to find time for a hypnotic treatment before—no, there wasn't time; he'd have to take a pill instead.

Sighing, he flipped the switches back on. His incoming basket started to fill up at once and all the communication instruments showed lights. But the lights were amber rather than blinking red; he ignored them and glanced through the stuff falling into his basket. Most of the items were for his information only: under doctrine his subordinates or their subordinates had taken action. Occasionally he would check a name and a suggested action and drop the sheet in the gaping mouth of the outgoing basket.

A radiotype came in that was not routine, in that it concerned a creature alleged to be extra-terrestrial but unclassified as to type and origin. The incident involved seemed unimportant—some nonsense in one of the native villages in the western part of the continent. But the factor of an extra-terrestrial creature automatically required the local police to report it to Spatial Affairs, and the lack of classification of the e.-t. prevented action under doctrine and resulted in the report being kicked upstairs.

Mr. Kiku had never seen Lummox and would have had no special interest if he had. But Mr. Kiku knew that each contact with "Out There" was unique. The universe was limitless in its variety. To assume without knowledge, to reason by analogy, to take the unknown for granted, all meant to invite disaster.

Mr. Kiku looked over his list to see whom he could send. Any of his career officers could act as a court of original and superior jurisdiction in any case involving extra-terrestrials, but who was on Earth and free? Hmm . . .

Sergei Greenberg, that was the man. System Trade Intelligence could get along without a chief for a day or two. He flipped a switch. "Sergei?"

"Yes, boss?"

"Busy?"

"Well, yes and no. I'm paring my nails and trying to figure a reason why the taxpayers should pay me more money."

"Should they, now? I'm sending a bluesheet down." Mr. Kiku checked Greenberg's name on the radiotype, dropped it in his outgoing basket, waited a few seconds until he saw Greenberg pick it out of his own incoming basket. "Read it."

Greenberg did so, then looked up. "Well, boss?"

"Phone the local justice that we are assuming tentative jurisdiction, then buzz out and look into it."

"Thy wish is my command, O King. Even money the critter is terrestrial after all, two to one I can identify if it isn't."

"No wager, not at those odds. You're probably right.

But it might be a 'special situation'; we can't take chances."

"I'll keep the local yokels in line, boss. Where is this hamlet? Westville? Or whatever it is?"

"How would I know? You have the sheet in front of you."

Greenberg glanced at it. "Hey! What do you know? It's in the mountains . . . this may take two or three weeks, boss. Hot enough for you?"

"Take more than three days and I'll charge it off your annual leave." Mr. Kiku switched off and turned to other matters. He disposed of a dozen calls, found the bottom of his incoming basket and lost it again, then noticed that it was time for the Rargyllian. Goose flesh crawled over him and he dug hastily into his desk for one of the special pills his doctor had warned him not to take too frequently. He had just gulped it when his secretary's light started blinking.

"Sir? Dr. Ftaeml is here."

"Show him in." Mr. Kiku muttered in a language his ancestors had used in making magic—against snakes, for example. As the door dilated he hung on his face the expression suitable for receiving visitors.

III

"—An Improper Question"

THE intervention by the Department of Spatial Affairs in the case of Lummox did not postpone the hearing; it speeded it up. Mr. Greenberg phoned the district judge, asked for the use of his courtroom, and asked him to have all parties and witnesses in court at ten o'clock the next morning—including, of course, the extra-terrestrial that was the center of the fuss. Judge O'Farrell questioned the last point.

"This creature . . . you need him, too?"

Greenberg said that he most decidedly wanted the e.-t. present, since his connection with the case was the reason for intervention. "Judge, we people in Dep-Space don't like to butt into your local affairs. After I've had a look at the creature and have asked half a dozen questions, I can probably bow out . . . which will suit us both. This alleged e.-t. is my only reason for coming out. So have the beastie present, will you?"

"Eh, he's rather too large to bring into the courtroom. I haven't seen him for several years and I understand he has grown a bit . . . but he would have been too large to bring indoors even then. Couldn't you look at him where he is?"

"Possibly, though I admit to a prejudice for having everything pertinent to a hearing in one spot. Where is he?"

"Penned up where he lives, with his owner. They have a suburban place a few miles out."

Greenberg thought about it. Although a modest man, one who cared not where he ate or slept, when it came to DepSpace business he operated on the rule of making the other fellow do the running around; otherwise the department's tremendous load of business would never get done. "I would like to avoid that trip out into the country, as I intend to hold my ship and get back to Capital tomorrow afternoon, if possible. It's rather urgent . . . a matter of the Martian treaty." This last was Greenberg's standard fib when he wanted to hurry someone not in the department.

Judge O'Farrell said that he would arrange it. "We'll rig a temporary pen on the lawn outside the courthouse."

"Swell! See you tomorrow, Judge. Thanks for everything."

Judge O'Farrell had been on a fishing trip two days earlier when Lummox had gone for his walk. The damage had been cleaned up by his return and, as a fixed principle, he avoided hearing or reading news reports or chitchat concerning cases he might have to try. When he phoned Chief-of-Safety Dreiser he expected no difficulty about moving Lummox.

Chief Dreiser went through the roof. "Judge, are you out of your head?"

"Eh? What's ailing you, Deacon?"

Dreiser tried to explain; the judge shrugged off his objections. Whereupon they both phoned the mayor. But the mayor had been on the same fishing trip; he threw his weight on O'Farrell's side. His words were: "Chief, I'm surprised at you. We can't have an important Federation official thinking that our little city is so backwoods that we can't handle a small thing like that." Dreiser groaned and called the Mountain States Steel & Welding Works.

Chief Dreiser decided to move Lummox before daylight, as he wished to get him penned up before the streets were crowded. But nobody had thought to notify John Thomas; he was awakened at four in the morning with a sickening shock; the wakening had interrupted a nightmare, he believed at first that something dreadful had happened to Lummox.

Once the situation was clear he was non-cooperative; he was a "slow starter," one of those individuals with a low morning blood-sugar count who is worth nothing until after a hearty breakfast—which he now insisted on.

Chief Dreiser looked angry. Mrs. Stuart looked mother-knows-best and said, "Now, dear, don't you think you had better . . ."

"I'm going to have my breakfast. And Lummox, too."

Dreiser said, "Young man, you don't have the right attitude. First thing you know you'll be in even worse trouble. Come along. You can get breakfast downtown."

John Thomas looked stubborn. His mother said sharply, "John Thomas! I won't have it, do you hear? You're being difficult, just like your father was."

The reference to his father rubbed him even more the wrong way. He said bitterly, "Why don't you stand up for me, Mum? They taught me in school that a citizen can't be snatched out of his home any time a policeman gets a notion. But you seem anxious to help *him* instead of *me*. Whose side are you on?"

She stared at him, astounded, as he had a long record of docile obedience. "John Thomas! You can't speak to your mother that way!"

"Yes," agreed Dreiser. "Be polite to your mother, or I'll give you the back of my hand—unofficially, of course. If there is one thing I can't abide it's a boy who is rude to his elders." He unbuttoned his tunic, pulled out a folded paper. "Sergeant Mendoza told me about the quibble you pulled the other day . . . so I came prepared. There's my warrant. Now, will you come? Or will I drag you?"

He stood there, slapping the paper against his palm, but did not offer it to John Thomas. But when John Thomas reached for it, he let him have it and waited while he read it. At last Dreiser said, "Well? Are you satisfied?"

"This is a court order," John Thomas said, "telling me to appear and requiring me to bring Lummox."

"It certainly is."

"But it says ten o'clock. It doesn't say I can't eat breakfast first . . . as long as I'm there by ten."

The Chief took a deep breath, expanding visibly. His face, already pink, got red, but he did not answer.

John Thomas said, "Mum? I'm going to fix my breakfast. Shall I fix some for you, too?"

She glanced at Dreiser, then back at her son and bit

her lip. "Never mind," she said grudgingly. "I'll get breakfast. Mr. Dreiser, will you have coffee with us?"

"Eh? That's kind of you, ma'am. I don't mind if I do. I've been up all night."

John Thomas looked at them. "I'll run out and take a quick look at Lummox." He hesitated, then added, "I'm sorry I was rude, Mum."

"We'll say no more about it, then," she answered coldly.

He had been intending to say several things, in self-justification, but he thought better of it and left. Lummox was snoring gently, stretched half in and half out of his house. His sentry eye was raised above his neck, as it always was when he was asleep; it swiveled around at John Thomas's approach and looked him over, but that portion of Lummox that stood guard for the rest recognized the youth; the star creature did not wake. Satisfied, John Thomas went back inside.

The atmosphere mellowed during breakfast; by the time John Thomas had two dishes of oatmeal, scrambled eggs and toast, and a pint of cocoa inside him, he was ready to concede that Chief Dreiser had been doing his duty and probably didn't kick dogs for pleasure. In turn, the Chief, under the influence of food, had decided that there was nothing wrong with the boy that a firm hand and an occasional thrashing would not cure . . . too bad his mother had to raise him alone; she seemed like a fine woman. He pursued a bit of egg with toast, captured it, and said, "I feel better, Mrs. Stuart, I really do. It's a treat to a widower to taste homecooking . . . but I won't dare tell my men."

Mrs. Stuart put a hand to her mouth. "Oh, I forgot about them!" She added, "I can have more coffee in a moment. How many are there?"

"Five. But don't bother, ma'am; they'll get breakfast when they go off duty." He turned to John Thomas. "Ready to go, young fellow?"

"Uh . . ." He turned to his mother. "Why not fix breakfast for them, Mum? I've still got to wake Lummox and feed him."

By the time Lummox had been wakened and fed and had had matters explained to him, by the time five patrolmen had each enjoyed a second cup of coffee after a hot meal, the feeling was more that of a social event than an arrest. It was long past seven before the procession was on the road.

It was nine o'clock before they got Lummox backed into the temporary cage outside the courthouse. Lummox had been delighted by the smell of steel and had wanted to stop and nibble it; John Thomas was forced to be firm. He went inside with Lummox and petted him and talked to him while the door was welded shut. He had been worried when he saw the massive steel cage, for he had never got around to telling Chief Dreiser that steel was less than useless against Lummox.

Now it seemed too late, especially as the Chief was proud of the pen. There had been no time to pour a foundation, so the Chief had ordered an open-work box of steel girders, top, bottom, and sides, with one end left open until Lummox could be shut in.

Well, thought John Thomas, they all knew so much and they didn't bother to ask me. He decided simply to warn Lummox not to eat a bite of the cage, under dire threats of punishment . . . and hope for the best.

Lummox was inclined to argue; from his point of view it was as silly as attempting to pen a hungry boy by stacking pies around him. One of the workmen paused, lowered his welding torch and said, "You know, it sounded just like that critter was talking."

"He was," John Thomas answered briefly.

"Oh." The man looked at Lummox, then went back to work. Human speech on the part of extra-terrestrials was no novelty, especially on stereo programs; the man seemed satisfied. But shortly he paused again. "I don't hold with animals talking," he announced. John Thomas did not answer; it did not seem to be a remark to which an answer could be made.

Now that he had time John Thomas was anxious to examine something on Lummox which had been worrying him. He had first noticed the symptoms on the morning following Lummox's disastrous stroll, two swellings located where Lummox's shoulders would have been had he been so equipped. Yesterday they had seemed larger, which disturbed him, for he had hoped that they were just bruises . . . not that Lummox bruised easily.

But they fretted him. It seemed possible that Lummox had hurt himself during the accidental gymkhana he had taken part in. The shot that Mr. Ito had taken at him had not damaged him; there had been a slight powder burn where the explosive charge had struck him but that was all; a charge that would destroy a tank was to Lummox about like a hearty kick to a mule . . . startling, but not harmful.

Lummox might have bruised himself in plunging through the greenhouses, but that seemed unlikely. More probably he had been hurt in falling off the viaduct. John Thomas knew that such a fall would kill any Earth animal big enough to have an unfavorable cube-square ratio, such as an elephant. Of course Lummox, with his unearthly body chemistry, was not nearly as fragile as an elephant . . . still, he might have bruised himself badly.

Dog take it! the swellings were bigger than ever, real tumors now, and the hide over them seemed softer and thinner, not quite the armor that encased Lummox elsewhere. John Thomas wondered if a person like Lummox could get cancer, say from a bruise? He did not know and he did not know anyone who would. Lummox had never been ill as far back as John Thomas could remember, nor had his father ever mentioned Lummox having anything wrong with him. Lummox was the same today, yesterday, and always—except that he kept getting bigger.

He would have to look over his grandfather's diary tonight and his great grandfather's notes. Maybe he had missed something . . .

He pressed one of the swellings, trying to dig his fingers in; Lummox stirred restlessly. John Thomas stopped and said anxiously, "Does that hurt?"

"No," the childish voice answered, "it *tickles*."

The answer did not reassure him. He knew that Lummox was ticklish, but it usually took something like a pickaxe to accomplish it. The swellings must be very sensitive. He was about to investigate farther when he was hailed from behind.

"John! Johnnie!"

He turned. Betty Sorenson was outside the cage. "Hi, Slugger," he called to her. "You got my message?"

"Yes, but not until after eight o'clock. You know the dorm rules. Hi, Lummox. How's my baby?"

"Fine," said Lummox.

"That's why I recorded," John Thomas answered. "The idiots rousted me out of bed before daylight. Silly."

"Do you good to see a sunrise. But what is all this rush? I thought the hearing was next week?"

"It was supposed to be. But some heavyweight from the Department of Space is coming out from Capital. He's going to try it."

"*What?*"

"What's the matter?"

"The matter? Why, everything! I don't know this man from Capital. I thought I was going to deal with Judge O'Farrell . . . I know what makes him tick. This new judge . . . well, I don't know. In the second place, I've got ideas I haven't had time to work out yet." She frowned. "We'll have to get a postponement."

"What for?" asked John Thomas. "Why don't we just go into court and tell the truth?"

"Johnnie, you're hopeless. If that was all there was to it, there wouldn't be any courts."

"Maybe that would be an improvement."

"But . . . Look, Knothead, don't stand there making silly noises. If we have to appear in less than an hour . . ." She glanced up at the clock tower on the ancient courthouse. "A good deal less. We've got to move fast. At the very least, we've got to get that homestead claim recorded."

"That's silly. They won't take it, I tell you. We can't homestead Lummox. He's not a piece of land."

"A man can homestead a cow, two horses, a dozen pigs. A carpenter can homestead his tools. An actress can homestead her wardrobe."

"But that's not 'homesteading.' I took the same course in commercial law that you did. They'll laugh at you."

"Don't quibble. It's section II of the same law. If you were exhibiting Lummie in a carnival, he'd be the 'tools of your trade,' wouldn't he? It's up to them to prove he isn't. The thing is to register Lummox as exempt from lien before somebody gets a judgment against you."

"If they can't collect from me, they'll collect from my mother."

"No, they won't. I checked that. Since your father put the money in a trust, legally she hasn't got a dime."

"Is that the law?" he asked doubtfully.

"Oh, hurry up! The law is whatever you can convince a court it is."

"Betty, you've got a twisted mind." He slid out between the bars, turned and said, "Lummie, I'll only be gone a minute. You stay right here."

"Why?" asked Lummox.

"Never mind 'why.' You wait for me here."

"All right."

There was a crowd on the courthouse lawn, people gawking at Lummox in his new notoriety. Chief Dreiser had ordered rope barriers erected and a couple of his men were present to see that they were respected. The two young people ducked under the ropes and pushed through the crowd to the courthouse steps. The county clerk's office was on the second floor; there they found his chief deputy, an elderly maiden lady.

Miss Schreiber took the same view of registering Lummox as free from judgment that John Thomas did. But Betty pointed out that it was not up to the county clerk to decide what was an eligible chattel under the law, and cited an entirely fictitious case about a man who homesteaded a multiple echo. Miss Schreiber reluctantly filled out forms, accepted the modest fee, and gave them a certified copy.

It was almost ten o'clock. John Thomas hurried out and started downstairs. He stopped when he saw that Betty had paused at a penny weighing machine. "Come on, Betty," he demanded. "This is no time for that."

"I'm not weighing myself," she answered while staring into the mirror attached to it. "I'm checking my make-up. I've got to look my best."

"You look all right."

"Why, Johnnie, a compliment!"

"It wasn't a compliment. Hurry up. I've got to tell Lummox something."

"Throttle back and hold at ten thousand. I'll bring you in." She wiped off her eyebrows, painted them back in the smart Madame Satan pattern, and decided that it made her look older. She considered adding a rolling-dice design on her right cheek, but skipped it as Johnnie was about to boil over. They hurried down and outdoors.

More moments were wasted convincing a policeman that they belonged inside the barrier. Johnnie saw that two men were standing by Lummox's cage. He broke into a run. "Hey! You two! Get away from there!"

Judge O'Farrell turned around and blinked. "What is your interest, young man?" The other man turned but said nothing.

"Me? Why, I'm his owner. He's not used to strangers. So go back of the rope, will you?" He turned to Lummox. "It's all right, baby. Johnnie's here."

"Howdy, Judge."

"Oh. Hello, Betty." The judge looked at her as if trying to decide why she was present, then turned to John Thomas. "You must be the Stuart boy. I'm Judge O'Farrell."

"Oh. Excuse me, Judge," John Thomas answered, his ears turning pink. "I thought you were a sightseer."

"A natural error. Mr. Greenberg, this is the Stuart boy . . . John Thomas Stuart. Young man, this is the Honorable Sergei Greenberg, Special Commissioner for the Department of Spatial Affairs." He looked around. "Oh yes . . . this is Miss Betty Sorenson, Mr. Commissioner. Betty, why have you done those silly things to your face?"

She ignored him with dignity. "Honored to meet you, Mr. Commissioner."

"Just 'Mr. Greenberg,' please, Miss Sorenson." Greenberg turned to Johnnie. "Any relation to *the* John Thomas Stuart?"

"I'm John Thomas Stuart the Eleventh," Johnnie answered simply. "I suppose you mean my great-great-great grandfather."

"I guess that would be it. I was born on Mars, almost within sight of his statue. I had no idea your family was mixed up in this. Perhaps we can have a gab about Martian history later."

"I've never been to Mars," Johnnie admitted.

"No? That's surprising. But you're young yet."

Betty listened, ears almost twitching, and decided

that this judge, if that was what he was, would be an even softer mark than Judge O'Farrell. It was hard to remember that Johnnie's name meant anything special ... especially since it didn't. Not around Westville.

Greenberg went on, "You've made me lose two bets, Mr. Stuart."

"Sir?"

"I thought this creature would prove not to be from 'Out There.' I was wrong; that big fellow is certainly not native to Earth. But I was equally sure that, if he *was* e.-t., I could attribute him. I'm not an exotic zoologist, but in my business one has to keep skimming such things ... look at the pictures at least. But I'm stumped. What is he and where did he come from?"

"Uh, why, he's just Lummox. That's what we call him. My great grandfather brought him back in the *Trail Blazer* ... her second trip."

"That long ago, eh? Well, that clears up some of the mystery; that was before DepSpace kept records ... in fact before there was such a department. But I still don't see how this fellow could have missed making a splash in the history books. I've read about the *Trail Blazer* and I remember she brought back many exotica. But I don't remember this fellow ... and, after all, extra-terrestrials were news in those days."

"Oh, that ... Well, sir, the captain didn't know Lummox was aboard. Great granddad brought him aboard in his jump bag and sneaked him off the ship the same way."

"In his *jump bag?*" Greenberg stared at Lummox's out-sized figure.

"Yes, sir. Of course Lummie was smaller then."

"So I am forced to believe."

"I've got pictures of him. He was about the size of a collie pup. More legs of course."

"Mmmm, yes. More legs. And he puts me more in

mind of a triceratops than a collie. Isn't he expensive to feed?"

"Oh, no, Lummie eats anything. Well, almost anything," John Thomas amended hastily, glancing self-consciously at the steel bars. "Or he can go without eating for a long time. Can't you, Lummie?"

Lummox had been lying with his legs retracted, exhibiting the timeless patience which he could muster when necessary. He was listening to his chum and Mr. Greenberg while keeping an eye on Betty and the judge. He now opened his enormous mouth. "Yes, but I don't like it."

Mr. Greenberg raised his eyebrows and said, "I hadn't realized that he was a speech-center type."

"A what? Oh, sure. Lummie's been talking since my father was a boy; he just sort of picked it up. I meant to introduce you. Here, Lummie . . . I want you to meet Mr. Commissioner Greenberg."

Lummox looked at Greenberg without interest and said, "How do you do, Mr. Commissioner Greenberg," saying the formula phrase clearly but not doing so well on the name and title.

"Uh, how do you do, Lummox." He was staring at Lummox when the courthouse clock sounded the hour. Judge O'Farrell turned and spoke to him.

"Ten o'clock, Mr. Commissioner. I suppose we had better get started."

"No hurry," Greenberg answered absent-mindedly, "since the party can't start until we get there. I'm interested in this line of investigation. Mr. Stuart, what is Lummox's R.I.Q. on the human scale?"

"Huh? Oh, his relative intelligence quotient. I don't know, sir."

"Good gracious, hasn't anyone ever tried to find out?"

"Well, no, sir . . . I mean 'yes, sir.' Somebody did run some tests on him back in my grandfather's time, but granddad got so sore over the way they were treating

Lummie that he chucked them out. Since then we've kept strangers away from Lummie, mostly. But he's real bright. Try him."

Judge O'Farrell whispered to Greenberg, "The brute isn't as bright as a good bird dog, even if he can parrot human speech a little. I know."

John Thomas said indignantly, "I heard that, Judge. You're just prejudiced!"

The judge started to answer but Betty cut across him. "Johnnie! You know what I told you . . . I'll do the talking."

Greenberg ignored the interruption. "Has any attempt been made to learn his language?"

"Sir?"

"Mmm, apparently not. And he may have been brought here before he was old enough to talk . . . his own language I mean. But he must have had one; it's a truism among xenists that speech centers are found only in nervous systems that use them. That is to say, he could not have learned human speech as speech, even poorly, unless his own breed used oral communication. Can he write?"

"How could he, sir? He doesn't have hands."

"Mmm, yes. Well, taking a running jump with the aid of theory, I'll bet on a relative score of less than 40, then. Xenologists have found that high types, equivalent to humans, always have three characteristics: speech centers, manipulation, and from these two, record keeping. So we can assume that Lummox's breed was left at the post. Studied any xenology?"

"Not much, sir," John Thomas admitted shyly, "except books I could find in the library. But I mean to major in xenology and exotic biology in college."

"Good for you. It's a wide open field. You'd be surprised how difficult it is to hire enough xenists just for DepSpace. But my reason for asking was this: as you know, the department has intervened in this case. Because of *him*." Greenberg gestured at Lummox. "There was a chance that your pet might be of a race having treaty rights with us. Once or twice, strange as it may seem, a foreigner visiting this planet has been mistaken for a wild animal, with . . . shall we say 'unfortunate' results?" Greenberg frowned, recalling the terrible hushed-up occasion when a member of the official family of the Ambassador from Llador had been found, dead and stuffed in a curiosity shop in the Virgin Islands. "But no such hazard exists here."

"Oh. I guess not, sir. Lummox is . . . well, he's just a member of our family."

"Precisely." The Commissioner spoke to Judge O'Farrell. "May I consult you a moment, Judge? Privately?"

"Certainly, sir."

The men moved away; Betty joined John Thomas. "It's a cinch," she whispered, "if you can keep from making more breaks."

"What did I do?" he protested. "And what makes you think it's going to be easy?"

"It's obvious. He likes you, he likes Lummox."

"I don't see how that pays for the ground floor of the Bon Marché. Or all those lamp posts."

"Just keep your blood pressure down and follow my lead. Before we are through, they'll be paying us. You'll see."

A short distance away Mr. Greenberg was saying to Judge O'Farrell, "Judge, from what I have learned it seems to me that the Department of Spatial Affairs should withdraw from this case."

"Eh? I don't follow you, sir."

"Let me explain. What I would like to do is to postpone the hearing twenty-four hours while I have my conclusions checked by the department. Then I can withdraw and let the local authorities handle it. Meaning you, of course."

Judge O'Farrell pursed his lips. "I don't like last-minute postponements, Mr. Commissioner. It has always seemed unfair to me to order busy people to gather together, to their expense and personal inconvenience, then tell them to come back another day. It doesn't have the flavor of justice."

Greenberg frowned. "True. Let me see if we can arrive at it another way. From what young Stuart tells me I am certain that this case is not one calling for intervention under the Federation's xenic policies, even though the center of interest is extra-terrestrial and therefore a legal cause for intervention if needed. Although the department has the power, that power is exercised only when necessary to avoid trouble with governments of other planets. Earth has hundreds of thousands of e.-t. animals; it has better than thirty thousand non-human xenians, either residents or visitors, having legal status under treaties as 'human' even though they are obviously non-human. Xenophobia being what it is, particularly in our cultural backwaters . . . no, I wasn't referring to Westville! Human nature being what it is, each of those foreigners is a potential source of trouble in our foreign relations.

"Forgive me for saying what you already know; it is a necessary foundation. The department can't go around wiping the noses of all our xenic visitors . . . even those that have noses. We haven't the personnel and certainly not the inclination. If one of them gets into trouble, it is usually sufficient to advise the local magistrate of our treaty obligations to the xenian's home planet. In rare cases the department intervenes. This, in my opinion, is not such a case. In the first place it seems that our friend Lummox here is an 'animal' under the law and . . ."

"Was there doubt?" the judge asked in astonishment.

"There might have been. That's why I am here. But, despite his limited ability to talk, his other limitations would keep such a breed from rising to a level where we could accept it as civilized; therefore he is an animal. Therefore he has only the usual rights of animals under our humane laws. Therefore the department need not concern itself."

"I see. Well, no one is going to be cruel to him, not in my court."

"Certainly. But for another quite sufficient reason the department is not interested. Let us suppose that this creature is 'human' in the sense that law and custom and treaty have attached to that word since we first made contact with the Great Race of Mars. He is not, but suppose it."

"Stipulated," agreed Judge O'Farrell.

"We stipulate it. Nevertheless he cannot be a concern of the department because . . . Judge, do you know the history of the *Trail Blazer?*"

"Vaguely, from grammar school days. I'm not a student of spatial exploration. Our own Earth is confusing enough."

"Isn't it, though? Well, the *Trail Blazer* made three of the first interspatial transition flights, when such flights were as reckless as the voyage Columbus attempted. They did not know where they were going and they had only hazy notions about how to get back . . . in fact the *Trail Blazer* never came back from her third trip."

"Yes, yes. I remember."

"The point is, young Stuart—I can't call him by his full name; it doesn't seem right—Stuart tells me that this loutish creature with the silly smile is a souvenir of the *Trail Blazer*'s second cruise. That's all I need to know. We have no treaties with any of the planets she visited, no trade, no intercourse of any sort. Legally they don't exist. Therefore the only laws that apply to Lummox are our own domestic laws; therefore the department should not intervene—and even if it did, a special master such as myself would be obliged to rule entirely by domestic law. Which you are better qualified to do than I."

Judge O'Farrell nodded. "Well, I have no objection to resuming jurisdiction. Shall we go in?"

"Just a moment. I suggested a delay because this case has curious features. I wanted to refer back to the department to make sure that my theory is correct and that I have not missed some important precedent or law. But I am willing to withdraw at once if you can assure me of one thing. This creature . . . I understand that, despite its mild appearance, it turned out to be destructive, even dangerous?"

O'Farrell nodded. "So I understand . . . unofficially of course."

"Well, has there been any demand that it be destroyed?"

"Well," the judge answered slowly, "again unofficially, I know that such a demand will be made. It has come to my attention privately that our chief of police intends to ask the court to order the animal's destruction as a public safety measure. I anticipate prayers from private sources as well."

Mr. Greenberg looked worried. "As bad as that? Well, Judge, what is your attitude? If you try the case, are you going to let the animal be destroyed?"

Judge O'Farrell retorted, "Sir, that is an improper question."

Greenberg turned red. "I beg your pardon. But I must get at it in some fashion. You realize that this specimen is unique? Regardless of what it has done, or how dangerous it may be (though I'm switched if I'm convinced of *that*), nevertheless its interest to science is such that it should be preserved. Can't you assure me that you will not order it destroyed?"

"Young man, you are urging me to prejudge a case, or a portion of a case. Your attitude is most improper!"

Chief Dreiser chose this bad time to come hurrying

up. "Judge, I've been looking all over for you. Is this hearing going to take place? I've got seven men who . . ."

O'Farrell interrupted him. "Chief, this is Mr. Commissioner Greenberg. Mr. Commissioner, our Chief of Safety."

"Honored, Chief."

"Howdy, Mr. Commissioner. Gentlemen, about this hearing. I'd like to know . . ."

"Chief," the judge interrupted brusquely, "just tell my bailiff to hold things in readiness. Now leave us in private, if you please."

"But . . ." The chief shut up and backed away, while muttering something excusable in a harassed policeman. O'Farrell turned back to Greenberg.

The Commissioner had had time during the interruption to recall that he was supposed to be without personal emotions. He said smoothly, "I withdraw the question, Judge. I had no intention of committing an impropriety." He grinned. "Under other circumstances I might have found myself slapped for contempt, eh?"

O'Farrell grudged a smile. "It is possible."

"Do you have a nice jail? I have over seven months leave saved up and no chance to take it."

"You shouldn't overwork, young man. I always find time to fish, no matter how full the docket. 'Allah does not subtract from man's allotted time those hours spent in fishing.'"

"That's a good sentiment. But I still have a problem. You know that I could insist on postponement while I consult the department?"

"Certainly. Perhaps you should. Your decision should not be affected by my opinions."

"No. But I agree with you; last-minute postponements are vexations." He was thinking that to refer to the department, in this odd case, meant to consult Mr. Kiku . . . and he could hear the Under Secretary making disgusted remarks about "initiative" and "responsibility" and "for heaven's sake, couldn't anyone else around this madhouse make a simple decision?" Greenberg made up his mind. "I think it is best for the department to continue intervention. I'll take it, at least through a preliminary hearing."

O'Farrell smiled broadly. "I had hoped that you would. I'm looking forward to hearing you. I understand that you gentlemen from the Department of Spatial Affairs sometimes hand out an unusual brand of law."

"Really? I hope not. I mean to be a credit to Harvard Law."

"Harvard? Why, so am I! Do they still shout for Reinhardt?"

"They did when I was there."

"Well, well, it's a small world! I hate to wish this case on a schoolmate; I'm afraid it is going to be a hot potato."

"Aren't they all? Well, let's start the fireworks. Why don't we sit *en banc*? You'll probably have to finish."

They started back to the courthouse. Chief Dreiser, who had been fuming some distance away, saw that Judge O'Farrell had forgotten him. He started to follow, then noted that the Stuart boy and Betty Sorenson were still on the other side of Lummox's cage. They had their heads together and did not notice that the two magistrates were leaving. Dreiser strode over to them.

"Hey! Inside with you, Johnnie Stuart! You were supposed to be in court twenty minutes ago."

John Thomas looked startled. "But I thought . . ." he began, then noticed that the judge and Mr. Greenberg had gone. "Oh! Just a minute, Mr. Dreiser . . . I've got something to say to Lummox."

"You've got nothing to say to that beast now. Come along."

"But, Chief . . ."

Mr. Dreiser grabbed his arm and started to move

away. Since he outweighed John Thomas by nearly one hundred pounds Johnnie moved with him. Betty interrupted with, "Deacon Dreiser! What a nasty way to behave!"

"That'll be enough out of you, young lady," Dreiser answered. He continued toward the courthouse with John Thomas in tow. Betty shut up and followed. She considered tripping the police chief, but decided not to.

John Thomas gave in to the inevitable. He had intended to impress on Lummox, at the very last minute, the necessity of remaining quiet, staying put, and not eating the steel bars. But Mr. Dreiser would not listen. It seemed to John that most of the older people in the world spent much of their time not listening.

Lummox had not missed their exit. He stood up, filling the enclosed space, and stared after John Thomas, while wondering what to do. The bars creaked as he brushed against them. Betty looked back and said, "Lummox! You wait there! We'll be back."

Lummox remained standing, staring after them and thinking about it. An order from Betty wasn't really an order. Or was it? There were precedents in the past to think over.

Presently he lay down again.

IV

The Prisoner at the Bars

As O'Farrell and Greenberg entered the room the bailiff shouted, "Order in the court!" The babble died down and spectators tried to find seats. A young man wearing a hat and hung about with paraphernalia stepped into the path of the two officials. "Hold it!" he said and photographed them. "One more . . . and give us a smile, Judge, like the Commissioner had just said something funny."

"One is enough. And take off that hat." O'Farrell brushed past him. The man shrugged but did not take off his hat.

The clerk of the court looked up as they approached. His face was red and sweaty, and he had his tools spread out on the justice's bench. "Sorry, Judge," he said. "Half a moment." He bent over a microphone and intoned, "Testing . . . one, two, three, four . . . Cincinnati . . . sixty-six." He looked up. "I've had more grief with this recording system today."

"You should have checked it earlier."

"So help me, Judge, if you can find anybody . . . Never mind. I did check it, it was running sweet. Then when I switched it on at ten minutes to ten, a transistor quit and it's been an endless job to locate the trouble."

"All right," O'Farrell answered testily, annoyed that it should happen in the presence of a distinguished visitor. "Get my bench clear of your implements, will you?"

Greenberg said hastily, "If it's all the same to you, I won't use the bench. We'll gather around a big table, court-martial style. I find it speeds things up."

O'Farrell looked unhappy. "I have always maintained the ancient formalities in this court. I find it worthwhile."

"Very likely. I suppose that those of us who have to try cases anywhere and everywhere get into sloppy habits. But we can't help it. Take Minatare for example; suppose you attempted, out of politeness, to conform to their customs in trying a case. They don't think a judge is worth a hoot unless he undergoes a cleansing fast before he mounts the judge's sphere . . . then he has to stay up there without food or drink until he reaches a decision. Frankly, I couldn't take it. Could you?"

Judge O'Farrell felt annoyed that this glib young man should imply that there could be a parallel between the seemly rituals of his court and such heathen practices. He recalled uneasily the three stacks of wheat cakes, adorned with sausage and eggs, with which he had started the day. "Well . . . 'other times, other customs,'" he said grudgingly.

"Exactly. And thanks for indulging me." Greenberg motioned to the bailiff; the two started shoving attorneys' tables together to make one big one before O'Farrell could make clear that he had quoted the old saw for the purpose of rebutting it. Shortly, about fifteen people were seated around the composite table and Greenberg had sent the bailiff out to find ash trays. He turned to the clerk, who was now at his control desk, wearing earphones and crouching over his instruments in the awkward pose of all electronics technicians. "Is your equipment working now?"

"The clerk pressed a thumb and forefinger together. "Rolling."

"Very well. Court's in session."

The clerk spoke into his mike, announcing time, date, place, nature and jurisdiction of the court, and the name and title of the special master presiding, reading the last and mispronouncing Sergei Greenberg's first name; Greenberg did not correct him. The bailiff came in, his hands full of ash trays, and said hastily, "Oyez! Oyez! Let all who have business before this court gather nigh and . . ."

"Never mind," Greenberg interrupted. "Thanks anyhow. This court will now hold a preliminary hearing on any and all issues relating to the actions last Monday of an extra-terrestrial creature locally resident and known as 'Lummox.' I refer to that big brute in a cage outside this building. Bailiff, go get a picture of him, please, and insert it in the record."

"Right away, your honor."

"The court wishes to announce that this hearing may be converted to a final determination on any or all issues at any time, if the court so announces and subject to objection and ruling at the time. In other words, don't hold your fire; this may be your only day in court. Oh yes . . . the court will receive petitions relating to this extra-terrestrial as well as hear issues."

"Question, your honor."

"Yes?"

"May it please the court: my client and I have no objection if all that we are engaged in is a preliminary inquiry. But will we return to accepted procedures if we go on to terminer?"

"This court, being convened by the Federation and acting in accordance with the body of law called 'Customs of Civilizations' in brief and consisting of agreements, treaties, precedents, et cetera, between two or more planets of the Federation, or with other civilizations with which member planets of the Federation have diplomatic relations, is not bound by local procedures. It is the purpose of this court to arrive at the truth and, from there, to reach equity . . . equity under the Law. The court will not trample on local law and custom except where they are hopelessly opposed to superior law. But where local custom is merely ritualistic, this court will ignore formality and get on with its business. Understand me?"

"Er, I believe so, sir. I may take exception later." The small, middle-aged man who spoke seemed embarrassed.

"Any one may object at any time for any reason and be heard. Also you may appeal from my decisions. However . . ." Greenberg grinned warmly. ". . . I doubt if it will do you much good. So far I have been pretty lucky in having my decisions upheld."

"I did not intend to imply," the man answered stiffly, "that the court was not properly . . ."

"Sure, sure! Let's get on with it." Greenberg picked up a stack of papers. "Here is a civil action. 'Bon Marché Merchandising Corporation versus 'Lummox,' John Thomas Stuart XI . . .'" ("*That name still bothers me*," he said in an aside to Judge O'Farrell.) ". . . Marie Brandley Stuart, et al., and another one like it for the Western Mutual Assurance Company, insurers of Bon Marché. Here is another, same defendants, brought by K. Ito and his insurance company, um, New World Casualty, Ltd., and one from the City of Westville, same defendants again . . . and still another brought by Mrs. Isabelle Donahue. Also some criminal matters . . . one is for harboring a dangerous animal, one for felonious harboring of same, another for negligence and another for maintaining a public nuisance."

John Thomas had been steadily turning white. Greenberg glanced at him and said, "They haven't skipped much, have they, son? Cheer up . . . the condemned man always eats a hearty breakfast." John Thomas managed a sickly grin. Betty found his knee under the table and patted it.

There was another paper in the stack; Greenberg shuffled it in with the others without reading it into the record. It was a petition signed by the Chief-of-Safety on behalf of the City of Westville praying the court to order the destruction of a dangerous animal known as "Lummox" and further identified as, etc. Instead Greenberg looked up and said, "Now who's who? You, sir?"

The man addressed was the lawyer who had questioned the court's methods; he identified himself as Alfred Schneider and stated that he was acting both for

Western Mutual and for the Bon Marché. "This gentleman beside me is Mr. deGrasse, manager of the store."

"Good. Now the next man, please." Greenberg established that all principals were present, with their attorneys; the roster included, besides himself, Judge O'Farrell, John Thomas, Betty, and Chief Dreiser, the following: Mrs. Donahue and her lawyer Mr. Beanfield, Messrs. Schneider and deGrasse for Bon Marché, Mr. Lombard, city attorney of Westville, the attorney for Mr. Ito's insurance company and Mr. Ito's son (acting for his father), Officers Karnes and Mendoza (witnesses), and John Thomas's mother with the Stuart family lawyer Mr. Postle.

Greenberg said to Postle, "I take it you are also acting for Mr. Stuart."

Betty interrupted with, "Heavens, no! I'm representing Johnnie."

Greenberg raised his eyebrows. "I was about to ask what you were doing here. Uh, you are an attorney?"

"Well . . . I'm his counsel."

O'Farrell leaned over and whispered, "This is preposterous, Mr. Commissioner. Of course she is not a lawyer. I know the child. I'm rather fond of her . . . but frankly, I don't think she is quite bright." He added severely, "Betty, you have no business here. Get out and quit making a fool of yourself."

"Now, see here, Judge . . ."

"One moment, young lady," Greenberg put in. "Do you have any qualifications to act as counsel for Mr. Stuart?"

"I certainly do. I'm the counsel he wants."

"Mmm, a very strong point. Though perhaps not sufficient." He spoke to John Thomas. "Is that correct?"

"Uh, yes, sir."

Judge O'Farrell whispered, "Don't do it, son! You'll be reversed."

Greenberg whispered back, "That's what I am afraid

of." He frowned, then spoke to Mr. Postle. "Are you prepared to act for both mother and son?"

"Yes."

"*No!*" Betty contradicted.

"Eh? Wouldn't Mr. Stuart's interests be better protected in the hands of an attorney than in yours? No, don't answer; I want Mr. Stuart to answer."

John Thomas turned pink and managed to mutter, "I don't want him."

"Why?"

John Thomas looked stubborn. Betty said scornfully, "Because his mother doesn't like Lummox, that's why. And . . ."

"That's not true!" Mrs. Stuart cut in sharply.

"It is true . . . and that old fossil Postle is stringing along with her. They want to get rid of Lummie, both of them!"

O'Farrell coughed in his handkerchief. Postle turned red. Greenberg said gravely, "Young lady, you will stand and apologize to Mr. Postle."

Betty looked at the Commissioner, dropped her eyes and stood up. She said humbly, "Mr. Postle, I'm sorry you're a fossil. I mean I'm sorry I said you were a fossil."

"Sit down," Greenberg said soberly. "Mind your manners hereafter. Mr. Stuart, no one is required to accept counsel not of his choice. But you place me in a dilemma. Legally you are a minor child; you have chosen as counsel another minor child. It won't look well in the record." He pulled at his chin. "Could it be that you . . . or your counsel . . . or both of you . . . are trying to cause a mistrial?"

"Uh, no, sir." Betty looked smugly virtuous; it was a possibility she had counted on but had not mentioned to Johnnie.

"Hmm . . ."

"Your honor . . ."

"Yes, Mr. Lombard?"

"This strikes me as ridiculous. This girl has no standing. She is not a member of the bar; obviously she can't function as an attorney. I dislike finding myself in the position of instructing the court but the obvious thing to do is to put her outside the bar and appoint counsel. May I suggest that the Public Defender is present and prepared?"

"You may so suggest. Is that all, Mr. City Attorney?"

"Uh, yes, your honor."

"May I say that the court also finds it distasteful for you to instruct the court; you will not do so again."

"Er . . . yes, your honor."

"This court will make its own mistakes in its own way. Under the customs by which this court is convened it is not necessary that a counsel be qualified formally . . . in your idiom, be a 'member of the bar,' a licensed lawyer. If you find that rule unusual, let me assure you that the herditary lawyer-priests of Deflai find it much more astonishing. But it is the only rule which can be applied everywhere. Nevertheless I thank you for your suggestion. Will the Public Defender stand up?"

"Here, your honor. Cyrus Andrews."

"Thank you. Are you prepared to act?"

"Yes. I'll need a recess to consult with my principal."

"Naturally. Well, Mr. Stuart? Shall the court appoint Mr. Andrews as your counsel? Or associate counsel?"

"No!" Again Betty answered.

"I was addressing Mr. Stuart, Miss Sorenson. Well?" John Thomas glanced at Betty. "No, your honor."

"Why not?"

"I'll answer that," Betty put in. "I talk faster than he does; that's why I'm counsel. We won't take Mr. Andrews because the City Attorney is against us on one of these silly things they've got about Lummox . . . and the City Attorney and Mr. Andrews are law partners when they are not fighting sham battles in court!"

Greenberg turned to Andrews. "Is that correct, sir?"

"Why, yes, we're law partners, your honor. You will understand that, in a town this size . . ."

"I quite understand. I also understand Miss Sorenson's objection. Thank you, Mr. Andrews. Stand down."

"Mr. Greenberg?"

"What is it now, young lady?"

"I can get you part way off the spot. You see, I had a dirty hunch that some busybody would try to keep me out of it. So we fixed it up ahead of time. I'm half owner."

"Half owner?"

"Of Lummox. See?" She took a paper from her bag and offered it. "A bill of sale, all legal and proper. At least it ought to be, I coped it out of the book."

Greenberg studied it. "The form appears correct. The date is yesterday . . . which would make you voluntarily liable to the extent of your interest, from a civil standpoint. It would not affect criminal matters of earlier date."

"Oh, pooh! There aren't any criminal matters."

"That remains to be determined. And don't say 'pooh'; it is not a legal term. The question here is whether or not the signer can vend this interest. Who owns Lummox?"

"Why, Johnnie does! It was in his father's will."

"So? Is that stipulated, Mr. Postle?"

Mr. Postle whispered with Mrs. Stuart, then answered, "So stipulated, your honor. This creature called 'Lummox' is a chattel of John Thomas Stuart, a minor child. Mrs. Stuart's interest is through her son."

"Very well." Greenberg handed the bill of sale to the clerk. "Read it into the record."

Betty settled back. "All right, your honor . . . appoint anybody you want to. Just as long as I can have my say."

Greenberg sighed. "Would it make any difference if I did?"

"Not much, I guess."

"Let the record show that you two, having been duly warned and advised, persist in acting as your own counsel. The court regretfully assumes the burden of protecting your rights and advising you as to the law."

"Oh, don't feel bad, Mr. Greenberg. We trust you."

"I'd rather you didn't," he said drily. "But let's move on. That gentleman down at the end . . . who are you?"

"Me, Judge? I'm the Galactic Press stringer around here. Name of Hovey."

"So? The clerk will supply a transcript for the press. I'll be available for the usual interview later, if anyone wants it. No pictures of me with this creature Lummox, however. Are there any more gentlemen of the press?"

Two others stood up. "The bailiff will place chairs for you just beyond the rail."

"Yes, Judge. But first . . ."

"Outside the rail, please." Greenberg looked around. "I think that's all . . . no, that gentleman down there. Your name, sir?"

The man addressed stood up. He was dressed in formal jacket and striped gray shorts and held himself with self-conscious dignity. "May it please the court, my name, sir, is T. Omar Esklund, Doctor of Philosophy."

"It neither pleases nor displeases the court, Doctor. Are you a party to any of these issues?"

"I am, sir. I appear here as *amicus curiae*, a friend of the court."

Greenberg frowned. "This court insists on choosing its own friends. State your business, Doctor."

"Sir, if you will permit me. I am state executive secretary of the Keep Earth Human League." Greenberg suppressed a groan but Esklund did not notice as he had looked down to pick up a large manuscript. "As is well known, ever since the inception of the ungodly practice of space travel, our native Earth, given to us by Divine law, has been increasingly overrun by creatures . . . 'beasts' rather let us say . . . of dubious origin. The pestilential consequences of this unholy traffic are seen on every . . ."

"Doctor Esklund!"

"Sir?"

"What is your business with this court? Are you a principal to any of the issues before it?"

"Well, not in so many words, your honor. In a broader sense, I am advocate for all mankind. The society of which I have the honor . . ."

"Do you have *any* business? A petition, perhaps?"

"Yes," Esklund answered sullenly, "I have a petition."

"Produce it."

Esklund fumbled among his papers, drew out one; it was passed to Greenberg, who did not look at it. "Now state briefly, for the record, the nature of your petition. Speak clearly and toward the nearest microphone."

"Well . . . may it please the court: the society of which I have the honor of being an officer . . . a league, if I may so say, embracing all mankind, prays . . . nay, *demands* that this unearthly beast which has already ravaged this fair community be destroyed. Such destruction is sanctioned and, yes, commanded by those sacred—"

"Is that your petition? You want this court to order the destruction of the e.-t. known as Lummox?"

"Yes, but more than that, I have here a careful documentation of the arguments . . . unanswerable arguments I may say, to . . ."

"Just a moment. That word 'demands' which you used; does it appear in the petition?"

"No, your honor, that came from my heart, from the fullness of . . ."

"Your heart has just led you into contempt. Do you wish to rephrase it?"

Esklund stared, then said grudgingly, "I withdraw the word. No contempt was intended."

"Very well. The petition is received; the clerk will record it. Decision later. Now as to that speech you wished to make: from the size of your manuscript I surmise that you will require about two hours?"

"I believe that will be ample, your honor," Esklund answered, somewhat mollified.

"Good. Bailiff!"

"Your honor?"

"Can you dig up a soap box?"

"Why, I believe so, sir."

"Excellent. Place it on the lawn outside. Doctor Esklund, everyone of us enjoys free speech . . . so enjoy yourself. That soap box is yours for the next two hours."

Dr. Esklund turned the color of eggplant. "You'll hear from us!"

"No doubt."

"We know your sort! Traitors to mankind. Renegades! Trifling with . . ."

"Remove him."

The bailiff did so, grinning. One of the reporters followed them out. Greenberg said gently, "We seem to have trimmed it down to indispensables now. We have several issues before us, but they have in common the same sheaf of facts. Unless there is objection, we will hear testimony for all issues together, then pass on the issues one at a time. Objection?"

The lawyers looked at each other. Finally Mr. Ito's attorney said, "Your honor, it would seem to me to be fairer to try them one at a time."

"Possibly. But if we do, we'll be here until Christmas. I dislike to make so many busy people go over the same ground repeatedly. But a separate trial of the facts to a jury is your privilege . . . bearing in mind, if you lose, your principal will have to bear the added costs alone."

Mr. Ito's son tugged at the sleeve of the lawyer and whispered to him. The lawyer nodded and said, "We'll go along with a joint hearing . . . as to facts."

"Very well. Further objection?" There was none. Greenberg turned to O'Farrell. "Judge, is this room equipped with truth meters?"

"Eh? Why, yes. I hardly ever use them."

"I like them." He turned to the others. "Truth meters will be hooked up. No one is required to use one, but anyone choosing not to will be sworn. This court, as is its privilege, will take judicial notice of and will comment on the fact if anyone refuses the use of a truth meter."

John Thomas whispered to Betty, "Watch your step, Slugger."

She whispered back, "I will, smarty! You watch yours."

Judge O'Farrell said to Greenberg, "It will take some time to rig them. Hadn't we better break for lunch?"

"Oh yes, lunch. Attention, everyone . . . this court does not recess for lunch. I'll ask the bailiff to take orders for coffee and sandwiches or whatever you like while the clerk is rigging the meters. We will eat here at the table. In the meantime . . ." Greenberg fumbled for cigarettes, fumbled again. ". . . has anybody got a match?"

Out on the lawn, Lummox, having considered the difficult question of Betty's right to give orders, had come to the conclusion that she possibly had a special status. Each of the John Thomases had introduced into his life a person equivalent to Betty; each had insisted that the person in question must be humored in every whim. This John Thomas had already begun the process with Betty; therefore, it was best to go along with what she wanted as long as it was not too much trouble. He lay down and went to sleep, leaving his watchman eye on guard.

He slept restlessly, disturbed by the tantalizing odor of steel. After a time he woke up and stretched, causing the cage to bulge. It seemed to him that John Thomas had been gone an unnecessarily long time. On second thought, he had not liked the way that man had taken John Thomas away . . . no, he hadn't liked it a bit. He wondered what he should do, if anything? What would John Thomas say, if he were here?

The problem was too complex. He lay down and tasted the bars of his cage. He refrained from eating them; he merely tried them for flavor. A bit grucky, he decided, but good.

Inside, Chief Dreiser had completed his testimony and had been followed by Karnes and Mendoza. No argument had developed and the truth meters had stayed steady; Mr. deGrasse had insisted on amplifying parts of the testimony. Mr. Ito's lawyer stipulated that Mr. Ito had fired at Lummox; Mr. Ito's son was allowed to describe and show photographs of the consequences. Only Mrs. Donahue's testimony was needed to complete the story of L-day.

Greenberg turned to her lawyer. "Mr. Beanfield, will you examine your client, or shall the court continue?"

"Go ahead, your honor. I may add a question or two."

"Your prvilege. Mrs. Donahue, tell us what happened."

"I certainly shall. Your honor, friends, distinguished visitors, unaccustomed as I am to public speaking, nevertheless, in my modest way, I believe I am . . ."

"Never mind that, Mrs. Donahue. Just the facts. Last Monday afternoon."

"But I was!"

"Very well, go ahead. Keep it simple."

She sniffed. "Well! I was lying down, trying to

snatch a few minutes rest . . . I have so many responsibilities, clubs and charitable committees and things . . ."

Greenberg was watching the truth meter over her head. The needle wobbled restlessly, but did not kick over into the red enough to set off the warning buzzer. He decided that it was not worth while to caution her.

". . . when suddenly I was overcome with a nameless dread."

The needle swung far into the red, a ruby light flashed and the buzzer gave out a loud rude noise. Somebody started to giggle; Greenberg said hastily, "Order in the court. The bailiff is instructed to remove any spectator making a disturbance."

Mrs. Donahue broke off suddenly when the buzzer sounded. Mr. Beanfield, looking grim, touched her sleeve and said, "Never mind that, dear lady. Just tell the court about the noise you heard and what you saw and what you did."

"He's leading the witness," objected Betty.

"Never mind," said Greenberg. "Somebody has to."

"But . . ."

"Objection overruled. Witness will continue."

"Well! Uh . . . well, I heard this noise and I wondered what in the world it was. I peeked out and there was this great ravening beast charging back and forth and . . ."

The buzzer sounded again; a dozen spectators laughed. Mrs. Donahue said angrily, "Will somebody shut that silly thing off? How anyone can be expected to testify with that going on is more than I can see."

"Order!" called Greenberg. "If there is more demonstration, the court will find it necessary to hold someone in contempt." He went on to Mrs. Donahue: "Once a witness has accepted the use of the truth meter the decision cannot be changed. But the data supplied by it is instructive merely; the court is not bound by it. Continue."

"Well, I should hope so. I never told a lie in my life."

The buzzer remained silent; Greenberg reflected that she must believe it. "I mean," he added, "that the court makes up its own mind. It does not allow a machine to do so for it."

"My father always said that gadgets like that were spawn of the devil. He said that an honest business man should not . . ."

"Please, Mrs. Donahue."

Mr. Beanfield whispered to her. Mrs. Donahue went on more quietly, "Well, there was that *thing*, that enormous beast kept by that boy next door. It was eating my rose bushes."

"And what did you do?"

"I didn't know what to do. I grabbed the first thing at hand . . . a broom, it was . . . and rushed out doors. The beast came charging at me and . . ."

Buzzzzzzz!"

"Shall we go over that again, Mrs. Donahue?"

"Well . . . anyhow, I rushed at it and began to beat it on the head. It snapped at me. Those great teeth . . ."

Buzzzzz!

"Then what happened, Mrs. Donahue?"

"Well, it turned away, the cowardly thing, and ran out of my yard. I don't know where it went. But there was my lovely garden, just *ruined*." The needle quivered but the buzzer did not sound.

Greenberg turned to the lawyer. "Mr. Beanfield, have you examined the damage to Mrs. Donahue's garden?"

"Yes, your honor."

"Will you tell us the extent of the damage?"

Mr. Beanfield decided that he would rather lose a client than be buzzed in open court by that confounded

68

toy. "Five bushes were eaten, your honor, in whole or in part. There was minor damage to the lawn and a hole made in an ornamental fence."

"Financial damage?"

Mr. Beanfield said carefully, "The amount we are suing for is before you, your honor."

"That is not responsive, Mr. Beanfield."

Mr. Beanfield shrugged mentally and struck Mrs. Donahue off his list of paying properties. "Oh, around a couple of hundred, your honor, in property damage. But the court should allow for inconvenience and mental anguish."

Mrs. Donahue yelped. "That's preposterous! My *prize* roses."

The needle jumped and fell back too quickly to work the buzzer. Greenberg said wearily, "What prizes, Mrs. Donahue?"

Her lawyer cut in, "They were right next to Mrs. Donahue's well-known champion plants. Her courageous action saved the more valuable bushes, I am happy to say."

"Is there more to add?"

"I think not. I have photographs, marked and identified, to offer."

"Very well."

Mrs. Donahue glared at her lawyer. "Well! I have something to add. There is one thing I insist on, absolutely *insist* on, and that is that that dangerous, bloodthirty beast be *destroyed!*"

Greenberg turned to Beanfield. "Is that a formal prayer, counsellor? Or may we regard it as rhetoric?"

Beanfield looked uncomfortable. "We have such a petition, your honor."

"The court will receive it."

Betty butted in with, "Hey, wait a minute! All Lummie did was eat a few of her measly old . . ."

"Later, Miss Sorenson."

"But . . ."

"Later, please. You will have your chance. The court is now of the opinion that it has all the pertinent facts. Does anyone have any new facts to bring out, or does anyone wish to question further any witness? Or bring forward another witness?"

"We do," Betty said at once.

"You do what?"

"We want to call a new witness."

"Very well. Do you have him here?"

"Yes, your honor. Just outside. Lummox."

Greenberg looked thoughtful. "Do I understand that you are proposing to put, uh, Lummox on the stand in his own defense?"

"Why not? He can talk."

A reporter turned suddenly to a colleague and whispered to him, then hurried out of the room. Greenberg chewed his lip. "I know that," he admitted. "I exchanged a few words with him myself. But the ability to talk does not alone make a competent witness. A child may learn to talk, after a fashion, before it is a year old, but only rarely is a child of tender years . . . less than five, let us say . . . found competent to give testimony. The court takes judicial notice that members of non-human races . . . non-human in the biological sense . . . may give evidence. But nothing has been presented to show that this particular extra-terrestrial is competent."

John Thomas whispered worriedly to Betty, "Have you slipped your cams? There's no telling what Lummie would say."

"Hush!" She went on to Greenberg. "Look, Mr. Commissioner, you've said a fancy lot of words, but what do they mean? You are about to pass judgment on Lummox . . . and you won't even bother to ask him a question. You say he can't give competent evidence. Well, I've seen others around here who didn't do

70

so well. I'll bet if you hook a truth meter to Lummie, it won't buzz. Sure, he did things he shouldn't have done. He ate some scrawny old rose bushes and he ate Mr. Ito's cabbages. What's horrible about that? When you were a kid, did you ever swipe a cookie when you thought nobody was looking?"

She took a deep breath. "Suppose when you swiped that cookie, somebody hit you in the face with a broom? Or fired a gun at you? Wouldn't you be scared? Wouldn't you run? Lummie is friendly. Everybody around here knows that . . . or at least if they don't they are stupider and more irresponsible than he is. But did anybody try to reason with him? Oh, no! They bullied him and fired off guns at him and scared him to death and chased him off bridges. You say Lummie is incompetent. Who is incompetent? All these people who were mean to him? Or Lummie? Now they want to kill him. If a little boy swiped a cookie, I suppose they'd chop his head off, just to be sure he wouldn't do it again. Is somebody crazy? What kind of a farce is this?"

She stopped, tears running down her cheeks. It was a talent which had been useful in school dramatics; to her own surprise she found that these tears were real.

"Are you through?" asked Greenberg.

"I guess so. For now, anyway."

"I must say that you put it very movingly. But a court should not be swayed by emotion. Is it your theory that the major portion of the damage . . . let us say everything but the rose bushes and the cabbages . . . arose from improper acts of human beings and therefore cannot be charged to Lummox or his owner?"

"Figure it yourself, your honor. The tail generally follows the dog. Why not ask Lummie how it looked to him?"

"We'll get to that. On another issue: I cannot grant that your analogy is valid. We are dealing here, not with a little boy, but with an animal. If this court

should order the destruction of this animal, it would not
be in spirit of vengeance nor of punishment, for an animal is presumed not to understand such values. The
purpose would be preventive, in order that a potential
danger might not be allowed to develop into damage
to life or limb or property. Your little boy can be re-
strained by the arms of his nurse . . . but we are dealing with a creature weighing several tons, capable of
crushing a man with a careless step. There is no parallel in your cookie-stealing small boy."

"There isn't, huh? That little boy can grow up and
wipe out a whole city by pushing one teeny little button. So off with his head!—before he grows up. Don't ask
him why he took the cookie, don't ask him anything!
He's a bad boy—chop his head off and save trouble."

Greenberg found himself again biting his lip. He
said, "It is your wish that we examine Lummox?"

"I said so, didn't I?"

"I'm not sure what you said. The court will consider
it."

Mr. Lombard said quickly, "Objection, your honor.
If this extraordinary . . ."

"Hold your objection, please. Court will recess for
ten minutes. All will remain." Greenberg got up and
walked away. He took out a cigarette, found again that
he had no light, stuck the pack back in his pocket.

Blast the girl! He had had it figured how to dispose
of this case smoothly, with credit to the department
and everybody satisfied . . . except the Stuart boy, but
that could not be helped . . . the boy and this preco-
cious preposterous young mammal who had him under
her wing. And under her thumb, too, he added.

He could not allow this unique specimen to be destroyed. But he had meant to do it suavely . . . deny
the petition of that old battle-axe, since it was obviously from malice, and tell the police chief privately
to forget the other one. The Save-the-World-for-the Nean-

derthals petition didn't matter. But this cocky girl, by talking when she should have listened, was going to make it appear that a departmental court could be pushed into risking public welfare over a lot of sentimental, anthropomorphic bosh!

Confound her pretty blue eyes!

They would accuse him of being influenced by those pretty blue eyes, too. Too bad the child wasn't homely.

The animal's owner was responsible for the damage; there were a thousand "strayed animal" cases to justify a ruling—since this was not the planet Tencora. That stuff about it being the fault of the persons who frightened him off was a lot of prattle. But the e.-t., as a specimen for science, was worth far more than the damage; the decision would not hurt the boy financially.

He realized that he had allowed himself to fall into a most unjudicial frame of mind. The defendant's ability to pay was not his business.

"Excuse me, your honor. Please don't monkey with those things."

He looked up, ready to snap somebody's head off, to find himself looking at the clerk of the court. He then saw that he had been fiddling with the switches and controls of the clerk's console. He snatched his hands away. "Sorry."

"A person who doesn't understand these things," the clerk said apologetically, "can cause an awful lot of trouble."

"True. Unfortunately true." He turned away sharply. "The court will come to order."

He sat down and turned at once to Miss Sorenson. "The court rules that Lummox is not a competent witness."

Betty gasped. "Your honor, you are being most unfair!"

"Possibly."

She thought for a moment. "We want a change of venue."

"Where did you learn that word? Never mind, you had one when the department intervened. That ends it. Now keep quiet for a change."

She turned red. "You ought to disqualify yourself!"

Greenberg had intended to be calm, positively Olympian, in his manner. He now found it necessary to take three slow breaths. "Young lady," he said carefully, "you have been trying to confuse the issue all day. There is no need for you to speak now; you have said too much already. Understand me?"

"I have not, I will too, and I didn't either!"

"What? Repeat that, please?"

She looked at him. "No, I had better take it back . . . or you will be talking about 'contempt.' "

"No, no. I wanted to memorize it. I don't think I have ever heard quite so sweeping a statement. Never mind. Just hold your tongue. If you know how. You'll be allowed to talk later."

"Yes, sir."

He turned to the others. "The court announced earlier that there would be due notice if we were to continue to terminer. The court sees no reason not to. Objection?"

The attorneys shifted uncomfortably and looked at each other. Greenberg turned to Betty. "How about you?"

"Me? I thought I wasn't allowed to vote."

"Shall we conclude these issues today?"

She glanced at John Thomas, then said dully, "No objection," then leaned to him and whispered, "Oh, Johnnie, I *tried!*"

He patted her hand under the table. "I know you did, Slugger."

Greenberg pretended not to hear. He went on in a cold, official voice. "This court has before it a petition

74

asking for the destruction of the extra-terrestrial Lummox on the grounds that it is dangerous and uncontrollable. The facts have not sustained that view; the petition is denied."

Betty gasped and squealed. John Thomas looked startled, then grinned for the first time. "Order, please," Greenberg said mildly. "We have here another petition to the same end, but for different reasons." He held up the one submitted by the Keep Earth Human League. "This court finds itself unable to follow the alleged reasoning. Petition denied.

"We have four criminal charges, I am dismissing all four. The law requires . . ."

The city attorney looked startled. "But, your honor—"

"If you have a point, will you save it? No criminal intent can be found here, which therefore would make it appear that there could be no crime. However, constructive intent may appear where the law requires a man to exercise due prudence to protect others and it is on this ground that these issues must be judged. Prudence is based on experience, personal or vicarious, not on impossible prescience. In the judgment of this court, the precautions taken were prudent in the light of experience . . . experience up to last Monday afternoon, that is to say." He turned and addressed John Thomas. "What I mean, young man, is this: your precautions were 'prudent' so far as you knew. Now you know better. If that beast gets loose again, it will go hard with you."

Johnnie swallowed. "Yessir."

"We have remaining the civil matters of damage. Here the criteria are different. The guardian of a minor, or the owner of an animal, is responsible for damage committed by that child or that animal, the law holding that it is better that the owner or guardian suffer than the innocent third party. Except for one point, which I will reserve for the moment, these civil actions fall under that rule. First, let me note that one or more of these issues ask for real, punitive, and exemplary damages. Punitive and exemplary damages are denied; there are no grounds. I believe that we have arrived at real damages in each case and counsels have so stipulated. As to costs, the Department of Spatial Affairs has intervened in the public interest; costs will be borne by the department."

Betty whispered, "A good thing we homesteaded him. Look at those insurance vultures grin."

Greenberg went on, "I reserved one point. The question has been raised indirectly that this Lummox may not be an animal . . . and therefore not a chattel . . . but may be a sentient being within the meaning of 'the Customs of Civilizations' . . . and therefore his own master." Greenberg hesitated. He was about to add his bit to the "Customs of Civilizations"; he was anxious not to be overruled. "We have long disavowed slavery; no sentient being may be owned. But if Lummox is sentient, what have we? May Lummox be held personally responsible? It would not appear that he has sufficient knowledge of our customs, nor does it appear that he is among us by his own choice. Are the putative owners in fact his guardians and in that way responsible? All these questions turn on this: is Lummox a chattel, or a free being?

"This court expressed its opinion when it ruled that Lummox might not testify . . . at this time. But this court is not equipped to render a final decision, no matter how strongly it may believe that Lummox is an animal.

"The court will therefore start proceedings on its own motion to determine the status of Lummox. In the meantime the local authorities will take charge of Lummox and will be held responsible both for his safety and for public safety with respect to him." Greenberg shut up and sat back.

A fly would have had his choice of open mouths. First to recover was the attorney for Western Mutual, Mr. Schneider. "Your honor? Where does that leave *us?*"

"I don't know."

"But . . . see here, your honor, let's face the facts. Mrs. Stuart hasn't any property or funds that can be attached; she's the beneficiary of a trust. Same for the boy. We expected to levy against the beast itself; he will bring a good price in the proper market. Now you have, if you will permit me, upset the apple cart. If one of those scientific . . . *hrrumph!* . . . persons starts a long series of tests, years long perhaps, or throws doubt on the beast's status as a chattel . . . well, where should we look for relief? Should we sue the city?"

Lombard was on his feet instantly. "Now, look here, you can't sue the city! The city is one of the damaged parties. On that theory . . ."

"Order," Greenberg said sternly. "None of those questions can be answered now. All civil actions will be continued until the status of Lummox is clarified." He looked at the ceiling. "There is another possibility. It would seem that this creature came to Earth in the *Trail Blazer*. If my memory of history serves, all specimens brought back by that ship were government property. If Lummox is a chattel, he may nevertheless not be private property. In that event, the source of relief may be a matter of more involved litigation."

Mr. Schneider looked stunned, Mr. Lombard looked angry, John Thomas looked confused and whispered to Betty, "What's he trying to say? Lummox belongs to me."

"Ssh . . ." Betty whispered. "I *told* you we would get out of it. Oh, Mr. Greenberg is a honey lamb!"

"But . . ."

"Hush up! We're ahead."

Mr. Ito's son had kept quiet except when testifying. Now he stood up. "Your honor?"

"Yes, Mr. Ito?"

"I don't understand any of this. I'm just a farmer. But I do want to know one thing. *Who's going to pay for my father's greenhouses?*"

John Thomas got to his feet. "I am," he said simply.

Betty tugged at his sleeve. "Sit down, you idiot!"

"You hush up, Betty. You've talked enough." Betty hushed up. "Mr. Greenberg, everybody else has been talking. Can I say something?"

"Go ahead."

"I've listened to a lot of stuff all day. People trying to make out that Lummox is dangerous, when he's not. People trying to have him killed, just for spite . . . yes, I mean you, Mrs. Donahue!"

"Address the court, please," Greenberg said quietly.

"I've heard you say a lot of things, too. I didn't follow all of them but, if you will pardon me, sir, some of them struck me as pretty silly. Excuse me."

"No contempt intended, I'm sure."

"Well . . . take this about whether Lummox is or isn't a chattel. Or whether he's bright enough to vote. Lummox is pretty bright, I guess nobody but me knows just how bright. But he's never had any education and he's never been anywhere. But that hasn't anything to do with who he belongs to. He belongs to *me*. Just the way I belong to him . . . we grew up together. Now I know I'm responsible for that damage last Monday . . . will you keep quiet, Betty! I can't pay for it now, but I'll pay for it. I . . ."

"Just a moment, young man. The court will not permit you to admit liability without counsel. If that is your intention, court will appoint counsel."

"You said I could have my say."

"Continue. Noted for the record that this is not binding."

"Sure, it's binding, because I'm going to do it. Pretty

soon my education trust comes due and it would about cover it. I guess I can . . ."

"John Thomas!" his mother called out sharply. "You'll do no such thing!"

"Mother, you had better keep out of this, too. I was just going to say . . ."

"You're not to say anything. Your honor, he is . . ."

"Order!" Greenberg interrupted. "None of this is binding. Let the lad speak."

"Thank you, sir. I was through, anyway. But I've got something to say to *you*, sir, too. Lummie is timid. I can handle him because he trusts me—but if you think I'm going to let a lot of strangers poke him and prod him and ask him silly questions and put him through mazes and things, you'd just better think again—because I won't stand for it! Lummie is sick right now. He's had more excitement than is good for him. The poor thing . . ."

Lummox had waited for John Thomas longer than he liked because he was not sure where John Thomas had gone. He had seen him disappear in the crowd without being sure whether or not Johnnie had gone into the big house nearby. He had tried to sleep after he woke up the first time, but people had come poking around, and he had had to wake himself up repeatedly because his watchman circuit did not have much judgment. Not that he thought of it that way; he was merely aware that he had come to with his alarms jangling time after time.

At last he decided that it was time he located John Thomas and went home. Figuratively, he tore up Betty's orders; after all, Betty was not Johnnie.

So he stepped up his hearing to "search" and tried to locate Johnnie. He listened for a long time, heard Betty's voice several times—but he was not interested in Betty. He continued to listen.

There was Johnnie now! He tuned out everything

else and listened. He was in the big house all right. Hey! Johnnie sounded just the way he did when he had arguments with his mother. Lummox spread his hearing a little and tried to find out what was going on.

They were talking about things he knew nothing about. But one thing was clear: somebody was being mean to Johnnie. His mother? Yes, he heard her once . . . and he knew that she had the privilege of being mean to Johnnie, just as Johnnie could talk mean to him and it didn't really matter. But there was somebody else . . . several others, and not a one of them had any such privilege.

Lummox decided that it was time to act. He heaved to his feet.

John Thomas got no farther in his peroration than "The poor thing . . ." There were screams and shouts from outside; everybody in court turned to look. The noises got rapidly closer and Mr. Greenberg was just going to send the bailiff to find out about it when suddenly it became unnecessary. The door to the courtroom bulged, then burst off its hinges. The front end of Lummox came in, tearing away part of the wall, and ending with him wearing the door frame as a collar. He opened his mouth. "Johnnie!" he piped.

"Lummox!" cried his friend. "Stand still. Stay right where you are. Don't move an inch!"

Of all the faces in the room, that of Special Commissioner Greenberg presented the most interesting mixed expression.

V

A Matter of Viewpoint

THE Right Honorable Mr. Kiku, Under Secretary for Spatial Affairs, opened a desk drawer and looked over his collection of pills. There was no longer any doubt; his stomach ulcer was acting up again. He selected one and turned wearily back to his tasks.

He read an order from the departmental Bureau of Engineering grounding all *Pelican*-class interplanetary ships until certain modifications were accomplished. Mr. Kiku did not bother to study the attached engineering report, but signed approval, checked "EFFECTIVE IMMEDIATELY" and dropped the papers in the outgoing basket. Engineering safety in space was the responsibility of BuEng; Kiku himself knew nothing of engineering and did not wish to; he would back up the decisions of his chief engineer, or fire him and get another one.

But he realized glumly that the financial lords who owned the *Pelican*-class ships would soon be knocking the ear of the Secretary . . . and, shortly thereafter, the Secretary, out of his depth and embarrassed by the political power wielded by those fine gentlemen, would dump them in his lap.

He was beginning to have his doubts about this new Secretary; he was not shaping up.

The next item was for his information only and had been routed to him because of standing orders that anything concerning the Secretary must reach his desk, no matter how routine. This item appeared routine and unimportant: according to the synopsis an organization calling itself "The Friends of Lummox" and headed by a Mrs. Beulah Murgatroyd was demanding an audience with the Secretary of Spatial Affairs; they were being shunted to the Special Assistant Secretary (Public Relations).

Mr. Kiku read no farther. Wes Robbins would kiss them to death and neither he nor the Secretary would be disturbed. He amused himself with the idea of punishing the Secretary by inflicting Mrs. Murgatroyd on him, but it was merely a passing fantasy; the Secretary's time must be reserved for really important cornerstone-layings, not wasted on crackpot societies. Any organization calling itself "The Friends of This or That" always consisted of someone with an axe to grind, plus the usual assortment of prominent custard heads and professional stuffed shirts. But such groups could be a nuisance . . . therefore never grant them the Danegeld they demanded.

He sent it to files and picked up a memorandum from BuEcon: a virus had got into the great yeast plant at St. Louis; the projection showed a possibility of protein shortage and more drastic rationing. Even starvation on Earth was no direct interest to Mr. Kiku. But he stared thoughtfully while the slide rule in his head worked a few figures, then he called as assistant. "Wong, have you seen BuEcon Ay0428?"

"Uh, I believe so, boss. The St. Louis yeast thing?"

"Yes. What have you don't about it?"

"Er, nothing. Not my pidgin, I believe."

"You believe, eh? Our out-stations are your business, aren't they? Look over your shipping schedules for the next eighteen months, correlate with Ay0428, and project. You may have to buy Australian sheep . . . and actually get them into our possession. We can't have our people going hungry because some moron in St. Louis dropped his socks in a yeast vat."

"Yes, sir."

Mr. Kiku turned back to work. He realized unhappily that he had been too brusque with Wong. His present frame of mind, he knew, was not Wong's fault, but that of Dr. Ftaeml.

No, not Ftaeml's fault . . . his own! He knew that he should not harbor race prejudice, not in *this* job. He was aware intellectually that he himself was relatively safe from persecution that could arise from differences of skin and hair and facial contour for the one reason that weird creatures such as Dr. Ftaeml had made the differences between breeds of men seem less important.

Still, there it was . . . he hated Ftaeml's very shadow. He could not help it.

If the so-and-so would wear a turban, it would help . . . instead of walking around with those dirty snakes on his head wiggling like a can of worms. But oh no! the Rargyllians were proud of them. There was a suggestion in their manner that anyone without them was not quite human.

Come now! . . . Ftaeml was a decent chap. He made a note to invite Ftaeml to dinner, not put it off any longer. After all, he would make certain of deep-hypnotic preparation; the dinner need not be difficult. But his ulcer gave a fresh twinge at the thought.

Kiku did not hold it against the Rargyllian that he had dropped an impossible problem in the department's tired lap; impossible problems were routine. It was just . . . well, why didn't the monster get a haircut?

The vision of the Chesterfieldian Dr. Ftaeml with a shingle cut, his scalp all lumps and bumps, enabled Mr. Kiku to smile; he resumed work feeling better. The next item was a brief of a field report . . . oh yes! Sergei Greenberg. Good boy, Sergei. He was reaching for his pen to approve the recommendation even before he had finished reading it.

Instead of signing, he stared for almost half a second, then punched a button. "Files! Send up the full report of Mr. Greenberg's field job, the one he got back from a few days ago."

"Do you have the reference number, sir?"

"That intervention matter . . . you find it. Wait . . . it's, uh, Rt0411, dated Saturday. I want it right now."

He had only time to dispose of half a dozen items when, seconds later, the delivery tube went *thwong!* and a tiny cylinder popped out on his desk. He stuck it into his reading machine and relaxed, with his right thumb resting on a pressure plate to control the speed with which the print fled across the screen.

In less than seven minutes he had zipped through not only a full transcript of the trial but also Greenberg's report of all else that had happened. Mr. Kiku could read at least two thousand words a minute with the aid of a machine; oral recordings and personal interviews he regarded as time wasters. But when the machine clicked off he decided on an oral report. He leaned to his interoffice communicator and flipped a switch. "Greenberg."

Greenberg looked up from his desk. "Howdy, boss."

"Come here, please." He switched off without politenesses.

Greenberg decided that the bossman's stomach must be bothering him again. But it was too late to find some urgent business outside the departmental building; he hurried upstairs and reported with his usual cheery grin. "Howdy, Chief."

"Morning. I've been reading your intervention report."

"So?"

"How old are you, Greenberg?"

"Eh? Thirty-seven."

"Hmm. What is your present rank?"

"Sir? Diplomatic officer second class . . . acting first." What the deuce? Uncle Henry knew the answers . . . he probably knew what size shoes he wore.

"Old enough to have sense," Kiku mused. "Rank

enough to be assigned as ambassador . . . or executive deputy to a politically-appointed ambassador. Sergei, how come you are so confounded stupid?"

Greenberg's jaw muscles clamped but he said nothing.

"Well?"

"Sir," Greenberg answered icily, "you are older and more experienced than I am. May I ask why you are so confounded rude?"

Mr. Kiku's mouth twitched but he did not smile. "A fair question. My psychiatrist tells me that it is because I am an anarchist in the wrong job. Now sit down and we'll discuss why you are so thick-headed. Cigarettes in the chair arm." Greenberg sat down, discovered that he did not have a light, and asked for one.

"I don't smoke," answered Kiku. "I thought those were the self-striking kind. Aren't they?"

"Oh. So they are." Greenberg lit up.

"See? You don't use your eyes and ears. Sergei, once that beast talked, you should have postponed the hearing until we knew all about him."

"Mmmm . . . I suppose so."

"You *suppose* so! Son, your subconscious alarms should have been clanging like a bed alarm on Monday morning. As it is, you let the implications be sprung on you when you thought the trial was over. And by a girl, a mere child. I'm glad I don't read the papers; I'll bet they had fun."

Greenberg blushed. He did read the papers.

"Then when she had you tangled up like a rang-tangtoo trying to find its own feet, instead of facing her challenge and meeting it . . . Meeting it how? By adjourning, of course, and ordering the investigation you should have ordered to start with, you . . ."

"But I *did* order it."

"Don't interrupt me; I want you browned on both sides. Then you proceeded to hand down a decision the like of which has not been seen since Solomon ordered the baby sawed in half. What mail-order law school did you attend?"

"Harvard," Greenberg answered sullenly.

"Hmm . . . Well, I shouldn't be too harsh on you; you're handicapped. But by the seventy-seven seven-sided gods of the Sarvanchil, what did you do next? First you deny a petition from the local government itself to destroy this brute in the interest of public safety . . . then you reverse yourself, grant the prayer and tell them to kill him . . . subject only to routine approval of this department. All in ten minutes. Exeunt omnes, laughing. Son, I don't mind you making a fool of yourself, but must you include the department?"

"Boss," Greenberg said humbly, "I made a mistake. When I saw the mistake, I did the only thing I could do; I reversed myself. The beast really is dangerous and there are no proper facilities for confining it in Westville. If it had not been beyond my power, I would have ordered it destroyed at once, without referring back for the department's approval . . . for your approval."

"Hummph!"

"You weren't sitting where I was, sir. You didn't see that solid wall bulge in. You didn't see the destruction."

"I'm not impressed. Did you ever see a city that had been flattened by a fusion bomb? What does one courthouse wall matter? . . . probably some thieving contractor didn't beef it up."

"But, boss, you should have seen the cage he broke out of first. Steel I-beams, welded. He tore them like straw."

"I recall that you inspected him in that cage. Why didn't you see to it that he was confined so that he couldn't get out?"

"Huh? Why, it's no business of the department to provide jails."

"Son, a factor concerning in any way anything from 'Out There' is the very personal business of this department. You know that. Once you know it awake and asleep, clear down to your toes, you'll begin to trot through a perfunctory routine, like an honorary chairman sampling soup in a charity hospital. You were supposed to be there with your nose twitching and your ears quivering, on the lookout for 'special situations.' You flubbed. Now tell me about this beast. I read the report, I saw his picture. But I don't *feel* him."

"Well, it's a non-balancing multipedal type, eight legs and about seven feet high at the dorsal ridge. It's . . ."

Kiku sat up straight. "Eight legs? Hands?"

"Hands? No."

"Manipulative organs of any sort? A modified foot?"

"None, chief . . . if there had been, I would have ordered a full-scale investigation at once. The feet are about the size of nail kegs, and as dainty. Why?"

"Never mind. Another matter. Go on."

"The impression is something like a rhinoceros, something like a triceratops, though the articulation is unlike anything native to this planet. 'Lummox' his young master calls him and the name fits. It's a rather engaging beast, but stupid. That's the danger; it's so big and powerful that it is likely to hurt people through clumsiness and stupidity. It does talk, but about as well as a four-year-old child . . . in fact it sounds as if it had swallowed a baby girl."

"Why stupid? I note that its master with the history-book name claims that it is bright."

Greenberg smiled. "He is prejudiced. I talked with it, boss. It's stupid."

"I can't see that you have established that. Assuming that an e.-t. is stupid because he can't speak our language well is like assuming that an Italian is illiterate because he speaks broken English. A non-sequitur."

"But look, boss, no *hands*. Maximum intelligence lower than monkeys. Maybe as high as a dog. Though not likely."

"Well, I'll concede that you are orthodox in xenological theory, but that is all. Some day that assumption is going to rise up and slap the classic xenist in the face. We'll find a civilization that doesn't need to pick at things with patty-paws, evolved beyond it."

"Want to bet?"

"No. Where is this 'Lummox' now?"

Greenberg looked flustered. "Boss, this report I am about to make is now in the microfilm lab. It should be on your desk any minute."

"Okay, so you were on the ball—this time. Let's have it."

"I got chummy with the local judge and asked him to keep me advised. Of course they couldn't throw this critter into the local Bastille; in fact they did not have anything strong enough to hold him . . . so they had learned, the hard way. And nothing could be built in a hurry that would be strong enough . . . believe me, that cage he crushed out of was *strong*. But the local police chief got a brain storm; they had an empty reservoir with sides about thirty feet high, reinforced concrete . . . part of the fire system. So they built a ramp and herded him down into it, then removed the ramp. It looked like a good dodge; the creature isn't built for jumping."

"Sounds okay."

"Yes, but that isn't all. Judge O'Farrell told me that the chief of police was so jittery that he decided not to wait for departmental okay; he went ahead with the execution.

"*What?*"

"Let me finish. He did not tell anybody—but accidentally-on-purpose the intake valve was opened that night and the reservoir filled up. In the morning there was Lummox, on the bottom. So Chief Dreiser assumed that his 'accident' had been successful and that he had drowned the beast."

"So?"

"It did not bother Lummox at all. He had been under water several hours, but when the water drained off, he woke up, stood up, and said, 'Good morning.'"

"Amphibious, probably. What steps have you taken to put a stop to this high-handedness?"

"Just a second, sir. Dreiser knew that firearms and explosives were useless . . . you saw the transcript . . . at least of power safe enough to use inside a town. So he tried poison. Knowing nothing about the creature, he used half a dozen sorts in quantities sufficient for a regiment and concealed in several kinds of food."

"Well?"

"Lummox gobbled them all. They didn't even make him sleepy; in fact it seemed to stimulate his appetite, for the next thing he did was to eat the intake valve and the reservoir started to fill up again. They had to shut it off from the pumping station."

Kiku snickered. "I'm beginning to like this Lummox. Did you say he *ate* the valve? What was it made of?"

"I don't know. The usual alloy, I suppose."

"Hmm . . . seems to like a bit of roughage in its diet. Perhaps it has a craw like a bird."

"I wouldn't be surprised."

"What did the Chief do next?"

"Nothing as yet. I asked O'Farrell to impress on Dreiser that he was likely to end up in a penal colony thirty light-years from Westville if he persisted in bucking the department. So he is waiting and trying to figure out his problem. His latest notion is to cast Lummox in concrete and let him die at his own convenience. But O'Farrell put the nix on that one—inhumane."

"So Lummox is still in the reservoir, waiting for us to act, eh?"

"I believe so, sir. He was yesterday."

"Well, he can wait there, I suppose, until other action can be taken." Mr. Kiku picked up Greenberg's short-form report and recommendation.

Greenberg said, "I take it that you are overruling me, sir?"

"No. What gave you that idea?" He signed the order permitting the destruction of Lummox and let it be swallowed by the outgoing basket. "I don't reverse a man's decision without firing him . . . and I have another job for you."

"Oh." Greenberg felt a twinge of compassion; he had been expecting, with relief, that the chief would reprieve Lummox's death sentence. Well . . . too bad . . . but the beast *was* dangerous.

Mr. Kiku went on, "Are you afraid of snakes?"

"No. I rather like them."

"Excellent! Though it's a feeling I can't imagine. I've always been deathly afraid of them. Once when I was a boy in Africa . . . never mind. Have you ever worked closely with Rargyllians? I don't recall."

Greenberg suddenly understood. "I used a Rargyllian interpreter in the Vega-VI affair. I get along all right with Rargyllians."

"I wish I did. Sergei, I have some business which involves a Rargyllian interpreter, a Dr. Ftaeml. You may have heard of him."

"Yes, of course, sir."

"I'll admit that, as Rargyllians go . . ." He made the noun sound like a swear word. ". . . Ftaeml is all right. But this involvement has the odor of trouble . . . and I find my own nose for trouble blanked out by this phobia of mine. So I'm putting you on as my assistant to sniff for me."

"I thought you didn't trust my nose, boss?"

"We'll let the blind lead the blind, if you'll forgive a

switch in metaphor. Perhaps between us we'll sniff it out."

"Yes, sir. May I ask the nature of the assignment?"

"Well . . ." Before Mr. Kiku could answer, his secretary's light flashed and her voice stated, "Your hypnotherapist is here, sir."

The Under Secretary glanced at his clock and said, "Where does the time go?" . . . then to the communicator: "Put him in my dressing room. I'll be in." He continued to Greenberg, "Ftaeml will be here in thirty minutes. I can't stop to talk, I've got to get braced for it. You'll find what there is . . . little enough! . . . in my 'pending-urgent' file." Mr. Kiku glanced at his incoming basket, which had filled to overflowing while they talked. "It won't take five minutes. Spend the rest of the time clearing up that stack of waste paper. Sign my name and hold anything that you think I must see . . . but it had better be no more than half a dozen items, or I'll send you back to Harvard!"

He got up hurriedly, while making a mental note to tell his secretary, from his dressing room, to note everything that went through in the next half hour and let him see it later . . . he wanted to see how the lad worked. Mr. Kiku was aware that he would die someday and he intended to see to it that Greenberg replaced him. In the meantime life should be as tough for the boy as possible.

The Under Secretary headed for his dressing room, the door ducked aside, contracted behind him; Greenberg was left alone. He was reaching for the pending-urgent file when a paper dropped into the incoming basket just as the light on it blinked red and a buzzer sounded.

He picked up the paper, ran his eye down the middle and had just realized that it really was urgent when a similar light-and-buzzer combination showed at the interoffice communicator and its screen came to life;

Greenberg recognized the chief of the bureau of system liaison. "Boss?" the image said excitedly.

Greenberg touched the two-way switch. "Greenberg here," he answered. "I'm keeping the chief's chair warm for him. Your memo just came in, Stan. I'm reading it."

Ibañez looked annoyed. "Never mind that. Get me the boss."

Greenberg hesitated. Ibañez's problem was simple, but sticky. Ships from Venus were regularly granted pratique without delay, each ship's doctor being a public health deputy. But the *Ariel*, already due at Port Libya, had suddenly been placed under quarantine by her doctor and was now waiting in a parking orbit. The Venerian foreign minister was aboard . . . most unfortunately, as Venus was expected to support Terra's position against Mars in the impending triangular conference.

Greenberg could stall the touchy problem until the boss was free; he could break in on the boss; he could go over the boss's head to the Secretary himself (which meant picking an answer and presenting it so as to get that answer approved); or . . . he could act, using Mr. Kiku's authority.

Mr. Kiku could not have predicted the emergency . . . but the boss had a pesky habit of pushing people off the deep end.

Greenberg's summing up had been quick. He answered, "Sorry, Stan, you can't talk to the boss. I am acting for him."

"Eh? Since when?"

"Just temporarily, but I am."

Ibañez frowned. "Look, chum, you had better find the boss. Maybe you are signing his name on routine matters . . . but this is not routine. We've got to bring that ship down in a hurry. Your neck would be out a yard if you took it upon yourself to authorize me to overlook a basic rule like quarantine. Use your head."

Break quarantine? Greenberg recalled the Great Plague of '51, back in the days when the biologist serenely believed that each planetary life group was immune to the ills of other planets. "We won't break quarantine."

Ibañez looked pained. "Sergei, we can jeopardize this conference . . . 'jeopardize?' What am I saying? We can't toss away ten years' work because some crewman has a slight fever. The quarantine *must* be broken. But I don't expect you to do it."

Greenberg hesitated. "He's under hypnosis, for a tough job coming up. It may be a couple of hours before you can see him."

Ibañez looked blank. "I'll have to tackle the Secretary. I don't dare wait two hours. That sacred cow from Venus is like as not to order his skipper to head home . . . we can't risk that."

"And we can't risk bringing in an epidemic, either. Here's what you do. Call him and tell him you are coming to get him in person. Use a fast scout. Get him aboard and leave the *Ariel* in quarantine orbit. Once you get him aboard the scout . . . and not before . . . tell him that both you and he will attend the conference in isolation suits." The isolation suit was a sealed pressure suit; its primary use was to visit planets whose disease hazards had not yet been learned. "The scout ship and crew will have to go into quarantine, too, of course."

"Isolation suit! Oh, he'll love that. Sergei, it would be less damaging to call off the conference. An indignity like that would put him against us for certain. The jerk is poisonously proud."

"Sure he'll love it," Greenberg explained, "once you suggest how to play it. 'Great personal self-sacrifice' . . . 'unwilling to risk the welfare of our beloved sister planet' . . . 'the call of duty takes precedence over any et cetera.' If you don't feel sure of it, take one of the public relations boys along. And look, all through the conference he must be attended by a physician . . . in a white suit . . . and a couple of nurses. The conference must stop every now and then while he rests . . . put a cot and hospital screens in the Hall of Heroes near the conference table. The idea is that he's come down with it himself but is carrying on as his dying act. Get it? Tell him before you land the scout ship . . . indirectly, of course."

Ibañez looked perturbed. "Do you think that will work?"

"It's up to you to make it work. I'm sending down your memo, ordering quarantine to continue but telling you to use your initiative to insure his presence at the conference."

"Well . . . all right." Ibañez suddenly grinned. "Never mind the memo. I'm on my way." He switched off.

Greenberg turned back to the desk, feeling exhilarated by the sensation of playing God. He wondered what the boss would have done? . . . but did not care. There might be many correct solutions, but this was one; it felt right. He reached again for the pending-urgent file.

He stopped. Something was gnawing at the back of his mind. The boss had not wanted to approve that death sentence; he had felt it. Shucks, the boss had *told* him that he was wrong; the proper action was a full investigation. But the boss, as a matter of loyalty to his subordinates, had not reversed him.

But he himself was sitting in the boss's chair at the moment. Well?

Was that why the boss had placed him there? To let him correct his own mistake? No, the boss was subtle but not omniscient; he could not have predicted that Greenberg would consider reopening the matter.

Still . . . He called the boss's private secretary. "Mildred?"

"Yes, Mr. Greenberg?"

"That brief-and-rec on that intervention I carried out . . . Rt0411, it was. It went out fifteen minutes ago. I want it back."

"It may have been dispatched," she said doubtfully. "The communications desk has been running only about seven minutes behind demand today."

"There is such a thing as too much efficiency. If the order has left the building, send a cancellation and a more-to-follow, will you? And get the original document back to me."

Finally he got to the pending-urgent file. As Mr. Kiku had said, the jacket marked "Ftaeml" was not large. He found it subtitled: "Beauty & the Beast" and wondered why. The boss had a sense of humor . . . but it veered so much that other people had a hard time following it.

Presently his eyebrows lifted. Those tireless interpreters, brokers, go-betweens, and expounders, the Rargyllians, were always popping up in negotiations between diverse races; the presence of Dr. Ftaeml on Earth had tipped Greenberg that something was up with a non-humanoid people . . . non-human in mentality, creatures so different psychologically that communication was difficult. But he had not expected the learned doctor was representing a race that he had never heard of . . . something termed "the *Hroshii*."

It was possible that Greenberg had simply forgotten these people with a name like a sneeze; they might be some unimportant breed, at a low cultural level, or economically inconsequential, or not possessing space travel. Or they might have been brought into the Community of Civilizations while Greenberg had been up to his ears in Solar System affairs. Once the human race had made contact with other races having interstellar travel the additions to the family of legal "humans" had come so fast that a man could hardly keep up; the more mankind widened its horizons the harder those horizons were to see.

Or perhaps he knew of the Hroshii under another name? Greenberg turned to Mr. Kiku's universal dictionary and keyed in the name.

The machine considered it, then the reading plate flashed: NO INFORMATION.

Greenberg tried dropping the aspirate on the assumption that the word might have degenerated in the mouths of non-Hroshii . . . still the same negative.

He dropped the matter. The universal dictionary in the British Museum was not more knowledgeable than the one in the Under Secretary's office; its working parts occupied an entire building in another part of Capital, and a staff of cyberneticists, semanticians and encyclopedists endlessly fed its hunger for facts. He could be sure that, whatever the "Hroshii" were, the Federation had never heard of them before.

Which was astounding.

Having let astonishment persist a full second Greenberg went on reading. He learned that the Hroshii were already here, not landed on Earth but within waving distance . . . in a parking orbit fifty thousand miles out. He let himself be astonished for two whole seconds before going on to discover that the reason he had not heard of their advent was that Dr. Ftaeml had urgently advised Mr. Kiku to keep patrol ships and such from challenging and attempting to board the stranger.

He was interrupted by the return of his report of the Lummox matter, bearing on it Mr. Kiku's confirmation of the sentence. He thought for a moment, then added to the endorsement so that it read: "Recommendation approved . . . but this action is not to be carried out until after a complete scientific analysis of this creature has been made. Local authorities will surrender custody when required to the Bureau of Xenic Science, which will arrange transportation and select the agency to pursue the evaluation."

Greenberg signed Kiku's name to the change and put it back into the system. He admitted sheepishly that the order was now weasel-worded . . . for it was a sure thing that once the xenobiologists got their hands on Lummox they would never let him go. Nevertheless his heart felt suddenly lighter. The other action was wrong; this one was *right*.

He turned his attention back to the Hroshii . . . and again his eyebrows went up. The Hroshii were not here to establish relations with Earth; they were here to rescue one of their own. According to Dr. Ftaeml, they were convinced that Terra was holding this Hroshia and were demanding that she be surrendered.

Greenberg felt as if he had blundered into a bad melodrama. These people with the asthmatic name had picked the wrong planet for cops-and-robbers nonsense. A non-human on Earth without a passport, without a dossier in the hands of the department, without an approved reason for visiting Earth, would be as helpless as a bride without a ration book. She would be picked up in no time . . . idiot's delight! she could not even get through quarantine.

Why didn't the boss simply tell them to take their wagon and go home?

Besides, how did they figure she had reached the surface of Earth? Walked? Or taken a swan dive? Star ships did not land; they were served by shuttles. He could just see her tackling the purser of one of those shuttles: "Excuse me, sir, but I am fleeing from my husband in a distant part of the Galaxy. Do you mind if I hide under this seat and sneak down to your planet?"

"No tickee, no washee" . . . that's what the purser would say. Those shuttle companies hated deadheads; Greenberg could feel it every time he presented his own diplomatic pass.

Something was niggling at him . . . then he remembered the boss's inquiry; did Lummox have hands? He realized that the boss must have been wondering whether Lummox could be the missing Hroshia, since Hroshii, according to Ftaeml, had eight legs. Greenberg chuckled. Lummox was not the boy to build and operate star ships, not he nor any of his cousins. Of course the boss had not seen Lummox and did not know how preposterous it was.

And besides that, Lummox had been here more than a hundred years. That would make him very late for supper.

The real question was what to do with the Hroshii now that we were in contact with them. Anything from "Out There" was interesting, educational, and profitable to mankind, once it was analyzed . . . and a race that had its own interstellar drive was sure to be all of that, squared and cubed. No doubt the boss was kidding them along while developing permanent relations. Very well, it was up to Greenberg to foster that angle and help the boss get past his emotional handicap in dealing through a Rargyllian.

He skimmed the rest of the report. What he had learned so far he had gotten from the synopsis; the rest was a transcript of Ftaeml's flowery circumlocutions. Then he handed the jacket back to the file and tackled the boss's work.

Mr. Kiku announced himself by looking over his shoulder and saying, "That basket is as full as ever."

"Oh. Howdy, boss. Yes, but think of the shape it would have been in if I hadn't torn up every second item without reading it." Greenberg moved from the chair.

Mr. Kiku nodded. "I know. Sometimes I just check 'disapproved' on all the odd-numbered ones."

"Feeling better?"

"Ready to spit in his face. What's a snake got that I haven't got more of?"

"That's the spirit."

"Dr. Morgan is very adept. Try him sometime if your nerves ever act up."

Greenberg grinned. "Boss, the only thing that bothers me is insomnia during working hours. I can't sleep at my desk the way I used to."

"That's the earliest symptom. The mind mechanics will get you yet." Mr. Kiku glanced at the clock. "No word from our friend with the animated hair?"

"Not yet." Greenberg told about the quarantine for the *Ariel* and what he had done. Mr. Kiku nodded, which was equivalent to a citation in front of the regiment in some circles; Greenberg felt a warm glow and went on to tell about the revision in the order for Lummox. He sidled up to it self-consciously.

"Boss, sitting in that chair puts a different slant on things."

"So I discovered, years ago."

"Um, yes. While I was there I got to thinking about that intervention matter."

"Why? We settled it."

"So I thought. Nevertheless . . . well, anyhow . . ." He blurted out his change in the order and waited.

Mr. Kiku nodded again. He considered telling Greenberg that it had saved him thinking up a face-saving way of accomplishing the same end, but decided not to. Instead he leaned to his desk. "Mildred? Heard anything from Dr. Ftaeml?"

"Just arrived, sir."

"Good. East conference room, please." He switched off and turned to Greenberg. "Well, son, now for some snake charming. Got your flute with you?"

VI

"Space Is Deep, Excellency"

"DR. FTAEML, this is my associate, Mr. Greenberg." The Rargyllian bowed low, his double knees and unhuman articulation making it an impressive rite. "I know the distinguished Mr. Greenberg by reputation, through a compatriot who was privileged to work with him. I am honored, sir."

Greenberg answered with the same sort of polite amphigory the cosmic linguist had selected. "I have long wished for the boon of experiencing in person the scholarly aura of Dr. Ftaeml, but I had never dared let the wish blossom into hope. Your servant and pupil, sir."

"Hrrump!" Mr. Kiku interrupted. "Doctor, this delicate affair you are negotiating is of such importance that I, with my constant housekeeping chores, have not been able to give it the close attention it demands. Mr. Greenberg is ambassador extraordinary and minister plenipotentiary of the Federation, commanded for this purpose."

Greenberg's eyes flicked toward his boss, but showed no surprise. He had noticed that the boss had earlier said "associate" rather than "assistant" and had spotted it as the elementary maneuver of enhancing the prestige of one's own negotiators for advantage in protocol—but he had not expected this sudden brevet. He was reasonably sure that Mr. Kiku had not bothered to have the rank approved by the Council; nevertheless the boss could make it stick and his credentials would probably show up on his desk. He wondered if his pay check would show it?

He decided that the boss must have a hunch that this

silly business had importance not evident. Or was he simply getting the medusoid off his back?

Dr. Ftaeml bowed again. "Most gratifying to work with his excellency." Greenberg suspected that the Rargyllian was not fooled; nevertheless it probably was really gratifying to him, since it implied that the medusoid was himself of ambassadorial rank.

A female aide brought in refreshments; they stopped for ritual. Ftaeml selected a French wine, while Greenberg and Kiku chose, by Hobson's choice, the only Rargyllian item available—some stuff called "wine" through failure of language but which looked like bread mushed into milk and tasted as if sulphuric acid had been added. Greenberg went throug the motions of enjoying it while not letting it pass his lips.

He noticed with respect that the boss actually consumed the stuff.

The rite common to seven out of ten civilizations gave Greenberg time to size up Ftaeml. The medusoid was dressed in an expensive parody of terrestrial formal clothes . . . cutaway jacket, lacy jabot, and striped shorts. It helped to hide the fact that, while he was a bifurcate humanoid with two legs, two arms, and head at the top of an elongated trunk, he was not remotely human in any but the legal sense.

But Greenberg had grown up in the presence of the Great Martians and had dealt with many other peoples since; he did not expect "men" to look like men and had no prejudice in favor of human form. Ftaeml was, to his eye, handsome and certainly graceful. His dry chitinous skin, purple with green highlights, was as neat as a leopard's pelt and as decorative. The absence of a nose was no matter and was made up for by the mobile, sensitive mouth.

Greenberg decided that Ftaeml must have his tail wrapped around him under his clothes in order to carry out the pretense that he looked like a terrestrial as well as being dressed like one—Rargyllians would go to any trouble to conform to the ancient, urbane rule that when in Rome, one should shoot Roman candles. The other Rargyllian Greenberg had worked with had worn no clothes at all (since the people of Vega-VI wore none) and had carried his tail aloft, like a proud cat. Thinking of Vega-VI made Greenberg shiver, he had found it necessary to bundle up to his ears.

He glanced at the medusoid's tendrils. Pshaw! they weren't snakelike. The boss must have a neurosis as big as a house. Sure, they were about a foot long and as thick as his thumb, but they didn't have eyes, they didn't have mouths or teeth—they were just tendrils. Most races had tendrils of some sort. What were fingers but short tendrils?

Mr. Kiku put down his cup when Dr. Ftaeml set down his glass. "Doctor, you have consulted with your principals?"

"Sir, I have had that honor. And may I take this opportunity to thank you for the scout ship you so graciously placed at my disposal for the unavoidable trips back and forth from the surface of your lovely planet to the vessel of the people I have the privilege of assisting? It is, I may say without casting any reflections on the great people I now serve, more suited to the purpose and more comfortable to one of my build than are the auxiliary craft of their vessel."

"Not at all. Glad to do a favor to a friend."

"You are gracious, Mr. Under Secretary."

"Well, what did they say?"

Dr. Ftaeml shrugged his whole body. "It pains me to inform you that they are unmoved. They insist that their she child be returned to them without delay."

Mr. Kiku frowned. "No doubt you explained that we don't have their missing child, have never heard of it, have no reason to think that she has ever been on this planet and strong reason to believe that she never could have been?"

"I did. You will pardon my inurbanity if I translate their answer in terms crude but unmistakable." He shrugged apologetically. "They say you are lying."

Mr. Kiku took no offense, being aware that a Rargyllian when acting as go-between was as impersonal as a telephone. "It would be better if I *were* lying. Then I could hand over their brat and the matter would be finished."

"*I* believe you," Dr. Ftaeml said suddenly.

"Thank you. Why?"

"You used the subjunctive."

"Oh. Did you tell them that there were over seven thousand varieties of non-terrestrial creatures on Earth, represented by some hundreds of thousands of individuals? That of these individuals some thirty thousand are sentient beings? But of these sentient beings only a very few have anything like the physical characteristics of your Hroshii? And that all those few we can account for as to race and planet of origin?"

"I am Rargyllian, sir. I told them all that and more, in their own language, putting it more clearly than you could explain it to another Earthmen. I made it live."

"I believe you." Mr. Kiku tapped the table top. "Do you have a suggestion?"

"Just a moment," put in Greenberg. "Don't you have a picture of a typical Hroshii? It might help."

" 'Hroshiu,' " corrected Ftaeml. "Or, in this case, 'Hroshia.' I am sorry. They do not use symbology of the picture type. Unfortunately I am not equipped to take one of your pictures."

"An eyeless race?"

"No, Excellency. Their sight is quite good, quite subtle. But their eyes and nervous systems abstract somewhat differently from yours. Their analog of 'picture' would be meaningless to you. Even I find it difficult and my race is admitted to be the most subtle of all in the interpretation of symbolic abstraction. If a Rargyllian . . ." He stopped and preened himself.

"Well . . . describe one to us. Use your justly famed semantic talents."

"A pleasure. The Hroshii manning this vessel are all about of a size, being of the military class . . ."

Mr. Kiku interrupted. "Military class? Doctor, is this a war vessel? You did not tell me this."

Dr. Ftaeml looked pained. "I considered the fact both obvious and distasteful."

"I suppose so." Mr. Kiku wondered if he should alert the Federation General Staff. Not now, he decided. Mr. Kiku was strongly prejudiced against the introduction of military might into negotiations, since he believed that a show of force not only was an admission of failure on the part of diplomats but also poisoned the chances of accomplishing anything more by negotiation. He could rationalize this opinion but he held it as an emotion. "Go on, please."

"The military class are of three sexes, the differences in the types being not readily apparent and need not concern us. My shipmates and hosts are perhaps six inches higher than this table and half again your height in length. Each has four pairs of legs and two arms. Their hands are small and supple and extremely dexterous. In my opinion the Hroshii are unusually beautiful, form serving function with rare grace. They are remarkably adroit with machines, instruments, and delicate manipulations of every sort."

Greenberg relaxed a little as Ftaeml talked. Despite everything, the vagrant notion had still been bothering him that this creature "Lummox" might be of the Hroshii . . . but he saw now that the thought came from nothing more than accidental similarity in leg number . . . as if an ostrich were a man because of two legs! His mind wanted to file Lummox into a category and no doubt would keep on trying, but this category did not fit.

Dr. Ftaeml was continuing: ". . . but the outstanding characteristic of the Hroshii, not covered by these mere facts of size, shape, body structure, and mechanical function, is an overwhelming impression of great mental power. So overwhelming, in fact . . ." The medusoid chuckled in embarrassment. ". . . that I was almost persuaded to waive my professional fee and serve them as a privilege."

Greenberg was impressed. These Hroshii really must have something; the Rargyllians, honest brokers though they were, would let a man die of thirst rather than tell him the local word for water, unless cash was in hand. Their mercenary attitude had the quality of devoutness.

"The only thing," Ftaeml added, "that saved me from this excess was the knowledge that in one thing I excelled them. They are not linguists. Rich and powerful as their own speech is, it is the only language they ever learn well. They are even less talented linguistically than is your own race." Ftaeml spread his grotesque hands in a gesture that was purely Gallic (or a perfect, studied imitation) and added, "So I repaired my self-esteem and charged twice my usual fee."

He ceased talking. Mr. Kiku stared glumly at the table and Greenberg merely waited. Finally Kiku said, "What do you suggest?"

"My esteemed friend, there is only one course that is of any use. The Hroshia they seek must be delivered up."

"But we do not have this Hroshia."

Ftaeml simulated a human sigh. "That is regrettable." Greenberg looked at him sharply; the sigh did not carry conviction. He felt that Ftaeml regarded the impasse as somehow tremendously exciting . . . which was ridiculous; a Rargyllian, having accepted the role of go-between, was invariably anxious that the negotiation be successful; anything less than success caused them to lose face in their own eyes.

So he spoke up. "Dr. Ftaeml, when you undertook this commission for the Hroshii, did you expect that we would be able to produce this, uh, Hroshia?"

The creature's tendrils suddenly slumped; Greenberg cocked an eyebrow and said drily, "No, I see that you did not. May I ask why, then, you accepted this commission?"

Ftaeml answered slowly and without his usual confidence: "Sir, one does not refuse a commission of the Hroshii. Believe me, one does not."

"Hmm . . . these Hroshii. Doctor, will you pardon me if I say that you have not yet conveyed to me a full understanding of these people? You tell us that they are mentally very powerful, so much so that a leading mind of a highly-advanced race . . . yourself . . . is almost 'overwhelmed' by them. You imply that they are powerful in other ways . . . that you, a member of a proud, free race, must obey their wishes. Now here they are in a single ship, facing an entire planet, a planet so powerful that it has been able to create hegemony more extensive than any before in this portion of space . . . yet you say that it would be 're-grettable' if we were not to satisfy their impossible demand."

"All that is true," Ftaeml answered carefully.

"When a Rargyllian speaks professionally I cannot disbelieve him. Yet this I have trouble believing. These superbeings . . . why have we never heard of them?"

"Space is deep, Excellency."

"Yes, yes. No doubt there are thousands of great races that we of Earth have never met, will never meet. Am I to infer that this is also the first contact of your race with the Hroshii?"

"No. We have long known of them . . . longer than we have known of you."

"Eh?" Greenberg glanced sharply at Mr. Kiku. He went on, "What are the relations of Rargyll with the Hroshii? And why has not this been reported to the Federation?"

"Excellency, is that last question a rebuke? If so, I must answer that I am not acting for my government."

"No," Greenberg assured him, "it was a simple inquiry. The Federation always seeks to extend its diplomatic linkage as far as possible. I was surprised to learn that your race, which claims friendship with ours, could know of a mighty civilization and not make that fact known to the Federation."

"May I say, Excellency, that I am surprised at your surprise? Space is deep . . . and my race have long been great travelers. Perhaps the Federation has not asked the right questions? As for the other, my people have no diplomatic relations, no relations of any sort, with the mighty Hroshii. They are a people who, as you say, mind their own business, and we are very happy to (as you would phrase it) . . . to stay out of their yard. It has been years, more than five of your centuries, since the last time a Hroshij ship appeared in our skies and demanded service from us. It is better so."

Greenberg said, "I seem to be getting more confused the more I know. They stopped at Rargyll to pick up an interpreter instead of coming straight here?"

"Not precisely. They appeared in our skies and asked if we had ever heard of you people. We answered that we knew you . . . for when the Hroshii ask, they are answered! We identified your star and I had the unsought honor to be chosen to represent them." He shrugged. "Here I am. Let me add that it was not until we were deep in space that I learned the object of their search."

Greenberg had made note earlier of a loose end. "Just a moment. They retained you, they started for

Earth, then told you that they were searching for a missing Hroshia. It must have been then that you decided that this mission would fail. Why?"

"Is it not evident? We Rargyllians, in your lovely and precise idiom, are the greatest gossips in space. Perhaps you would say 'historians'. but I mean something more lively than that. Gossips. We go everywhere, we know everyone, we speak all languages. I did not need to 'check the files' to know that men of Earth had never been to the capital planet of the Hroshii. Had you made such contact you would have forced your attentions on them and started a war. It would have been a 'scandal to the jaybirds' . . . a lovely phrase, that; I must see a jaybird while I am here. It would have been discussed with many a fine anecdote wherever two Rargyllians got together. So I knew that they must be mistaken; they would not find what they sought."

"In other words," Greenberg answered, "you people identified the wrong planet . . . and wished this problem on us."

"Please," protested Dr. Ftaeml. "Our identification was perfect, I assure you—not of your planet, for the Hroshii did not know where you came from—but of you yourself. The creatures they wished to locate were men of Earth, in every possible detail—down to your fingernails, your internal organs."

"Yet you knew they were mistaken. Doctor, I am not the semantician you are. I seem to see a contradiction . . . or a paradox."

"Permit me to explain. We who deal professionally in words know how cheap words are. A paradox can exist only in words, never in the facts behind the words. Since the Hroshii described exactly the men of Earth and since I knew that the men of Earth knew not the Hroshii, I concluded what I must conclude—that there is another race in this galaxy as like to your race as twin Sornia in their shell—as two peas in the pod. Peas? You like beans better?"

" 'Peas' is the correct idiom," Mr. Kiku answered soberly.

"Thank you. Your language is rich; I must refresh myself of it while I am here. Would you believe it? . . . the man from whom I first learned it intentionally taught me idioms unacceptable in your polite society. For example 'as cold as . . .' "

"Yes, yes," Mr. Kiku said hastily. "I can believe it. Some of our compatriots have an odd sense of humor. You concluded that there is somewhere in this star cloud a race so like ours as to be our twin brothers? I find that notion statistically unlikely to the point of impossibility."

"The entire universe, Mr. Under Secretary, is wildly unlikely to the point of ridiculousness. Therefore, we of Rargyll know that God is a humorist." The medusoid made a gesture peculiar to his breed, then politely repeated it in idiom by making one of the most common Earthly gestures of reverence.

"You explained this conclusion to your clients?"

"I did . . . and I repeated it most carefully in my lastest consultation. The result was foreseeable."

"Yes?"

"Each race has its talent, each its weakness. The Hroshii, once having with mighty intellect arrived at an opinion, are not easily swayed. 'Pig-headed' is your precise term."

"Pig-headedness breeds pig-headedness, Dr. Ftaeml."

"Please, my dear sir! I hope that you will not be so tempted. Let me report, if I must, that you have been unable to find their treasured one, but that you are instituting new and more thorough searches. I am your friend . . . do not admit that this negotiation has failed."

"I never broke off a negotiation in my life," Mr. Kiku

answered sourly. "If you can't outargue the other fellow, sometimes you can outlive him. But I do not see what more we have to offer them. Except for that one possibility we spoke of last time . . . did you bring the coordinates of their planet? Or did they refuse?"

"I have them. I told you that they would not refuse; the Hroshii are not in the least afraid of having other races know where to find them . . . they are merely indifferent." Dr. Ftaeml opened a brief case which was either an imitation of a terrestrial one, or might have been purchased on Earth. "Nevertheless it was not easy. The where-and-when had to be translated from their concepts to those using Rargyll as the true center of the universe, for which purpose it required that I first convince them of the necessity, then explain to them spacetime units as used on Rargyll. Now, since I must shame myself by admitting that I am not skilled in your methods of reckoning the shape of the universe, it is necessary that I have help in translating our figures into yours."

"No need to feel shamefaced," Mr. Kiku answered, "for I don't know anything about our astrogation methods myself. We use specialists for that sort of thing. Just a moment." He touched an ornamental knob on the conference table. "Get me BuAstro."

"They've all gone home for the day," a disembodied female voice answered, "except the astrogation duty officer."

"Then that's who I want. Hurry it up."

Very shortly a male voice said, "Dr. Warner, night duty officer."

"Kiku here. Doctor, you solve space-time correlations?"

"Of course, sir."

"Can you do it from Rargyllian data?"

"Rargyllian?" The duty officer whistled softly. "That's a tough one, sir. Dr. Singh is the man for that."

"Get him up here, right away."

"Uh, why, he's gone home, sir. He'll be here in the morning."

"I didn't ask where he was; I said, 'Get him up here . . . right away.' Use police alarm and general call, if necessary. I want him *now*."

"Er . . . yes, sir."

Mr. Kiku turned back to Dr. Ftaeml. "I expect to be able to show that no terrestrial starship ever visited the Hroshii. Fortunately we do have astrogation records for every interstellar trip. My thought is this: it is time that the principals met face to face in this negotiation. With your skillful interpretation we can show them that we have nothing to hide, that the facilities of our civilization are at their disposal, and that we would like to help them find their missing sibling . . . but that she is not here. Then, if they have any thing to suggest, we will . . ." Mr. Kiku broke off as a door at the end of the room opened. He said tonelessly, "How do you do, Mr. Secretary?"

The Most Honorable Mr. Roy MacClure, Secretary for Spatial Affairs for the Federated Community of Civilizations, was entering. His eye seemed to light only on Mr. Kiku. "There you are, Henry! Been looking all over. That stupid girl didn't know where you had gone, but I found that you had not left the building. You must . . ."

Mr. Kiku took him firmly by the elbow and said loudly, "Mr. Secretary, allow me to present Dr. Ftaeml, Ambassador *de facto* of the mighty Hroshii."

Mr. MacClure met the occasion. "How do you do, Doctor? Or should I say 'Excellency'?" He had the grace not to stare.

" 'Doctor' will do nicely, Mr. Secretary. I am well, thank you. May I enquire as to your health?"

"Oh, good enough, good enough . . . if everything didn't pop at once. Which reminds me . . . can you spare me my chief assistant? I'm awfully sorry but something urgent has come up."

"Certainly, Mr. Secretary. Your pleasure is my greatest wish."

Mr. MacClure looked sharply at the medusoid but found himself unable to read his expression . . . if the thing had expressions, he amended. "Uh, I trust you are being well taken care of, Doctor?"

"Yes, thank you."

"Good. I really am sorry, but . . . Henry, if you please?"

Mr. Kiku bowed to the Rargyllian, then left the table while wearing an expression so masklike that Greenberg shivered. Kiku spoke in a whisper to MacClure as soon as they were away from the table.

MacClure glanced back at the other two, then answered in a whisper that Greenberg could catch. "Yes, yes! But this is crucially important, I tell you. Henry, what in the world possessed you to ground those ships without consulting me first?"

Mr. Kiku's reply was inaudible. MacClure went on, "Nonsense! Well, you will just have to come out and face them. You can't . . ."

Mr. Kiku turned back abruptly. "Dr. Ftaeml, was it your intention to return to the Hroshii ship tonight?"

"There is no hurry. I am at your service, sir."

"You are most gracious. May I leave you in Mr. Greenberg's care? We speak as one."

The Rargyllian bowed. "I shall count it an honor."

"I look forward to the pleasure of your company tomorrow."

Dr. Ftaeml bowed again. "Until tomorrow. Mr. Secretary, Mr. Under Secretary . . . your servant."

The two left. Greenberg did not know whether to laugh or cry; he felt embarrassed for his whole race. The medusoid was watching him silently.

Greenberg grinned with half his mouth and said,

"Doctor, does the Rargyllian tongue include swear words?"

"Sir, I can use profanity in more than a thousand tongues . . . some having curses that will addle an egg at a thousand paces. May I teach you some of them?"

Greenberg sat back and laughed heartily. "Doctor, I like you. I really like you . . . quite aside from our mutual professional duty to be civil."

Ftaeml shaped his lips in a good imitation of a human smile. "Thank you, sir. The feeling is mutual . . . and gratifying. May I say without offense that the reception given my sort on your great planet is sometimes something that one must be philosophical about?"

"I know. I'm sorry. My own people, most of them, are honestly convinced that the prejudices of their native village were ordained by the Almighty. I wish it were different."

"You need not be ashamed. Believe me, sir, that is the one conviction which is shared by all races everywhere . . . the only thing we all have in common. I do not except my own race. If you knew languages . . . All languages carry in them a portrait of their users and the idioms of every language say over and over again, 'He is a stranger and therefore a barbarian.'"

Greenberg grinned wryly. "Discouraging, isn't it?"

"Discouraging? Why, sir? It is sidesplitting. It is the only joke that God ever repeats, because its humor never grows stale." The medusoid added, "What is your wish, sir? Are we to continue to explore this matter? Or is your purpose merely to stetch the palaver until the return of your . . . associate?"

Greenberg knew that the Rargyllian was saying as politely as possible that Greenberg could not act without Kiku. Greenberg decided that there was no sense in pretending otherwise . . . and besides, he was hungry. "Haven't we worked enough today, Doctor? Would you do me the honor of having dinner with me?"

"I would be delighted! But . . . you know our peculiarities of diet?"

"Certainly. Remember, I spent some weeks with one of your compatriots. We can go to the Hotel Universal."

"Yes, of course." Dr. Ftaeml seemed unenthusiastic.

"Unless there is something you would like better?"

"I have heard of your restaurants with entertainment . . . would it be possible? Or is it . . . ?"

"A night club?" Greenberg thought. "Yes! The Club Cosmic. Their kitchen can do anything the Universal can."

They were about to leave when a door dilated and a slender, swarthy man stuck his head in. "Oh. Excuse me. I thought Mr. Kiku was here."

Greenberg remembered suddenly that the boss had summoned a relativity mathematician. "Just a moment. You must be Dr. Singh."

"Yes."

"Sorry. Mr. Kiku had to leave, I am here for him."

He introduced the two and explained the problem. Dr. Singh looked over the Rargyllian's scroll and nodded. "This will take a while."

"May I help you, Doctor?" asked Ftaeml.

"It won't be necessary. Your notes are quite complete." Thus assured, Greenberg and Ftaeml went out on the town.

The floor show at the Club Cosmic included a juggler, which delighted Ftaeml, and girls, which delighted Greenberg. It was late by the time Greenberg left Ftaeml in one of the special suites reserved for non-human guests of DepSpace at Hotel Universal. Greenberg was yawning as he came down the lift, but decided that the evening had been worth while in the interest of good foreign relations.

Tired though he was, he stopped by the department. Dr. Ftaeml had spilled one item during the evening that he thought the boss should know . . . tonight if he could reach him, or leave it on his desk if not. The Rargyllian, in an excess of pleasure over the juggler, had expressed regret that such things must so soon cease to be.

"What do you mean?" Greenberg had asked.

"When mighty Earth is volatilized . . ." the medusoid had begun, then stopped.

Greenberg had pressed him about it. But the Rargyllian insisted that he had been joking.

Greenberg doubted if it meant anything. But Rargyllian humor was usually much more subtle; he decided to tell the boss about it as quickly as possible. Maybe that strange ship needed a shot of paralysis frequencies, a "nutcracker" bomb, and a dose of vacuum.

The night guard at the door stopped him. "Mr. Greenberg . . . the Under Secretary has been looking for you for the past half hour."

He thanked the guard and hurried upstairs. Mr. Kiku he found bent over his desk; the incoming basket was clogged as always but the Under Secretary was paying no attention. He glanced up and said quietly, "Good evening, Sergei. Look at this." He passed over a report.

It was Dr. Singh's rework of Dr. Ftaeml's notes. Greenberg picked out at the bottom the geocentric coordinates and did a quick sum. "Over nine hundred light-years!" he commented. "And out in *that* direction, too. No wonder we've never encountered them. Not exactly next door neighbors, eh?"

"Never mind that," Mr. Kiku admonished. "Not the date. This computation is the Hroshii's claim as to when and where they were visited by one of our ships."

Greenberg looked and felt his eyebrows crawl up toward his scalp. He turned to the answer machine and started to code an inquiry. "Don't bother," Kiku told him. "Your recollection is correct. The *Trail Blazer*. Second trip."

"The *Trail Blazer*," Greenberg repeated foolishly.

"Yes. We never knew where she went, so we couldn't have guessed. But we know exactly *when* she went. It matches. Much simpler hypothesis than Dr. Ftaeml's twin races."

"Of course." He looked at his boss. "Then it is—Lummox."

"Yes, it's Lummox."

"But it *can't* be Lummox. No hands. Stupid as a rabbit."

"No, it can't be. But it is."

VII

"Mother Knows Best"

LUMMOX was not in the reservoir. He had got tired and had gone home. It had been necessary to tear a notch in the reservoir to get out comfortably, but he had damaged it no more than was needful. He did not care to have any arguments with John Thomas over such silly matters—not any more arguments, that is.

Several people made a fuss over his leaving, but he ignored them. He was careful not to step on anybody and their actions he treated with dignified reserve. Even when they turned loose hated spray things on him he did not let them herd him thereby, the way they had herded him out of that big building the day he had gone for a walk; he simply closed his eyes and his rows of nostrils, put his head down and slogged for home.

John Thomas met him on the way, having been fetched by the somewhat hysterical chief of safety.

Lummox stopped and made a saddle for John Thomas, after mutual greetings and reassurances, then resumed his steady march homeward.

Chief Dreiser was almost incoherent. "Turn that brute around and head him back!" he screamed.

"You do it," Johnnie advised grimly.

"I'll have your hide for this! I'll—I'll—"

"What have I done?"

"You— It's what you haven't done. That beast broke out and—"

"I wasn't even there," John Thomas pointed out while Lummox continued plodding.

"Yes, but . . . That's got nothing to do with it! He's out now; it's up to you to assist the law and get him penned up again. John Stuart, you're getting in serious trouble."

"I don't see how you figure. You took him away from me. You got him condemned and you say he doesn't belong to me any longer. You tried to kill him . . . you know you did, without waiting to see if the government would okay it. If he belongs to me, I ought to sue you. If he doesn't belong to me, it's no skin off my nose if Lummox climbs out of that silly tank." John Thomas leaned over and looked down. "Why don't you climb into your car, Chief, instead of running along beside us and getting yourself winded?"

Chief Dreiser ungraciously accepted the advice and let his driver pick him up. By the time this was done he had somewhat recovered his balance. He leaned out and said, "John Stuart, I won't bandy words with you. What I have or have not done hasn't anything to do with the case. Citizens are required to assist peace officers when necessary. I am demanding officially—and I've got this car's recorder going while I ask it—that you assist me in returning that beast to the reservoir."

John Thomas looked innocent. "Then can I go home?"

"Huh? Of course."

"Thanks, Chief. Uh, how long do you figure he will stay in the reservoir after I put him in it and go home? Or were you planning on hiring me in as a permanent member of your police force?"

Chief Dreiser gave up; Lummox went home.

Nevertheless Dreiser regarded it as only a temporary setback; the stubbornness that made him a good police officer did not desert him. He admitted to himself that the public was probably safer with the beast penned up at home while he figured out a surefire way to kill him. The order from the Under Secretary for Spatial Affairs, permitting him to destroy Lummox arrived and that made Dreiser feel better . . . old Judge O'Farrell had been pretty sarcastic about his jumping the gun.

The cancellation of that order and the amended order postponing Lummox's death indefinitely never reached him. A new clerk in the communications office of DepSpace made a slight error, simply a transposition of two symbols; the cancellation went to Pluto . . . and the amended order, being keyed to the cancellation, followed it.

So Dreiser sat in his office with the death order clutched in his hand and thought about ways to kill the beast. Electrocution? Maybe . . . but he could not even guess at how much of a jolt it would take to do it. Cut his throat like butchering a hog? The Chief had serious doubts about what sort of knife to use and what the brute would be doing in the meantime.

Firearms and explosives were no good. Wait a minute! Get the monster to open its mouth, wide, then shoot straight down its throat, using an explosive charge that would blow his innards to bits. Kill him instantly—yes, sir! Lots of animals had armor—turtles, rhinos, armadillos, and things—but always outside, not inside. This brute was no exception; Chief Dreiser had had several looks down inside that big mouth the time he had tried poison. The beast might be armor plate outside; inside he was pink and moist and soft like everybody else.

Not let's see; he'd have the Stuart boy tell the brute to hold its mouth open and . . . no, that wouldn't do. The boy would see what was up and like as not would order the beast to charge . . . and then some cops' widows would draw pensions. That boy was going bad, no doubt of it . . . funny how a good boy could take a wrong turn and wind up in prison.

No, the thing to do was to get the kid downtown on some excuse and carry out the order while he wasn't around. They could entice the brute into saying "ah!" by offering him food . . . "tossing it to him," Dreiser amended.

He glanced at his clock. Today? No, he wanted to choose the weapon and then rehearse everybody so that it would go like clockwork. Tomorrow early . . . better have the boy picked up right after breakfast.

Lummox seemed contented to be home, ready to let bygones be bygones. He never said a word about Chief Dreiser and, if he realized that anyone had tried to harm him, he did not mention it. His naturally sunny disposition displayed itself by wanting to put his head in Johnnie's lap for cuddling. It had been a long time since his head was small enough for this; he merely placed the end of his muzzle on the boy's thigh, carrying the weight himself, while Johnnie stroked his nose with a brickbat.

Johnnie was happy only on one side. With the return of Lummox he felt much better, but he knew that nothing had been settled; presently Chief Dreiser would again try to kill Lummox. What to do about it was an endless ache in his middle.

His mother had added to his unhappiness by raising a loud squawk when she saw "that beast!" returned to the Stuart home. John Thomas had ignored her demands, threats, and orders and had gone ahead stabling his friend and feeding and watering him; after a while she had stormed back into the house, saying that she was going to phone Chief Dreiser. Johnnie had expected that and was fairly sure that nothing would come of it . . . and nothing did; his mother remained in the house. But Johnnie brooded about it; he had a life-long habit of getting along with his mother, deferring to her, obeying her. Bucking her was even more distressing to him than it was to her. Every time his father had left (including the time his ship had not come back) he had told Johnnie, "Take care of your mother, son. Don't cause her any trouble."

Well, he had *tried* . . . he really had! But it was sure that Dad had never expected Mum to try to get rid of Lummox. Mum ought to know better; she had married Dad knowing that Lummox was part of the package. Well, hadn't she?

Betty would never switch sides like that.

Or would she?

Women were very strange creatures. Maybe he and Lum ought to bach it together and not take chances. He continued to brood until evening, spending his time with the star beast and petting him. Lummie's tumors were another worry. One of them seemed very tender and about to burst; John Thomas wondered if it ought to be lanced? But no one knew any more about it than he did and he did not know.

On top of everything else, here Lummie was ill . . . it was just too much!

He did not go in to dinner. Presently his mother came out with a tray. "I thought you might like to picnic out here with Lummox," she said blandly.

Johnnie looked at her sharply. "Why, thanks, Mum . . . uh, thanks."

"How is Lummie?"

"Uh, he's all right, I guess."

"That's good."

He stared after her as she went in. Mum angry was bad enough, but Mum with that secret, catlike look, all sweetness and light, he was even more wary of. Nevertheless he polished off the excellent dinner, not having eaten since breakfast. She came out again a half hour later and said, "Finished, dear?"

"Uh, yes . . . thanks, it was good."

"Thank you, dear. Will you bring the tray in? And come in yourself; there is a Mr. Perkins coming to see you at eight."

"Mr. Perkins? Who's he?" But the door was closing behind her.

He found his mother downstairs, resting and knitting socks. She smiled and said, "Well? How are we now?"

"All right. Say, Mum, who is this Perkins? Why does he want to see *me*?"

"He phoned this afternoon for an appointment. I told him to come at eight."

"But didn't he say what he wanted?"

"Well . . . perhaps he did, but mother thinks it is better for Mr. Perkins to explain his errand himself."

"Is it about Lummox?"

"Don't cross-examine Mum. You'll know quickly enough."

"But, look here, I . . ."

"We'll say no more about it, do you mind? Take off your shoe, dear. I want to measure for the foot."

Baffled, he started to remove his shoe. Suddenly he stopped. "Mum, I wish you wouldn't knit socks for me."

"What, dear? But mother enjoys doing it for you."

"Yes, but . . . Look, I don't *like* hand-knit socks. They make creases on the soles of my feet . . . I've showed you often enough!"

"Don't be silly! How could soft wool do your feet

any harm? And think what you would have to pay for real wool, real handwork, if you bought it. Most boys would be grateful."

"But I don't *like* it, I tell you!"

She sighed. "Sometimes, dear, I don't know what to do with you, I really don't." She rolled up her knitting and put it aside. "Go wash your hands . . . yes, and your face, too . . . and comb your hair. Mr. Perkins will be here any moment."

"Say, about this Mr. Perkins . . ."

"Hurry, dear. Don't make things difficult for mother."

Mr. Perkins turned out to be pleasant; John Thomas liked him despite his supiscions. After a few polite inanities, with coffee served for ritual hospitality, he came to the point.

He repesented the Exotic Life Laboratory of the Museum of Natural History. As a result of the news picture of Lummox in connection with the story of the trial the beast had come to the attention of the Museum . . . which now wanted to buy him.

"To my surprise," he added, "in searching the files I discovered that on another occasion the Museum attempted to buy this specimen . . . from your grandfather, I believe. The name was the same as yours and the date fitted. Are you any relation to . . ."

"My great great great grandfather . . . sure," John Thomas interrupted. "And it was probably my grandfather they tried to buy Lummox from. But he was not for sale then—and he's not for sale now!"

His mother looked up from knitting and said, "Be reasonable, dear. You are in no position to take that attitude."

John Thomas looked stubborn. Mr. Perkins went on with a warm smile, "I sympathize with your feelings, Mr. Stuart. But our legal department looked into the matter before I came out here and I am familiar with your present problems. Believe me, I'm not here to make them worse; we have a solution that will protect your pet and clear up your troubles."

"I'm not going to sell Lummox," John Thomas persisted.

"Why not? If it turns out to be the only solution?"

"Well . . . because I can't. Even if I wanted to. He wasn't left to me to sell, he was left to me to keep and take care of. He was in this family before I was . . . before my mother was, for that matter." He looked sternly at his mother. "Mum, I don't know what's gotten into you."

She answered quietly, "That will be enough of that, dear. Mother does what is best for you."

Mr. Perkins changed the subject smoothly as John Thomas began to cloud up. "In any case, now that I've come all this way, may I see the creature? I'm terribly interested."

"Uh, I suppose so." Johnnie got up slowly and led the stranger outside.

Mr. Perkins looked up at Lummox, took a deep breath and let it out. "Marvelous!" He walked around him, admiring. "Absolutely marvelous! Unique . . . and the biggest e.-t. specimen I've ever seen. How in the world was he shipped?"

"Why, he's grown some," John Thomas admitted.

"I understand he parrots human speech a bit. Can you coax him to do it?"

"Huh? He doesn't 'parrot' . . . he *talks*."

"Really?"

"Of course. Hey, Lummie, how are you, boy?"

"I'm all right," Lummox piped. "What does *he* want?"

"Oh, nothing, nothing. He just wanted to see you."

Mr. Perkins stared. "He talks! Mr. Stuart, the laboratory *must* have this specimen."

"That's out, I told you."

"I'm prepared to go much higher, now that I've seen him . . . and heard him."

John Thomas started to say something rude, checked himself and said instead, "Look, Mr. Perkins, are you married?"

"Why, yes. Why?"

"Any kids?"

"One, a little girl. She's just five." His face softened.

"I'll make you a deal. We'll swap even. No questions asked and each of us does as he likes with his 'specimen.'"

Perkins started to flare up, then suddenly grinned. "Touché! I'll shut up. But," he went on, "you were taking a chance. One or two of my colleagues would have taken you up. You can't understand what a temptation a specimen like this is to a man of science. Really." He looked longingly at Lummox and added, "Shall we go in?"

Mrs. Stuart looked up as they came in; Mr. Perkins shook his head briefly. They sat down and Mr. Perkins fitted his finger tips together. "Mr. Stuart, you have forbidden me to discuss a possible sale, but if I tell the director of the Lab that I didn't even put the proposition, I will look foolish. Would you let me state what the museum has in mind . . . just for the record?"

"Well . . ." John Thomas frowned. "I guess there's no harm in that."

"Thanks. I must do something to justify my travel expenses. Let me analyze the situation. That creature . . . your friend Lummox . . . or let's say 'our friend Lummox' for I liked him as soon as I saw him. Our friend Lummox is under sentence of death, isn't he? A court order."

"Yes," John Thomas admitted. "But it hasn't been confirmed by the Space Department yet."

"I know. But the police have already made attempts to kill him, without waiting for final approval. Right?"

John started to use bad language, then glanced at

his mother and refrained. "The stupid idiots! Anyhow, they can't kill Lummox; they're too dumb."

"I agree with your sentiments . . . privately. That buffoon chief of police ought to have his commission taken away. Why, he might have destroyed an absolutely unique specimen. Imagine!"

Mrs. Stuart said crisply, "Chief Dreiser is a fine gentleman."

Mr. Perkins turned to her and said, "Mrs. Stuart, I did not mean to cast slurs on a friend of yours. But I stick by my guns; the Chief had no right to take things into his own hands. Such behavior is worse on the part of a public official than it is when done by a lay citizen."

"He had public safety to think about," she insisted.

"True. Perhaps that is an extenuating circumstance. I take back my remarks. They are off the subject and I did not intend to start an argument."

"I'm glad to hear you did not, Mr. Perkins. Shall we get back to the subject?"

John Thomas felt himself warming a little to the scientist—Mum had slapped Perkins down just the way she did him—and, besides, he liked Lummox. Mr. Perkins continued, "Any time now, tomorrow, or even today, the Department of Spatial Affairs will approve the destruction of Lummox and . . ."

"Maybe they'll turn it down."

"Can you risk Lummox's life on that unjustified hope? The Chief of Police will show up again—and this time he'll kill Lummox."

"No, he won't! He doesn't know how. We'll laugh at him!"

Mr. Perkins shook his head slowly. "That's not your head talking, that's your heart. The Chief will make sure this time. He's been made to look silly; he won't let it happen again. If he can't figure out a sure way himself, he'll get expert advice. Mr. Stuart, any biologist could run a rough analysis on Lummox and tell almost offhand two or three certain ways to kill him . . . kill him quickly and safely. I've already thought of one, just from seeing him."

John Thomas looked at him in alarm. "You won't tell Chief Dreiser?"

"Of course not! I'd be strung up by the thumbs first. But there are thousands of others who can advise him. Or he may hit on a method himself. Be sure of this: if you wait until that death sentence is approved, it will be too late. They'll kill Lummox. And that would be a great pity."

John Thomas did not answer. Mr. Perkins added quietly, "You can't oppose the forces of society singlehanded. If you are stubborn you yourself will make certain that Lummox will be killed."

John Thomas pushed his fist hard against his mouth. Then he said almost inaudibly, "What can I *do?*"

"Much, if you let me help you. First, let me make this clear. If you entrust your pet to us, he will never be harmed in any way. You hear talk about vivisection and such . . . well, forget it. Our object is to put specimens into environments as much like their home planets as possible, then study them. We want them to be healthy and happy, and we go to a lot of trouble to accomplish those ends. Eventually Lummox will die a natural death . . . then we'll mount the hide and skeleton, as a permanent exhibit."

"How would you like to be stuffed and exhibited?" Johnnie asked bitterly.

"Eh?" Perkins looked surprised, then laughed. "It wouldn't bother me at all; I'm leaving my carcass to the medical school of my alma mater. And it won't bother Lummox. The point is to get him out of the clutches of the police . . . so that he can live to a ripe old age."

"Wait a minute. If you buy him, that doesn't get him off. They'll still kill him. Won't they?"

"Yes and no. Mostly no. Selling him to the Museum doesn't cancel the order to destroy him, but, believe me, it will never be carried out. I've been coached by our legal department as to what to do. First, we agree on terms and you give me a bill of sale; that gives the Museum legal standing. At once, tonight, I get hold of your local judge and get a temporary order postponing the execution for a few days; it is definitely within his discretion to postpone it while this new factor of a change in ownership is considered. That's all we need. We can get straight to the Secretary for Spatial Affairs if we need to . . . and I promise you that, once the Museum holds title, Lummox will never be destroyed."

"You're *sure?*"

"Sure enough to risk the Museum's money. If I'm wrong, I might be out of a job." Perkins grinned. "But I'm not wrong. Once I have the temporary order and have phoned the Museum to get busy on a permanent order my next step is to settle all the damage. I'll carry cash, enough to do it . . . cash has a convincing effect. That done, we'll have only the Chief of Safety against us . . . and, while he may seem an obstacle to you, he will never be able to stand up against the weight that the Museum can bring to bear, when needed. And everybody lives happily ever after!" Perkins smiled. "Anything wrong with it?"

John Thomas traced out a pattern on the rug with his toe, then looked up. "Look, Mr. Perkins, I know I have to do something to save Lummox. But up to now I haven't seen any way . . . and I guess I haven't had the courage to look the facts in the face."

"Then you'll do it?"

"Just a minute, please! This isn't any good either. Lummie would be miserable with loneliness. He'd never get used to it. It would just be swapping death for life imprisonment. I'm not sure but what he'd rather be dead . . . than to be all alone, with a lot of strangers and them poking him and bothering him and making tests of him. But I can't even ask him what he wants because I'm not sure Lummie understands about death. But he does understand about strangers."

Mr. Perkins chewed his lip and reflected that it was very hard to do this young man a favor. "Mr. Stuart? If you were to go with Lummox, would it make a difference?"

"Huh? How?"

"I think I can promise you a job as an animal handler . . . In fact I have a vacancy in my own department; I could hire you tonight and we could sort the red tape later. After all, there is a real advantage in having an exotic animal cared for by someone who knows his ways."

Before Johnnie could answer his mother said, "No!"

"Eh? What, Mrs. Stuart?"

"Out of the question. Mr. Perkins, I had hoped that you would provide a rational way out of this silly unpleasantness. But I cannot agree to that last suggestion. My son is to go to college. I will not have him waste his life sweeping out that beast's cage . . . like a roustabout! No indeed!"

"Now look here, Mother . . ."

"John Thomas! If you please! The subject is closed."

Mr. Perkins looked from the boy's smoldering face to his mother's set expression. "After all," he said, "that is no business of the Museum. Let me put it this way, Mrs. Stuart. I'll keep that job open for, oh, say six months . . . no, please, Mrs. Stuart! Whether or not your son takes it is your problem . . . and I am sure you don't need my advice. I just want to assure your son that the Museum won't keep him away from his pet. Is that fair?"

Her needles were clicking like machinery. "I suppose so," she admitted.

"Mr. Stuart?"

"Wait a minute. Mother, you don't think I'd . . ."

"Please, Mr. Stuart! The Museum of Natural History has no place in a family discussion. You know our offer. Will you accept?"

Mrs. Stuart interrupted. "I don't believe you mentioned the price, Mr. Perkins."

"Why, so I didn't! Shall we say twenty thousand?"

"Net?"

"Net? Oh, no . . . subject to the claims we'll have to settle, of course."

" 'Net,' Mr. Perkins," she said firmly.

He shrugged. "Net."

"We accept."

"Good."

"Hey, wait a minute!" protested John Thomas. "We don't either. Not if this other thing isn't settled. I'm not going to turn Lummox over to . . ."

"Quiet! Dear, I've been patient but we'll have no more of this nonsense. Mr. Perkins, he accepts. Do you have the papers with you?"

"We don't either accept!"

"Just a moment," Mr. Perkins appealed. "Ma'am, am I correct in thinking that I must have your son's signature for a valid bill of sale?"

"You'll get it."

"Hmm. Mr. Stuart?"

"I'm not going to sign unless it's settled that Lummox and I stay together."

"Mrs. Stuart?"

"This is ridiculous."

"I think so, too. But there is nothing I can do." Perkins stood up. "Good night, Mr. Stuart. Thanks for letting me speak my piece—and for letting me see Lummox. No, don't get up; I can find the door."

He started to leave, while the Stuarts were busy not looking at each other. He paused at the door. "Mr. Stuart?"

"Huh? Yes, Mr. Perkins?"

"Would you do me a favor? Get as many pictures of Lummox as possible? Color-stereo-motion-sound if you can. I would have a professional crew flown here . . . but there may not be time. You know. It would be a shame indeed if there were not some scientific record left of him. So do what you can." He turned away again.

John Thomas gulped and was up out of his chair. "Mr. Perkins! Hey! Come back."

A few minutes later he found himself signing a bill of sale. His signature was shaky but legible. "Now Mrs. Stuart," Mr. Perkins said smoothly, "if you will sign underneath, where it says 'Guardian' . . . thanks! Oh yes! I must scratch out that part about 'subject to settlement of claim.' I don't have the cash with me; I got here after the banks had closed, so I'll pass over a nominal sum to bind it and we'll settle the rest before we move the specimen."

"No," said John Thomas.

"Eh?"

"I forgot to tell you. The Museum can settle the claims, since I can't and after all Lummox did it. But I'm not going to take any money. I'd feel like Judas."

His mother said sharply, "John Thomas! I won't let you . . ."

"Better not say it, Mum," he said dangerously. "You know what Dad would have thought."

"Hrrumph!" Mr. Perkins cleared his throat loudly. "I'm going to fill in the usual legal fiction of a nominal sum. I won't stay longer; Judge O'Farrell told me that he goes to bed at ten. Mrs. Stuart, I consider the Museum bound by my offer. Mr. Stuart, I'll leave you to settle with your mother in your own way. Good night all!" He shoved the bill of sale in his pocket and left quickly.

An hour later they were still facing each other wearily and angrily across the living room. John Thomas had let himself be bullied into conceding that his mother could take the money, as long as he was not required to touch it. He had given this in exchange, he thought, for permission to accept the job with Lummox.

But she shook her head. "Quite out of the question. After all, you are about to go to college. You couldn't take that beast along. So you had no reason to expect to keep him with you anyhow."

"Huh? But I thought you had meant to take care of him . . . the way you promised Dad . . . and I would have seen him on week ends."

"Keep your father out of this! I might as well tell you right now that I made up my mind long ago that the day you went away to school this household would cease to be a zoo. This present mix-up has simply moved up the date a few days."

He stared at her, unable to answer.

Presently she came over and put a hand on his shoulder. "Johnnie? Johnnie dear . . ."

"Huh?"

"Look at me, darling. We've had some bitter words and I'm sorry they were ever spoken . . . I'm sure you did not mean them. But Mum has only been thinking of your welfare, you know that? Don't you?"

"Uh, I suppose so."

"That's all Mum ever thinks about . . . what's best for her big boy. You're young, and when a person is young, things seem important that aren't. But as you grow older, you will find that Mum knew best. Don't you see that?"

"Well . . . Mum, about that job. If I could only . . ."

"Please, dear. Mother has a splitting headache. We'll say no more about it now. Get a good night's sleep and tomorrow you'll see things differently." She patted his cheek, bent down and kissed him. "Good night, dear."

"G'night."

He sat there long after she had gone up, trying to figure things out. He knew that he should feel good . . . he'd saved Lummie, hadn't he?

But he did not feel good; he felt like an animal that has chewed a leg off to escape a trap . . . shock and misery, not relief.

At last he got up and went outside to see Lummox.

VIII

The Sensible Thing To Do

JOHN THOMAS stayed with Lummox a short time only, as he could not bear to tell him the truth and there was nothing else to talk about. Lummox sensed his distress and asked questions; at last John Thomas pulled himself together and said, "There's nothing wrong I tell you! Shut up and go to sleep. And be darn sure you stay in the yard, or I'll beat you bow-legged."

"Yes, Johnnie. I don't like it outside anyway. People did funny things."

"Just remember that and don't do it again."

"I won't Johnnie. Cross my heart."

John Thomas went in and up to bed. But he did not go to sleep. After a while he got up, dressed in part, and went up to the attic. The house was very old and had a real garret, reached by a ladder and scuttle hole in an upper hallway closet. Once there had been a proper staircase but it had been squeezed out when the landing flat was built on the roof, as the space had been needed for the lazy lift.

But the attic was still there and it was John Thomas's only private place. His room his mother "tidied" sometimes, even though it was his duty (and wish) to do it himself. Anything might happen when Mum tidied. Papers might be lost, destroyed, or even read, for Mum believed that there should be no secrets between parents and children.

So anything he wanted to keep to himself he kept in the attic; Mum never went there—ladders made her dizzy. He had a small, almost airless and very dirty room there which he was supposed to use only for "storage." Its actual uses were varied: he had raised snakes there some years before; there he kept the small collection of books which every boy comes by but does not discuss with parents; he even had a telephone there, an audio extension run from the usual sound & sight instrument in his bedroom. This last was a practical result of his high-school course in physics and it had been real work to wire it, as it not only had to be rigged when Mum was out of the house and in such a way that she would not notice it but also it had to be done so as not to advertise its presence to the phone company's technicians.

But it worked, jury-rigged though it was, and he had added a "servant" circuit which flashed a warning light if anyone was listening from any other instrument in the house.

Tonight he had no wish to call anyone and it was past the hour when direct messages were permitted at the dormitory where Betty lived. He simply wanted to be alone . . . and to look over some papers he had not looked at in a long time. He fumbled under his work table, flipped a toggle; a panel opened in what appeared to be blank wall. In the cupboard thus exposed were books and papers. He took them out.

One item was a thin-paper notebook, his great grandfather's diary of the *Trail Blazer*'s second voyage of exploration. It was more than a hundred years old and showed the wear of many hands. John Thomas had read it a dozen times; he supposed that his father and his grandfather had done the same. All the pages were fragile, many had been repaired.

He thumbed through it, turned the pages carefully, but browsing rather than reading. His eye lit on one remembered item:

. . . *"Some of the lads are panicky, especially the married men. But they should of thought of it before they signed up. Everybody knows the score now; we burst through and came out somewhere not close to home. Who cares? We meant to travel, didn't we?"*

John Thomas turned a few more pages. He had always known the story of the *Trail Blazer;* it produced in him neither awe nor wonder. One of the first interstellar ships, her crew had plied the profession of discovery with the same acceptance of the unknown that had marked the golden days of the fifteenth century, when men had braved uncharted seas in wooden vessels. The *Trail Blazer* and her sisters had gone out the same way, burst through the Einstein barrier, taken their chances on getting back. John Thomas Stuart VIII had been aboard her that second voyage, had come home in one piece, married, begat a male child, and settled down . . . it was he who had built the landing flat on the roof.

Then one night he had heard the call of the wild goose, signed up again. He had not come back.

John Thomas located the first mention of Lummox:

"This planet is a fair imitation of good old Terra, which is a relief after the last three, since we can hit dirt without suiting up. But evolution must

have been playing double-or-nothing here, instead of the four-limbed arrangement considered stylish at home practically everything here has at least eight legs . . . 'mice' that look like centipedes, rabbitlike creatures with six short legs and one pair of tremendous jumping legs, all sorts up to things as big as giraffes. I caught one little fellow (if you can call it that . . . fact is, he came up and crawled into my lap) and I was so taken with him that I am going to try to keep him as a mascot. He puts me in mind of a dachshund puppy, only better engineered. Cristy had the airlock watch, so I was able to get him aboard without turning him over to Biology."

The next day's entry did not mention Lummox, being concerned with a more serious matter:

"We hit the jackpot this time . . . Civilization. The officers are so excited they are almost off their heads. I've seen one of the dominant race at a distance. The same multi-legged pattern, but otherwise making you wonder what would have happened to Earth if the dinosaurs had made good."

Still further on . . . :

"I've been wondering what to feed Cuddlepup. I needn't have worried. He likes everything I've sneaked out of the mess for him . . . but he will eat anything that is not riveted down. Today he ate my Everlasting stylus and it has me worried. I don't suppose the ink cartridge will poison him but how about the metal and plastic? He's just like a baby; everything he can reach goes in his mouth.

"Cuddlepuppy gets cuter every day. The little

tyke seems to be trying to talk; he whines at me and I whine back at him. Then he crawls into my lap and tells me that he loves me, plain as anything. I'll be switched if I'll let Biology have him, even if they catch me. Those birds would likely as not cut him up just to see what makes him tick. He trusts me and I'm not going to let him down."

John Thomas, Junior, had not gone to sea. Instead he had killed himself flying a boxkite affair termed an "aeroplane." That had been before the first of the World Wars; for several years thereafter the house had received "paying guests."

J. T. Stuart III had died to greater purpose; the submarine of which he was gunnery officer had penetrated Tsushima Straits to the Sea of Japan, but had failed to return.

John Thomas Stuart IV was killed on the first trip to the Moon.

John Thomas V had emigrated to Mars; his son, the famous name in the family, Johnnie skipped over quickly; he had long since grown tired of being reminded that he bore the same name as General Stuart, first governor of the Martian Commonwealth after the revolution. Johnnie wondered what would have happened to his great great great grandfather if the revolution had failed? Would they have hanged him? . . , instead of putting up statues of him?

Much of the book was devoted to an attempt by Johnnie's grandfather to clear the name of his own grandfather—for the son of General Stuart was no public hero; instead he had sweated out his last fifteen years of life in the Triton penal colony. His wife had returned to her family on Earth and taken back her maiden name, for herself and her son.

But her son had gone proudly into court the day he was of age and had had his name changed from "Carlton Gimmidge" to "John Thomas Stuart VIII." It was he who had fetched Lummox back and he had used his bonus money from the second trip of the *Trail Blazer* to buy back the old homestead. He had apparently impressed on his own son that his son's grandfather had gotten a dirty deal; the son had made a great point of it in this record.

Johnnie's grandfather could himself have used an advocate to defend his name. The record stated simply that John Thomas Stuart IX had resigned from the service and had never gone into space again, but Johnnie knew that it had been a choice of that or a court martial; his own father had told him . . . but he had told him also that his grandfather could have got off scot-free had he been willing to testify. His father had added, "Johnnie, I'd rather see you loyal to your friends than with your chest decked out in medals."

The old man had still been living at the time Johnnie's father told him this. On a later occasion, while Johnnie's father was out on patrol, Johnnie had tried to let him know that he knew.

Granddad had been furious. "Poppycock!" he had shouted. "They had me dead to rights."

"But Dad said your skipper was actually the one who . . ."

"Your Dad wasn't there. Captain Dominic was the finest skipper that ever trod steel . . . may his soul rest in peace. Set up the checkers, son. I'm going to beat you."

Johnnie had tried to get the straight of it after his grandfather died, but his father's answer was not direct. "Your grandfather was a romantic sentimentalist, Johnnie. It's the flaw in our make-up. Hardly sense enough in the whole line to balance a check book." He had puffed his pipe and added, "But we do have fun."

Johnnie put the books and papers away, feeling dully that it had not done him much good to read about his forebears; Lummox was still on his mind. He guessed he ought to go down and try to get some sleep.

He was turning away as the phone flashed; he grabbed it before the light could change to sound signal; he did not want his mother to wake. "Yes?"

"That you, Johnnie?"

"Yeah. I can't see you, Betty; I'm up in the attic."

"That isn't the only reason you can't. I haven't got my face on, so I've got the video switched off. Besides it's pitch dark in this hallway, since I'm not allowed to phone this time o' night. Uh, the Duchess isn't listening, is she?"

Johnnie glanced at his warning signal. "No."

"I'll make this brief. My spies report that Deacon Dreiser got the okay to go ahead."

"*No!*"

"Yes. Point is, what do we do about it? We can't sit still and let him."

"Uh, I've done something."

"What? Nothing silly, I hope. I shouldn't have been away today."

"Well, a Mr. Perkins . . ."

"Perkins? The chap who went to see Judge O'Farrell tonight?"

"Yes. How did you know?"

"Look, don't waste time. I always know. Tell me your end."

"Well . . ." John Thomas gave a confused report. Betty listened without comment, which made him defensive; he found himself expounding the viewpoints of his mother and of Mr. Perkins, rather than his own. "So that's how it was," he finished lamely.

"So you told them to go climb a tree? Good. Now here is our next move. If the Museum can do it, we can do it. It's just a case of getting Grandpa O'Farrell to . . ."

"Betty, you don't understand. I sold Lummox."

"What? You *sold* Lummox?"

"Yes. I had to. If I didn't . . ."

"*You* sold *Lummox*."

"Betty, I couldn't help my . . ."

But she had switched off on him.

He tried to call back, got a recorded voice that said, "This instrument is out of direct service until tomorrow morning at eight. If you wish to record a message stand by for . . ." He switched off.

He sat holding his head and wishing he were dead. The worst of it was, Betty was right. He had let himself be badgered into doing something he *knew* was wrong, just because it had seemed that there was nothing else he could do.

Betty had not been fooled. Maybe what she wanted to try wasn't any good either . . . but she had known a wrong answer when she heard it.

He sat there, flailing himself but not knowing what to do. The more he thought, the angrier he got. He had let himself be talked into something that wasn't *right* . . . just because it was reasonable . . . just because it was logical . . . just because it was common sense.

The deuce with common sense! His ancestors hadn't used common sense, any of 'em! Who was he to start such a practice?

None of them had ever done the sensible thing. Why, take his great great great grandfather . . . he'd found a situation he hadn't liked and he had turned a whole planet upside down through seven bloody years. Sure, they called him a hero . . . but does starting a revolution come under the head of common sense?

Or take . . . Oh, shucks, take any of 'em! There hadn't been a "good" boy in the bunch. Would granddad have sold Lummox? Why, granddad would have torn down the courthouse with his bare hands. If granddad was here, he'd be standing guard over Lummox with a gun and daring the world to touch one spine.

He certainly wasn't going to take any of Perkins' dirty money; he knew that.

But what could he *do*?

He could go to Mars. Under the Lafayette Law he was a citizen and could claim land. But how could he get there? Worse, how could he get Lummox there?

The trouble with that, he told himself savagely, is that it almost makes sense. And sense is no use to me.

At last he hit on a plan. It had the one virtue of having no sense to it at all; it was compounded of equal parts of folly and of risk. He felt that granddad would have liked it.

IX

Customs and an Ugly Duckling

HE went down to the upper hallway and listened at his mother's door. He did not expect to hear anything as her bedroom was sound-proofed; the action was instinctive. Then he returned to his own room and made rapid preparations, starting by dressing in camping clothes and mountain boots. His sleeping bag he kept in a drawer of his desk; he got it out, tucked it in a side pocket of his coat and shoved its power pack in a breast pocket. Other items of hiking and camping gear he distributed among other pockets and he was almost ready to go.

He counted his cash and swore softly; his other assets were in a savings account and now he would have no chance to draw from it. Well, it couldn't be helped . . . he started downstairs, then remembered an important matter. He went back to his desk.

"Dear Mum," he wrote. *"Please tell Mr. Perkins that the deal is off. You can use my college money to pay back the insurance people. Lum and I are going away and it won't do any good to try to find us. I'm sorry but we have to."* He looked at the note, decided that there was no more to be said, added *"love,"* and signed it.

He started a note to Betty, tore it up, tried again, and finally told himself that he would send her a letter when he had more to say. He went downstairs, left the note on the dining table, then went to the pantry and picked out supplies. A few minutes later, carrying a large sack crammed with tins and packages, he went out to Lummox's house.

His friend was asleep. The watchman eye accepted him; Lummox did not stir. John Thomas hauled back and kicked him as hard as possible. "Hey, Lum! Wake up."

The beast opened his other eyes, yawned daintily, and piped, "Hello, Johnnie."

"Pull yourself together. We're going for a hike."

Lummox extended his legs and stood up, letting a ripple run from head to stern. "All right."

"Make me a seat—and leave room for this." Johnnie held up the bag of groceries. Lummox complied without comment; John Thomas chucked the sack up on the beast, then scrambled up himself. Soon they were on the road in front of the Stuart home.

Almost irrational as he was, John Thomas nevertheless knew that running away and hiding Lummox was a project almost impossible; Lummox anywhere would be about as conspicuous as a bass drum in a bathtub. However there was a modicum of method in his madness; concealing Lummox near Westville was not quite the impossibility it would have been some places.

Westville lay in an open mountain valley; immediately west the backbone of the continent shoved its gaunt ridges into the sky. A few miles beyond the city commenced one of the great primitive areas, thousands of square miles of up-and-down country almost the same as it had been when the Indians greeted Columbus. During a short season each year it swarmed with red-coated sportsmen, blazing away at deer and elk and each other; most of the year it was deserted.

If he could get Lummox there without being seen, it was barely possible that they could avoid being caught—until his food supplies ran out. When that time came—well, he might live off the country just as Lummox would . . . eat venison, maybe. Or maybe go back to town without Lummox and argue it out again from the strong position of being able to refuse to tell where Lummox was until they listened to reason. The possibilities were not thought out; he simply intended to get Lummox under cover and then think about it . . . get him somewhere where that old scoundrel Dreiser couldn't try out ways to hurt him!

John Thomas could have turned Lummox to the west and set off across country toward the mountains, Lummox being no more dependent on pavement than is a tank . . . but Lummox left a track in soft earth as conspicuous as that of a tank. It was necessary to stay on paved road.

Johnnie had a solution in mind. In an earlier century a transcontinental highway had crossed the mountains here, passing south of Westville and winding ever higher toward the Great Divide. It had long since been replaced by a modern powered road which tunneled through the wall of rock instead of climbing it. But the old road remained, abandoned, overgrown in many places, its concrete slabs heaved and tilted from frost and summer heat . . . but still a paved road that would show little sign of Lummox's ponderous progress.

He led Lummox by back ways, avoiding houses and

working toward a spot three miles west where the expressway entered the first of its tunnels and the old highway started to climb. He did not go quite to the fork, but stopped a hundred yards short, parked Lummox in front of a vacant lot, warned him not to move, and scouted the lay of the land. He did not dare take Lummox onto the expressway to reach the old road; not only might they be seen but also it would be dangerous to Lummox.

But John Thomas found what he thought he remembered: a construction road looping around the junction. It was not paved but was hard-packed granite gravel and he judged that even Lummox's heavy steps would not leave prints. He went back and found Lummox placidly eating a "For Sale" sign. He scolded him and took it away, then decided that he might as well get rid of the evidence and gave it back. They continued while Lummox munched the sign.

Once on the old highway John Thomas relaxed. For the first few miles it was in good repair, for it served homes farther up the canyon. But there was no through traffic, it being a dead end, and no local traffic at this hour. Once or twice an air car passed overhead, party or theater goers returning home, but if the passengers noticed the great beast plodding on the road below they gave no sign.

The road meandered up the canyon and came out on a tableland; here was a barrier across the pavement: ROAD CLOSED . . . VEHICULAR PASSAGE FORBIDDEN BEYOND THIS POINT. Johnnie got down and looked it over. It was a single heavy timber supported at the chest height. "Lummie, can you walk over that without touching it?"

"Sure, Johnnie."

"All right. Take it slowly. You mustn't knock it down. Don't even brush against it."

"I won't, Johnnie." Nor did he. Instead of stepping over it as a horse might step over a lower barrier Lummox retracted pairs of legs in succession and flowed over it.

Johnnie crawled under the barrier and joined him. "I didn't know you could do that."

"Neither did I."

The road was rough ahead. Johnnie stopped to lash down the groceries with a line under Lummox's keel, then added a bight across his own thighs. "All right, Lummie. Let's have some speed. But don't gallop; I don't want to fall off."

"Hang on, Johnnie!" Lummox picked up speed, retaining his normal foot pattern. He rumbled along at a fast trot, his gait smoothed out by his many legs. Johnnie found that he was very tired, both in body and spirit. He felt safe, now that they were away from houses and traveled roads, and fatigue hit him. He leaned back and Lummox adjusted his contours to him. The swaying motion and steady pounding of massive feet had soothing effect. Presently he slept.

Lummox went on surefootedly over the broken slabs. He was using his night sight and there was no danger of stumbling in the dark. He knew that Johnnie was asleep and kept his gait as smooth as possible. But in time he got bored and decided on a nap, too. He had not slept well the nights he had spent away from home . . . always some silliness going on and it had fretted him not to know where Johnnie was. So now he rigged out his guardian eye, closed his others and shifted control over to the secondary brain back in his rump. Lummox proper went to sleep, leaving that minor fraction that never slept to perform the simple tasks of watching for road hazards and of supervising the tireless pounding of his eight great legs.

John Thomas woke as the stars were fading in the morning sky. He stretched his sore muscles and shivered. There were high mountains all around and the road crawled along the side of one, with a sheer drop to a stream far below. He sat up. "Hey, Lummie!"

No answer. He shouted again. This time Lummox answered sleepily, "What's the matter, Johnnie?"

"You've been asleep," he accused.

"You didn't say not to, Johnnie."

"Well . . . all right. Are we on the same road?"

Lummox consulted his alter ego and answered. "Sure. Did you want another road?"

"No. But we've got to get off this one. It's getting light."

"Why?"

John Thomas did not know how to answer that question; trying to explain to Lummox that he was under sentence of death and must hide did not appeal to him. "We have to, that's why. But just keep going now. I'll let you know."

The stream climbed up to meet them; in a mile or so the road lay only a few feet above it. They came to a place where the stream bed widened out into a boulder field, with water only in a central channel. "Whoa!" called out Johnnie.

"Breakfast?" inquired Lummox.

"Not yet. See those rocks down there?"

"Yes."

"I want you to step wide onto those rocks. Don't put your big feet on that soft shoulder dirt. Step from the pavement to the rocks. Get me?"

"Don't leave tracks?" Lummox asked doubtfully.

"That's right. If anybody comes along and sees tracks, you'll have to go back downtown again—because they'll follow the tracks and find us. See?"

"I won't leave any tracks, Johnnie."

Lummox went down onto the dry stream bed like a gargantuan inchworm. The maneuver caused John Thomas to grab for his safety line with one hand and for his supplies with the other. He yelped.

Lummox stopped and said, "You all right, Johnnie?"

"Yes. You just surprised me. Upstream now and stay on the rocks." They followed the stream, found a place to cross, then followed it on the other side. It swung away from the road and soon they were several hundred yards from it. It was now almost broad daylight and John Thomas was beginning to worry about air reconnaissance, even though it was unlikely that the alarm would be out so soon.

Up ahead a grove of lodgepole pines came down to the bank. It seemed dense enough; even if Lummox were not invisible in it, nevertheless holding still he would look like a big, mountain-country boulder. It would have to do; there was no time to pick a better place. "Up the bank and into those trees, Lum, and don't break the bank down. Step easy."

They entered the grove and stopped; Johnnie dismounted. Lummox tore down a branch of pine and started to eat. It reminded John Thomas that he himself had not eaten lately but he was so dead tired that he was not hungry. He wanted to sleep, really sleep . . . not half awake and clutching a safety line.

But he was afraid that if he let Lummox graze while he slept the big stupid lunk would wander into the open and be spotted. "Lummie? Let's take a nap before we have breakfast."

"Why?"

"Well, Johnnie's awful tired. You just lie down here and I'll put my sleeping bag beside you. Then when we wake up, we'll eat."

"Not eat until you wake up?"

"That's it."

"Well . . . all right," Lummox said regretfully.

John Thomas took his sleeping bag out of his picket, flipped the light membrane open, and plugged in the power pack. He set the thermostat and switched it on, then while it heated he inflated the mattress side. The thin mountain air made it heavy work; he stopped with it only partly blown up and peeled off all his clothes. Shivering in the frosty air he slid inside, closed it to a nose hole. "G'night, Lummie."

"G'night, Johnnie."

Mr. Kiku slept badly and was up early. He breakfasted without disturbing his wife and went to the Spatial Affairs hall, arriving while the great building was quiet except for the handful on night duty. Seated at his desk, he tried to think.

His subconscious had been nagging him all night, telling him that he had missed something important. Mr. Kiku had high respect for his subconscious, holding a theory that real thinking was never done at the top of the mind, which he regarded merely as a display window for results arrived at elsewhere, like the "answer" windows in a calculator.

Something young Greenberg had said . . . something about the Rargyllian believing that the Hroshii, with only one ship, were a serious menace to Earth. Mr. Kiku had discounted it as a clumsy attempt by the snake boy to bluff from weakness. Not that it mattered; the negotiation was about over . . . the one remaining detail being to set up permanent relations with the Hroshii.

His subconscious had not thought so.

He leaned to his desk and spoke to the night communications supervisor. "Kiku. Call the Hotel Universal. There's a Dr. Ftaeml there, a Rargyllian. As soon as he orders breakfast I want to talk a him. No, don't wake him, a man is entitled to his rest."

Having done what could be done, he turned to the mind-soothing routine of clearing up accumulated work.

His incoming basket was empty for the first time in some days and the building was beginning to stir when his desk communicator showed a blinking red light.

"Kiku here."

"Sir," the face said anxiously, "on that call to Hotel Universal. Dr. Ftaeml did not order breakfast."

"Sleeping late perhaps. His privilege."

"No, sir. I mean he skipped breakfast. He's on his way to space port."

"How long ago?"

"Five to ten minutes. I just found out."

"Very well. Call space port, tell them not to clear his ship. Make certain that they understand that it has diplomatic clearance and that they must actually do something . . . not just scratch its clearance on the board and go back to sleep. Then reach Dr. Ftaeml himself—my compliments to the Doctor and will he do me the honor of waiting a few minutes to see me? I am on my way to the port."

"Yes, sir!"

"That done, there is a matter of a special efficiency report for you . . . uh, Znedov, is it? Make out the form and grade yourself; I want to see your opinion of yourself."

"Yes, sir."

Mr. Kiku switched off and called Transportation. "Kiku. I am leaving for the space port as quickly as I can reach the roof. Provide a dart and a police escort."

"Yes, sir!"

Mr. Kiku stopped only to tell his secretary where he was going, then stepped into his private lift to the roof.

At the space port Dr. Ftaeml was waiting out on the passengers' promenade, watching the ships and pretending to smoke a cigar. Mr. Kiku came up and bowed. "Good morning, Doctor. It was most gentle of you to wait for me."

The Rargyllian tossed the cigar aside. "The honor is mine, sir. To be attended at the port by a person of your rank and pressing duties . . ." He finished with a shrug which expressed both surprise and pleasure.

"I will not keep you long. But I had promised myself the pleasure of seeing you today and I had not known that you intended to leave."

"My fault, Mr. Under Secretary I had intended to pop up and pop back and then to wait your pleasure this afternoon."

"Good. Well, perhaps by tomorrow I shall be able to present an acceptable solution of this problem."

Ftaeml was plainly surprised. "Successful?"

"I hope so. The data you provided yesterday has given us a new clue."

"Do I understand that you have *found* the missing Hroshia?"

"Possibly. Do you know the fable of the Ugly Duckling?"

" 'Ugly Duckling'?" The Rargyllian seemed to be searching his files. "Yes, I know the idiom."

"Mr. Greenberg, following the clue you provided, has gone to fetch the Ugly Duckling. If by wild chance it turns out to be the swan that we are seeking, then . . ." Mr. Kiku gave a shrug unconsciously like that of Ftaeml.

The Rargyllian seemed to have trouble believing it. "And is it the . . . 'swan,' Mr. Under Secretary?"

"We will see. Logic says that it must be; probability says that it cannot be."

"Mmmm . . . and may I report this to my clients?"

"Suppose we wait until I hear from Mr. Greenberg. He has left Capital to investigate. Can I reach you through the scout ship?"

"Certainly, sir."

"Uh, Doctor . . . there was one more thing."

"Yes, sir?"

"You made an odd remark to Mr. Greenberg last night

. . . supposedly a joke . . . or perhaps an accident. You said something about Earth being 'volatilized'."

For a moment the Rargyllian said nothing. When he did speak he changed the subject. "Tell me, sir, in what way does logic state that your 'Ugly Duckling' is a swan?"

Mr. Kiku spoke carefully. "A Terran ship visited a strange planet at the time defined by your data. The dominant race could have been Hroshii; the identification is not exact except as to time. A life form was removed and brought here. This being is still alive after more than one hundred twenty years; Mr. Greenberg has gone to fetch it for identification by your principals."

Dr. Ftaeml said softly, "It must be. I did not believe it but it *must* be." He went on, louder and quite cheerfully, "Sir, you have made me happy."

"Indeed?"

"Very. You have also made it possible for me to speak freely."

"You have always been free to speak, Doctor, so far as we were concerned. I do not know what instructions you have from your clients."

"They have placed no check on my tongue. But . . . You are aware, sir, that the customs of a race are implicit in its speech?"

"I have sometimes had cause to suspect so," Mr. Kiku answered drily.

"To be sure. If you visited a friend in a hospital, knowing him to be dying, knowing that you could not help him, would you speak to him of his doom?"

"No. Not unless he brought up the subject."

"Precisely! Speaking to you and to Mr. Greenberg I was perforce bound by your customs."

"Dr. Ftaeml," Mr. Kiku said slowly, "let us be blunt. Am I to believe that you are convinced that this single foreign ship could do a serious damage to this planet, with its not inconsiderable defenses?"

"I will be blunt, sir. Should the Hroshii eventually conclude that, through the actions of this planet or some member of its culture, their Hroshia had died or was forever lost, Earth would not be damaged; Earth would be destroyed."

"By this one ship?"

"Unassisted."

Mr. Kiku shook his head. "Doctor, I am sure that you are convinced of what you say. I am not. The extent and thoroughness of the defenses of this, the leading planet of the Federation, cannot possibly be known to you. But should they be so foolish they will learn that we have teeth."

Ftaeml looked sorrowful. "In all the many tongues of civilization I find no words to convince you. But believe me . . . anything that you could do against them would be as futile as throwing stones at one of your modern warships."

"We shall see. Or, fortunately, we shall not see. I do not like weapons, Doctor; they are the last resort of faulty diplomacy. Have you spoken to them of the willingness of the Federation to accept them into the Community of Civilizations?"

"I have had grave difficulty in explaining to them the nature of your offer."

"Are they, then, so hopelessly warlike?"

"They are not warlike at all. How can I put it? Are you warlike when you smash . . . strike . . . swat . . . yes, swat a fly? The Hroshii are practically immortal by your standards, and even by mine. They are so nearly invulnerable to all ordinary hazards that they tend to look down . . . how is your idiom? . . . 'Olympian' . . . they look down on us from Olympian heights. They cannot see any purpose in relations with lesser races;

therefore your proposal was not taken seriously, though, believe me, I put it."

"They sound stupid," Kiku answered sourly.

"Not true, sir. They evaluate your race and mine most exactly. They know that any culture possessing star travel has at least some minor skill in the physical arts. They know therefore that you will regard yourselves as powerful. For that reason they are even now contemplating a display of force, to convince you that you must forthwith deliver up their Hroshia . . . they think of this as being like a goad to a draft animal, a sign which he will be able to understand."

"Hmm . . . You know the nature of this demonstration?"

"I do. My trip this morning to their ship is to persuade them to wait. They intend to touch lightly the face of your satellite, leave on it an incandescent mark perhaps a thousand miles long, to convince you that they . . . uh . . . 'ain't foolin'.'"

"I am not impressed. We could order a force of ships and make such a sign ourselves. Not that we would."

"Could you do it with one ship, in a matter of seconds, without fuss, from a distance of a quarter million miles?"

"You think they could?"

"I am sure of it. A minor demonstration. Mr. Under Secretary, there are novae in their part of the sky which were not accidents of nature."

Mr. Kiku hesitated. If it all were true, then such a demonstration might serve his own needs by causing the Hroshii to show their hand. The loss of a few worthless lunar mountains would not matter . . . but it would be difficult to evacuate such an area of even the few who might be in it. "Have you told them that our Moon is inhabited?"

"It is not inhabited by their Hroshia, which is all that matters to them."

"Hmm . . . I suppose so. Doctor, could you suggest to them, first, that you may be about to find their Hroshia, and second, that their Hroshia may be somewhere on our satellite, which is why the search has taken so long?"

The Rargyllian simulated a wide human grin. "Sir, I salute you. I shall be happy to convey such a suggestion. I am sure there will be no demonstration of force."

"Good health, Doctor. I'll be in touch with you."

"Your good health, sir."

On his way back Mr. Kiku realized that he had felt not a single twinge in the presence of the medusoid . . . why, the blighter was rather likable, in a horrid way. Dr. Morgan was certainly an adroit hypnotherapist.

His work basket was choked as usual; he put the Hroshii out of mind and worked happily. Late that afternoon communications informed him that they were hoding a circuit for Mr. Greenberg. "Put him on," Mr. Kiku said, feeling that at last the pieces were falling into place.

"Boss?" Greenberg began.

"Eh? Yes, Sergei. What the deuce are you looking upset about?"

"Because I'm wondering how I'm going to like it as a private in the Outer Legion."

"Quit trying to break it gently. What happened?"

"The bird has flown."

"Flown? Where?"

"I wish I knew. The most likely place is a forest preserve west of here."

"Then why are you wasting time telling me? Get in there and find it."

Greenberg sighed. "I knew you would say that. Look, boss, this haystack has over ten million acres in it, tall trees, tall mountains, and no roads. And the local police chief is there ahead of me, with all his own men and half the sheriff's deputies in the state. He's ordered them to kill on sight and has posted a reward for the ship making the kill."

"*What?*"

"Just what I said. Your authorization to carry out the judgment of the court came through; the cancellation of it got lost . . . how, I don't know. But the acting chief is an old relic with the soul of a file clerk; he points to the order and won't budge . . . he won't even let me call them on police frequency. With our intervention withdrawn I haven't an ounce of authority to force him."

"You are accepting that, I suppose?" Mr. Kiku said bitterly. "Just waiting for it to blow up in your face?"

"Just about. I've got a call in for the mayor—he's out of town. Another for the governor—he's in a closed grand jury session. And another for the chief forest ranger . . . I think he's out after the reward. As soon as I switch off I'm going to twist the arm of the acting chief until he sees the light and . . ."

"You should be doing that now."

"I won't dally. I called to suggest that you turn on heat from back there. I need help."

"You'll get it."

"Not just to reach the governor, not just to start a fresh intervention. Even after we reach this wild police chief and persuade him to call off his dogs I'll still need help. Ten million acres of mountains, boss . . . it means men and ships, lots of men, lots of ships. It's no job for one man with a brief case. Besides, I'm going to join the Outer Legion."

"We'll both join," Kiku said glumly. "All right, get on it. Move."

"It's been nice knowing you."

Mr. Kiku switched off, then moved very fast, initiating a fresh departmental intervention, sending an emergency-priority message to the state governor, another to the mayor of Westville, another to the Westville district court. Formal action completed, he sat for a few seconds, bracing himself for what he must do next . . . then went in to tell the Secretary that they must ask for help from the military authorities of the Federation.

X

The Cygnus Decision

WHEN John Thomas woke up he had trouble remembering where he was. The sleeping bag was toasty warm, he felt good, rested but lazy. Gradually the picture of where he was and why he was there built up and he poked his head out. The sun was high and it was pleasantly warm. Lummox was nearby. "Hi, Lummie."

"Hi, Johnnie. You slept a long time. You were noisy, too."

"Was I?" He crawled out and pulled his clothes on, switched off the sleeping bag. He folded it and turned to Lummox—and started. "What's *that?*"

Near Lummox's head, lying squashed out as if it had been stepped on, was a very dead grizzly bear . . . about a six-hundred-pound male. Blood had gushed from mouth and nostrils, then dried. Lummox glanced at it. "Breakfast," he explained.

John Thomas looked at it with distaste. "Not for me, it's not. Where did you get it?"

"I catched it," Lummox answered and simpered.

"Not 'catched it' . . . 'caught it.' "

"But I did catch it. It tried to get in with you and I catched it."

"Well, all right. Thanks." John Thomas looked at the bear again, turned away and opened his food bag. He selected a can of ham and eggs, twisted off the top, and waited for it to heat.

Lummox took this as a signal that it was now all right for him to breakfast, too, which he did—first the bear, then a couple of small pine trees, a peck or so of gravel for crunchiness, and the empty container of John Thomas's breakfast. They went down to the stream afterwards, with Johnnie going first to search the sky; Lummox washed down his meal with a few hogsheads of clear mountain water. Johnnie knelt and drank, then washed his face and hands and wiped them on his shirt. Lummox asked, "What do we do now, Johnnie? Go for a walk? Catch things, maybe?"

"No," Johnnie denied. "We go back up in those trees and lie low until dark. You've got to pretend you're a rock." He went up the bank, Lummox followed. "Settle down," John Thomas ordered. "I want to look at those bumps."

Lummox did so; it brought the tumors down where his master could inspect them without stretching. Johnnie looked them over with increasing worry. They were larger and seemed to have lumps and bumps inside; Johnnie tried to remember whether such a development was a sign of malignancy. The skin over them had stretched and thinned until it was hardly more than thick leather, not in the least like the rest of Lummox's armor. It was dry and hot to his touch. Johnnie kneaded the left one gently; Lummox pulled away.

"Is it that tender?" Johnnie asked anxiously.

"I can't *stand* it," Lummox protested. He extended his legs and walked over to a large pine tree, started rubbing the tumor against it.

"Hey!" said Johnnie. "Don't do that! You'll hurt yourself."

"But it *itches*." Lummox went on scratching.

John Thomas ran to him, intending to be firm. But

just as he reached him the tumor split open. He watched in horror.

Something dark and wet and writhing emerged, caught on the ruptured skin, held there inchoate, then burst free to dangle and flop like a jungle snake from a branch. For an agonized moment all that Johnnie could think was that it was indeed something like that . . . some giant, parasitic worm eating its way out of its unlucky host. He thought with dumb self-blame that he had forced Lummie to climb over the mountains . . . when he was sick to death with *that*.

Lummox sighed and wiggled. "Gee!" he said with satisfaction. "That *feels* better!"

"Lummox! Are you all right?"

"Huh? Why shouldn't I be, Johnnie?"

"Why? Why, *that!*"

"What?" Lummox looked around; the strange growth bent forward and he glanced at it. "Oh, that . . ." he answered, dismissing the matter.

The end of the thing opened out like a blossoming flower . . . and Johnnie realized at last what it was.

Lummox had grown an arm.

The arm dried rapidly, lightened in color and seemed to firm. Lummox did not have much control over it yet, but John Thomas could begin to see its final form. It had two elbows, a distinct hand with thumbs on each side. There were five fingers, seven digits in all, and the middle finger was longer and fully flexible, like an elephant's trunk. The hand did not resemble a human hand much but there was no doubt that it was at least as useful—or would become so; at the moment the digits wiggled aimlessly.

Lummox let him examine it, but did not himself seem especially interested in the development; Lummox acted as if it were something he always did right after breakfast.

Johnnie said, "Let me have a look at the other bump," and walked around Lummox. The rightside tumor was still more bloated. When John Thomas touched it Lummox shrugged away and turned as if to rub it against the tree. "Hold it!" Johnnie called out. "Stand still."

"I've *got* to scratch."

"You might lame yourself for life. Hold still, I want to try something." Lummox sulkily complied; Johnnie took out his belt knife and gently nicked the center of the swelling.

The nick spread and Lummox's right arm came out almost in Johnnie's face. He jumped back.

"Thanks, Johnnie!"

"Any time, any time." He sheathed the knife and stared at the newborn arms, his face thoughtful.

He could not figure all the implications of Lummox's unexpected acquisition of hands. But he did realize that it was going to change things a lot. In what way, he did not know. Perhaps Lummie would not need so much care after this. On the other hand he might have to be watched or he would be forever getting into things he shouldn't. He remembered uneasily someone saying what a blessing it was cats did not have hands . . . well, Lummie had more curiosity than any cat.

But he felt without knowing why that such things were side issues; this was *important*.

In any case, he decided fiercely, this doesn't change one thing: Chief Dreiser isn't going to get another crack at him!

He searched the sky through the branches and wondered if they could be spotted. "Lum . . ."

"Yes, Johnnie?"

"Haul in your legs. It's time to play like a rock."

"Aw, let's go for a walk, Johnnie."

"We'll go for a walk tonight. But until it gets dark I want you to stay put and hold still."

"Aw, Johnnie!"

"Look, you don't want to go downtown again, do you? All right, then, quit arguing."

"Well, if you feel that way about it." Lummox settled to the ground. John Thomas sat down, leaned against him, and thought.

Maybe there was a way in this for Lummie and him to make a living . . . in a carnival or something. E.-t.s were big stuff in carnivals; they couldn't run without them—even though half of them were fakes—and Lummie wasn't a fake. Probably he could learn to do tricks with his hands, play something or something. Maybe a circus was still better.

No, that wasn't the thing for Lummie; crowds made him nervous. Uh, what could the two of them do to make a living? . . . after this mess with the authorities was straightened out, of course. A farm, maybe? Lummie would be better than a tractor and with hands he would be a farm hand, too. Maybe that was the ticket, even though he had never thought about farming.

In his mind's eye he saw himself and Lummox growing great fields of grain . . . and hay . . . and vegetables and . . . unaware that he had fallen asleep.

He was awakened by a cracking noise and knew vaguely that he had heard several of them. He opened his eyes, looked around and found that he was lying beside Lummox. The creature had not left the spot . . . but he was moving his arms. One arm flailed past Lummox's head, there was a blur and another crack . . . and a small aspen some distance away suddenly came down. Several others were down near it.

John Thomas scrambled to his feet. "Hey, stop that!"

Lummox stopped. "What's the matter, Johnnie?" he asked in a hurt voice. There was a pile of rocks in front of him; he was just reaching for one.

"Don't throw rocks at trees."

"But you do, Johnnie."

"Yes, but I don't ruin them. It's all right to eat trees, but don't just spoil them."

"I'll eat them. I was going to."

"All right." Johnnie looked around. It was dusk, they could start again in a few minutes. "Go ahead and have them for supper. Here, wait a minute." He examined Lummox's arms. They were the same color as the rest of him, and beginning to get armor hard. But the most striking change was that they were twice as thick as they had been at first—as big around as Johnnie's thighs. Most of the loose hide had sloughed off; Johnnie found that he could tear off the rest. "Okay. Chow time."

Lummox finished the aspens in the time it took John Thomas to prepare and eat his simple meal, and was ready to eat the empty container as a sweet. It was dark by then; they took to the road.

The second night was even less eventful than the first. It grew steadily colder as they wound even higher; presently Johnnie plugged the power pack of his sleeping bag into his suit. Shortly he was warm and drowsy. "Lum—if I go to sleep, call me when it starts to get light."

"Okay, Johnnie." Lummox stored the order in his after brain, just in case. Cold did not bother him, he was not conscious of it, as his body thermostat was more efficient than was Johnnie's—even more efficient than the one controlling the power pack.

John Thomas dozed and woke up and dozed. He was dozing when Lummox called him, just as the first rays brushed distant peaks. Johnnie sat up and began watching for a place to pull out and hide. Luck was against him; it was straight up on one side and the other side swung over a deep, dismal drop. As minutes wore away and it turned broad daylight he began to get panicky.

But there was nothing to do but plod ahead.

A stratoship passed in the distance. He could hear the thunderclap, but he could not see it; he could only hope that it was not scanning for him. A few minutes later, while searching all around, he spotted behind them a dot that he hoped was an eagle.

Very soon he was forced to admit that it was a single human in a flight harness. "Stop, Lummox! Pull over to the wall. You're a landslide."

"A landslide, Johnnie?"

"Shut up and do it!" Lummox shut up and did it. John Thomas slid down and hid behind Lummox's head, making himself small. He waited for the flier to pass over.

The flier did not pass, but swooped in a familiar shoot-the-works style and came in for a landing. Johnnie sighed with relief as Betty Sorenson landed on the spot he had just vacated. She called out, "Howdy, Lummie," then turned to Johnnie, put her hands on her hips and said, "Well! Aren't you a pretty sight! Running off without telling me!"

"Uh, I meant to, Slugger, I really did. But I didn't have a chance to . . . I'm sorry."

She dropped her fierce expression and smiled. "Never mind. I think better of you than I have in some time. At least you did *something*. Johnnie, I was afraid you were just a big lummox yourself—pushed around by anybody."

John Thomas decided not to argue, being too pleased to see her to take offense. "Uh . . . well, anyway, how did you manage to spot us?"

"Huh? Knothead, you've been gone two nights and you are still only a short flight from town . . . how could you expect not to be spotted?"

"Yes, but how did you know where to look?"

She shrugged. "The old rule: I thought like a mule and went where the mule would. I knew you would be along this road, so I started out at barely 'can-see' and swooped along it. And if you don't want to be caught in the next few minutes we had better boost out of here and get under cover. Come on! Lummie old boy, start your engines."

She put down a hand and Johnnie swung aboard; the procession started up. "I've been trying to get off the road," Johnnie explained nervously, "but we haven't come to a spot."

"I see. Well, hold your breath, 'cause around this bend is Adam-and-Eve Falls and we can get off the road just above them."

"Oh, is that where we are?"

"Yes." Betty leaned forward in a futile attempt to see around a rock shoulder ahead. So doing, she caught her first glimpse of Lummox's arms. She grabbed John Thomas. "Johnnie! There's a boa constrictor on Lummie!"

"What? Don't be silly. That's just his right arm."

"His *what?* Johnnie, you're ill."

"Level off and quit grabbing me. I said 'arms'—those tumor things were arms."

"The tumors . . . were arms?" She sighed. "I got up too early and I haven't had breakfast. I can't take shocks like that. All right, tell him to stop. I got to see this."

"How about getting under cover?"

"Oh. Yes, you're right. You're usually right, Johnnie —two or three weeks late."

"Don't strain yourself. There are the falls."

They passed the falls; the floor of the canyon thereby came up to meet them. John Thomas took the first chance to get off the road, a spot like their bivouac of the day before. He felt much better to have Lummox back under thick trees again. While he prepared breakfast, Betty examined Lummox's brand-new arms.

"Lummox," she said reprovingly, "you didn't tell mama about this."

"You didn't ask me," he objected.

"Excuses, always excuses. Well, what can you do with them?"

"I can throw rocks. Johnnie, is it all right?"

THE CYGNUS DECISION

"No!" John Thomas said hastily. "Betty, how do you want your coffee?"

"Just bare-footed," she answered absently and went on inspecting the limbs. There was a notion hovering in her mind about them, but it would not light . . . which annoyed her, as she expected her mind to work for her with the humming precision of a calculator and no nonsense, please! Oh, well . . . breakfast first.

After they had fed the dirty dishes to Lummox, Betty lounged back and said to John Thomas, "Problem child, have you any idea what a storm you have stirred up?"

"Uh, I guess I've got Chief Dreiser's goat."

"No doubt and correct. But you might as well turn it loose; there won't be room in the pen."

"Mr. Perkins?"

"Right. Keep trying."

"Mum, of course."

"Of course. She alternates between weeping for her lost baby and announcing that you are no son of hers."

"Yeah. I know Mum," he admitted uneasily. "Well, I don't care. I knew they'd all be sore at me. But I had to."

"Of course you had to, Knothead darling, even though you did it with the eager grace of a hippopotamus. But I don't mean them."

"Huh?"

"Johnnie, there is a little town in Georgia named Adrian. It's too small to have a regular safety force, just a constable. Do you happen to know that constable's name?"

"Huh? Of course not."

"Too bad. For as near as I was able to find out, that constable is the only cop who isn't looking for you, which is why I rallied around—even though you, you dirty name, ran off without bothering to alert me."

"I told you I was sorry!"

"And I forgave you. I'll let you forget it in ten years or so."

"What's this nonsense about this constable? And why should everybody be out after me? Aside from Chief Dreiser, I mean?"

"Because he has put out a general alarm and offered a reward for Lummie, alive or dead . . . preferably dead. They are serious about it, Johnnie . . . terribly serious. So whatever plan you had we now junk and shift to a good one. What did you have in mind? Or did you?"

John Thomas turned pale and answered slowly, "Well . . . I meant to keep on like this for a night or two, until we reached a place to hide."

She shook her head. "No good. In their stumbling official way they will have concluded by now that this is where you would head . . . since it is the only place near Westville where a creature the size of Lummox could possibly hide. And . . ."

"Oh, we'd get off the road!"

"Of course. And they will search this forest tree by tree. They really mean it, chum."

"You didn't let me finish. You know that old uranium mine? The Power and Glory? You go over Dead Wolf Pass and then take off north on a gravel road. That's where we're heading. I can put Lummox completely out of sight there; the main tunnel is big enough."

"Flashes of sense in that. But not good enough for what you are up against."

She was silent. Johnnie stirred uneasily and said, "Well? If that's no good, what do we do?"

"Pipe down. I'm thinking." She lay still, staring up at the deep blue mountain sky. At last she said, "You didn't solve anything by running away."

"No . . . but I sure mixed it up."

"Yes, and so far so good. Everything ought to be turned

upside down occasionally; it lets in air and light. But now we've got to see that the pieces fall back where we want them. To do that we've got to gain time. Your notion of the Power and Glory Mine isn't too bad; it will do until I can make better arrangements."

"I don't see why they would ever find him there. It's about as lonely as you can get."

"Which is why it is sure to be searched. Oh, it might fool Deacon Dreiser; I doubt he could find his own hat without a search warrant. But he's dug up an air posse the size of a small army; they are certain to find you. You took your sleeping bag and food; therefore you are camping out. I found you, they will find you. I did it by knowing what makes you tick, whereas they have to work by logic, which is slower. But just as certain. They'll find you . . . and that's the end of Lummox. They won't take chances . . . bomb him, probably."

John Thomas considered the dismal prospect. "Then what's the sense of hiding him in the mine?"

"Just to gain a day or so, because I'm not ready to take him out yet."

"Huh?"

"Of course. We'll hide him in town."

"What? Slugger, the altitude has got you."

"In town and under cover . . . because it is the only place in the wide, wide world they won't look for him." She added, "Maybe in Mr. Ito's greenhouses."

"Huh? Now I know you're crazy."

"Can you think of a safer place? Mr. Ito's son is not hard to reason with; I had a nice talk with him just yesterday. I stood short and looked up at him and let him explain things. One of his greenhouses would be perfect . . . snug, maybe, but this is an emergency. You can't see through that milky glass they are built out of and nobody would dream that Lummie might be inside."

"I don't see how you can do it."

"You let me handle it. If I don't get the greenhouse
. . . but I will! . . . then I'll get an empty warehouse
or something. We'll put Lummie in the mine tonight,
then I'll fly back and arrange things. Tomorrow night
Lummie and I will go back to town and . . ."

"Huh? It took us two nights to get this far—and it
will take us most of tonight to get to the mine. You can't
ride him back in one night."

"How fast can he go when he tries?"

"But nobody can ride him when he gallops. Not even
me."

"I won't ride him; I'll fly over him, pacing him and
making him slow down for curves. Three hours, maybe? . . . and another hour to sneak him into the greenhouse."

"Well . . . maybe it would work."

"It will because it's got to. Then you get caught."

"Huh? Why don't I just go home?"

"No, that would be a giveaway. They catch you,
you've been doing amateur uranium prospecting . . .
I'll fetch out a radiation counter. You don't know where
Lummox is; you kissed him goodbye and turned him
loose, then came up here to forget your sorrows. You'll
have to be convincing . . . and *don't* let them use a truth
meter."

"Yes, but . . . Look, Slugger, what's the good? Lummie can't stay in a greenhouse forever."

"We're simply buying time. They are ready to kill
him on sight . . . and they will. So we keep him out of
sight until we can change that."

"I suppose I should have gone through with the sale
to the Museum," John Thomas answered miserably.

"No! Your instincts are sound, Johnnie, even though
you've got less brains than a door knob. Look . . . do
you remember the Cygnus Decision?"

"The Cygnus Decision? We had it in elementary
Customs of Civilization?"

"Yes. Quote it."

"What is this? A mid-semester quiz?" John Thomas frowned and dug into his memory. " 'Beings possessed of speech and manipulation must be presumed to be sentient and therefore to have innate human rights, unless conclusively proved otherwise.' " He sat up. "Hey! They can't kill Lummox—he's got hands!"

XI

"It's Too Late, Johnnie"

"MIND your air speed," she cautioned. "Do you know the old one about the man whose lawyer assured him that they could not put him in jail for *that?*"

"What was 'that'?"

"Never mind. His client answered, 'But, counsellor, I'm *speaking* from the jail.' Point is, the Cygnus Decision is just theory; we've got to keep Lummox out of sight until we can get the court to change its mind."

"Unh, I see. I guess you're right."

"I'm always right," Betty admitted with dignity. "Johnnie, I'm dying of thirst; thinking is dry work. Did you bring any water up from the creek?"

"No, I didn't."

"Got a bucket?"

"Yeah, somewhere." He felt in his pockets, found it and pulled it out. He stopped to blow it up to semi-rigidity, then said, "I'll fetch it."

"No, give it to me. I want to stretch my legs."

" 'Ware fliers!"

"Don't teach your grandmother." She took it and went down hill, keeping to the trees until she reached the bank. Johnnie watched her slim figure catching shafts of cathedral light among the pines and thought how pretty she was . . . very nearly as good a head on her as a man and pretty to boot. Aside from being bossy the way females always were, Slugger was all right.

She came back carrying the plastic bucket carefully. "Help yourself," she offered.

"Go ahead."

"I drank from the creek."

"All right." He drank deeply. "You know, Betty, if you weren't knock-kneed, you'd be pretty good-looking."

"Who's knock-kneed?"

"And there's always your face, of course," he went on pleasantly. "Aside from those two shortcomings you're not—"

He did not finish—she dived and hit him low. The water went all down his front and partly on her. The scuffle continued until he got her right arm locked up behind her, holding her helpless. "Say 'Pretty please,' " he advised.

"Darn you, Johnnie Stuart! 'Pretty please.' "

"With sugar on it?"

"With sugar on it—and spit, too. Let me up."

"All right."

He got to his feet. She rolled to a sitting position, looked up at him and laughed. They were both dirty, scratched, and somewhat bruised and they both felt very fine indeed. Lummox had watched the mock fight with interest but no alarm, since Johnnie and Betty could never really be mad at each other. He commented, "Johnnie's all wet."

"He certainly is, Lummie—more ways than one." She looked him over. "If I had two clothes pins, I'd hang you on a tree. By your ears, of course."

"We'll be dry in five minutes, a day like this."

"I'm not wet, not through a flying suit. But you look like a dunked cat."

"I don't mind." He lay down, found a pine needle and bit it. "Slugger, this is a swell place. I wish I didn't have to go on up to the mine."

"Tell you what—after we get this mess straightened out and before we start school, we'll come back up here and camp a few days. We'll bring Lummox, too—won't we, Lummie?"

"Sure," agreed Lummox. "Catch things. Throw rocks. Fun."

John Thomas looked at her reprovingly. "And get me talked about all over town? No, thanks."

"Don't be prissy. We're here now, aren't we?"

"This is an emergency."

"You and your nice-nice reputation!"

"Well, somebody ought to watch such things. Mum says that boys had to start worrying when girls quit. She says things used to be different."

"Of course they were—and they will be again. They run the whole program over and over again." She looked thoughtful. "But, Johnnie, you pay too much attention to what your mother says."

"I suppose so," he admitted.

"You had better break yourself of it. Otherwise no girl is going to take a chance on marrying you."

He grinned. "That's my insurance policy."

She dropped her eyes and blushed. "I wasn't speaking for myself! I don't want you—I'm just taking care of you for practice."

He decided not to pursue that angle. "Honestly," he said, "a person gets in the habit of behaving a certain way and it's hard to stop. For instance, I've got an aunt—my Aunt Tessie, remember her?—who believes in astrology."

"No! She *doesn't!*"

"Surest thing. She doesn't look nutty, does she? But she is and it's embarrassing because she just will talk about it and mother insists that I have to be polite.

If I could just tell her she has holes in her head, it wouldn't matter. But oh no! I have to listen to her rave and pretend that she's a sane, responsible adult—when she can't count above ten without an abacus."

"An 'abacus'?"

"You know—a slipstick with beads. I said 'abacus' because there isn't a prayer that she could ever learn to read a slipstick. She *likes* being a lame brain—and I have to cater to it."

"Don't do it," Betty said suddenly. "Pay no attention to what your mother says."

"Slugger, you are a subversive influence."

"Sorry, Johnnie," she answered mildly. She added, "Did I ever tell you why I divorced my parents?"

"No, you never did. That's your business."

"So it is. But I think I'll tell you, you might understand me better. Bend down." She grabbed him by an ear, whispered into it.

As John Thomas listened he took on an expression of extreme surprise. "Not really?"

"Fact. They didn't contest it so I never had to tell anyone. But that's why."

"I don't see how you put up with it."

"I didn't. I stood up in court and divorced them and got a professional guardian who doesn't have nutty ideas. But look, Johnnie, I didn't bare my soul just to make your chin drop. Heredity isn't everything; I'm myself, an individual. You aren't your parents. You're not your father, you are not your mother. But you are a little late realizing it." She sat up straight. "So be yourself, Knothead, and have the courage to make your own mess of your life. Don't imitate somebody else's mess."

"Slugger, when you talk that stuff, you make it sound rational."

"That's because I'm always rational. How well fixed are you for groceries? I'm hungry."

"You're as bad as Lummox. The grub sack is over there."

"Lunch?" inquired Lummox, hearing his name.

"Umm . . . Betty, I don't want him tearing down trees, not in daylight. How long will it take them to track me down?"

"I wouldn't count on over three days, big as this place is."

"Well . . . I'll hold back food for five, just in case." He selected a dozen canned rations and gave them to Lummox. He did not open them as Lummox rather liked having the packages suddenly become hot when he bit into them. He finished them off before Betty had their own lunches opened.

After they ate Johnnie started to bring up the subject again. "Betty, do you really think that—" He broke off suddenly. "Hear anything?"

She listened, then nodded solemnly.

"How fast?"

"Not over two hundred."

He nodded. "Then they are scanning. Lummox! Don't more a muscle!"

"I won't, Johnnie. Why not move a muscle?"

"Do it!"

"Don't get excited," Betty advised. "They are probably just laying out their search pattern. Chances are they couldn't identify us either in the scope or visually with these trees to break up the image." But she looked worried. "I wish Lummie were already in the mine tunnel, though. If anyone is smart enough to run a selective scan straight down that road while we're on it tonight . . . well, we've had it."

John Thomas was not really listening. He was leaning forward, cupping his ears with both hands. "Hush!" he whispered, "Betty—they're coming back!"

"Don't panic. It's probably the other leg of the search pattern."

But even as she said it she knew that she was wrong. The sound came over them, hovered and dropped in pitch. They looked up, but the denseness of the forest and the altitude of the craft kept them from seeing it.

Suddenly there was a light so bright that it made the sharp sunlight seem dusky when it passed. Betty gulped. "What was *that?*"

"Ultraflash photo," he answered soberly. "They're checking what they picked up on the scope."

The sound above them squealed higher, then dropped; the eyeburning flash occurred again. "Stereoed it," Johnnie announced solemnly. "They'll really see us now, if they only suspected before."

"Johnnie, we've got to get Lummox out of here!"

"How? Take him up on the road and let them pin-point him with bomb? No, kid, our only hope now is that they decide he is a big boulder—I'm glad I made him stay tucked in." He added, "We mustn't move, either. They may go away."

Even that outside hope passed. One after another, four more ships were heard. Johnnie ticked them off. "That one has taken station to the south. The third one was north, I think. Now they'll cover to the west . . . a pinwheel guard. They've got us boxed, Slugger."

She looked at him, her face dead white. "What do we do, Johnnie?"

"Huh? Why, noth— No, Betty look. You duck down through the trees to the creek. Take your flight harness with you. Then follow the stream a good distance and take to the air. Keep low until you get out from under their umbrella. They'll let you go—they don't want you."

"And what will *you* be doing?"

"Me? I stay here."

"And so do I."

Johnnie said fretfully, "Don't make me any trouble, Slugger. You'd just be in the way."

"What do you think you can do? You don't even have a gun."

"I have this," John Thomas answered grimly, touching his sheath knife, "—and Lummox can throw rocks."

She stared at him, then laughed wildly. "What? Rocks indeed! Oh, Johnnie—"

"They're not going to take us without a fight. Now will you get out of here—fast!—and quit being a nuisance?"

"No!"

"Look, Slugger, there isn't time to argue. You get clear and fast. I stay with Lummox; that's my privilege. He's mine."

She burst into tears. "And you're *mine*, you big stupid oaf."

He tried to answer her and could not. His face began to break in the spasmodic movements of a man trying to control tears. Lummox stirred uneasily. "What's the matter, Johnnie?" he piped.

"Huh?" John Thomas replied in a choked voice. "Nothing." He reached up and patted his friend. "Nothing at all, old fellow. Johnnie's here. It's all right."

"All right, Johnnie."

"Yes," agreed Betty faintly. "It's all right, Lummie." She added in a low voice to John Thomas. "It'll be quick, won't it, Johnnie? We won't feel it?"

"Uh, I guess so! Hey! None of that—in just one half second I'm going to punch you right on the button . . . and then dump you off the bank. That ought to protect you from the blast."

She shook her head slowly, without anger nor fear. "It's too late, Johnnie. You know it is. Don't scold me—just hold my hand."

"But—" He stopped. "Hear that?"

"More of them."

"Yeah. They're probably building an octagon . . . to make sure we don't get out."

A sudden thunderclap spared her the need to answer. It was followed by the squeal of a hovering ship; this time they could see it, less than a thousand feet over their heads. Then an iron voice rumbled out of the sky. "Stuart! John Stuart! Come out in the open!"

Johnnie took out his sheath knife, threw back his head and shouted, "Come and get me!"

Betty looked up at him, her face shining, and patted his sleeve. "Tell 'em, Johnnie!" she whispered. "That's my Johnnie."

The man behind the giant voice seemed to have a directional mike trained on him; he was answered: "We don't want you and we don't want to hurt anybody. Give up and come out."

He threw back a one-word defiance and added, "We aren't coming out!"

The thundering voice went on, "Final warning, John Stuart. Come out with your hands empty. We'll send a ship down for you."

John Thomas shouted back, "Send it down and we'll wreck it!" He added hoarsely to Lummox, "Got some rocks, Lummie?"

"Huh? Sure! Now, Johnnie?"

"Not yet. I'll tell you."

The voice remained silent; no ship came down to them. Instead a ship other than the command ship dropped swiftly, squatted a hundred feet above the pines and about the same distance from them laterally. It started a slow circle around them, almost a crawl.

Immediately there was a rending sound, then a crash as a forest giant toppled to the ground. Another followed at once. Like a great invisible hand a drag field from the ship knocked over trees and swept them aside. Slowly it cut a wide firebreak around them. "Why are they doing that?" Betty whispered.

"It's a forestry service ship. They're cutting us off."

"But why? Why don't they just do it and get it over with?" She began to shake, he put an arm around her.

"I don't know, Slugger. They're driving."

The ship closed the circle, then faced them and seemed to settle back on its haunches. With the delicate care of a dentist pulling a tooth the operator reached in, selected one tree, plucked it out of the ground, and tossed it aside. He picked another—and still another. Gradually a wide path was being cut through the timber to the spot where they waited.

And there was nothing to do but wait. The ranger's ship removed the last tree that shielded them; the tractor field brushed them as he claimed it, making them stagger and causing Lummox to squeal with terror. John Thomas recovered himself and slapped the beast's side. "Steady, boy. Johnnie is here."

He thought about having them retreat back from the clearing now in front of them, but there seemed no use in it.

The logging ship lay off; an attack ship moved in. It dropped suddenly and touched ground at the end of the corridor. Johnnie gulped and said, "*Now*, Lummox. Anything that comes out of that ship—see if you can hit it."

"You bet, Johnnie!" Lummox reached with both hands for ammunition.

But he never picked up the rocks. John Thomas felt as if he had been dumped into wet concrete up to his chest; Betty gasped and Lummox squealed. Then he piped, "Johnnie! The rocks are stuck!"

John Thomas labored to speak. "It's all right, boy. Don't struggle. Just hold still. Betty, you all right?"

"Can't breathe!" she gasped.

"Don't fight it. They've got us."

Eight figures poured out of the door of the ship. They looked not human, being covered head to foot with heavy metal mesh. Each wore a helmet resembling a fencer's mask and carried as a back pack a field anti-generator. They trotted confidently in open double file toward the passage through the trees; as they struck the field they slowed slightly, sparks flew, and a violet nimbus formed around each. But on they came.

The second four were carrying a large metal-net cylinder, high as a man and of equal width. They balanced it easily up in the air. The man in the lead called out, "Swing wide of the beast. We'll get the kids out first, then dispose of him." He sounded quite cheerful.

The squad came up to the odd group of three, cutting around without passing close to Lummox. "Easy! Catch them both," the leader called out. The barrellike cage was lowered over Betty and John Thomas, setting slowly until the man giving orders reached inside and flipped a switch—whereupon it struck sparks and dropped to the ground.

He gave them a red-faced grin. "Feels good to get the molasses off you, doesn't it?"

Johnnie glared at him with his chin quivering, and replied insultingly while he tried to rub cramps out of his leg muscles. "Now, now!" the officer answered mildly. "No good to feel that way. You made us do it." He glanced up at Lummox. "Good grief! He *is* a big beast, isn't he? I'd hate to meet him in a dark alley, without weapons."

Johnnie found that tears were streaming down his face and that he could not stop them. "Go ahead!" he cried, his voice misbehaving. "Get it over with!"

"Eh?"

"He never meant any harm! So kill him quickly . . . don't play cat-and-mouse with him." He broke down and sobbed, covering his face with his hands. Betty put her hands on his shoulders and sobbed with him.

The officer looked distressed. "What are you talking about, son? We aren't here to hurt him. We have orders to bring him in without a scratch on him—even if we lost men in the process. Craziest orders I ever had to carry out."

XII

Concerning Pidgie-Widgie

MR. KIKU was feeling good. Breakfast was not a burning lump in his middle; he felt no need to shop in his pill drawer, nor even a temptation to get out his real estate folders. The Triangular Conference was going well and the Martian delegates were beginning to talk sense. Ignoring the various amber lights on his desk he began singing: *"Frankie and Johnnie were lovers . . . and oh boy how they could love . . . swore to be true to each other . . ."*

He had a fair baritone voice and no sense of pitch.

Best of all that silly, confused Hroshian affair was almost over . . . and no bones broken. Good old Doc Ftaeml seemed to think that there was an outside chance of establishing diplomatic relations, so delighted the Hroshii had been at recovering their missing Hroshia.

With a race as powerful as the Hroshii diplomatic relations were essential . . . they must be allies, though that might take a while. Perhaps not too long, he decided; they certainly did nip-ups at the sight of Lummox . . . almost idolatrous.

Looking back, the things that had confused them were obvious. Who would have guessed that a creature half as big as a house and over a century old was a baby? Or that this race attained hands only when old enough to use them? For that matter, why was this Hroshia so much bigger than its co-racials? Its size had misled

Greenberg and himself as much as anything. Interesting point . . . he'd have the xenologists look into it.

No matter. By now Lummox was on his . . . *her* way to the Hroshian ship. No fuss, no ceremony, no publicity, and the danger was over. Could they actually have volatilized Terra? Just as well not to have found out. All's well that ends well. He went back to singing.

He was still singing when the "urgent" light began jittering and he delivered the last few bars into Greenberg's face: ". . . *just as true as the stars above!*" He added. "Sergei, can you sing tenor?"

"Why should you care, boss? That wasn't a tune."

"You're jealous. What do you want, son? See them off okay?"

"Unh, boss, there's a slight hitch. I've got Dr. Ftaeml with me. Can we see you?"

"What is it?"

"Let's wait until we are alone. One of the conference rooms?"

"Come into the office," Mr. Kiku said grimly. He switched off, opened a drawer, selected a pill and took it.

Greenberg and the medusoid came in at once: Greenberg flopped down in a chair as if exhausted, pulled out a cigarette, felt in his pockets, then put it away. Mr. Kiku greeted Dr. Ftaeml formally, then said to Greenberg, "Well?"

"Lummox didn't leave."

"Eh?"

"Lummox refused to leave. The other Hroshii are boiling like ants. I've kept the barricades up and that part of the space port around their landing craft blocked off. We've got to do something."

"Why? This development is startling, but I fail to see that it's our responsibility. Why the refusal to embark?"

"Well . . ." Greenberg looked helplessly at Ftaeml.

The Rargyllian said smoothly, "Permit me to explain, sir. The Hroshia refuses to go aboard without her pet."

"Pet?"

"The kid, boss. John Thomas Stuart."

"Exactly," agreed Ftaeml. "The Hroshia states that she has been raising 'John Thomases' for a long time; she refuses to go home unless she can take her John Thomas with her. She was quite imperious about it."

"I see," agreed Kiku. "To put it in more usual language the boy and the Hroshia are attached to each other. That's not surprising; they grew up together. But Lummox will have to put up with the separation, just as John Thomas Stuart had to. As I recall, he made a bit of fuss; we told him to shut up and shipped him home. That's what the Hroshia must do: tell her to shut up, force her, if necessary, into their landing craft and take her along. That's what they came here for."

The Rargyllian answered, "Permit me to say, sir, that by putting it into 'more usual language' you have missed the meaning. I have been discussing it with her in her own tongue."

"Eh? Has she learned so quickly?"

"She has long known it. The Hroshii, Mr. Under Secretary, know their own language almost from the shell. One may speculate that this use of language almost on the instinctive level is one reason, perhaps *the* reason, why they find other languages difficult and never learn to use them well. The Hroshia speaks your language hardly as well as one of your four-year-old children, though I understand that she began acquiring it one of your generations ago. But in her own language she is scathingly fluent . . . so I learned, much to my sorrow."

"So? Well, let her talk. Words can't hurt us."

"She *has* talked . . . she has given orders to the commander of the expedition to recover her pet at once. Otherwise, she states, she will remain here and continue raising 'John Thomases.'"

179

"And," Greenberg added, "the commander has handed us an ultimatum to produce John Thomas Stuart at once . . . or else."

" 'Or else' meaning what I think it means?" Kiku answered slowly.

"The works," Greenberg said simply. "Now that I've seen their ground craft I'm not sure but what they can."

"You must understand, sir," Ftaeml added earnestly, "that the commander is as distressed as you are. But he must attempt to carry out the wishes of the Hroshia. This mating was planned more than two thousand of your years ago; they will not give it up lightly. He cannot allow her to remain . . . nor can he force her to leave. He is very much upset."

"Aren't we all?" Mr. Kiku took out two more pills. "Dr. Ftaeml, I have a message for your principals. Please convey it exactly."

"I shall, sir."

"Please tell them that their ultimatum is rejected with contempt. Please . . ."

"Sir! I beg of you!"

"Attend me. Tell them that and do not soften it. Tell them that we tried in every way to help them, that we succeeded, and that they have answered kindness with threats. Tell them that their behavior is unworthy of civilized people and that the invitation to join the Community of Civilizations is withdrawn. Tell them that I spit in their faces . . . find an idiom of equal strength. Tell them that free men may die, but they are never bullied."

Greenberg was grinning widely and clasping both hands in the ancient sign of approval. Dr. Ftaeml seemed to grow pale under his outer chitin.

"Sir," he said, "I greatly regret being required to deliver this message."

Kiku smiled icily. "Deliver it as given. But before you

do, find opportunity to speak to the Hroshia Lummox. You can do so?"

"Most assuredly, sir."

"Tell her that the commander of the expedition, in his zeal, seems bent on killing the human, John Thomas Stuart. See that she understands what is threatened."

The Rargyllian arranged his mouth in a broad smile. "Forgive me, sir; I underestimated you. Both messages will be delivered, in the proper order."

"That is all."

"Your good health, sir." The Rargyllian turned to Greenberg, put a loose-jointed arm around his shoulders. "My brother Sergei, we have already found our way together out of one tight maze. Now, with the help of your spiritual father, we shall find our way out of another. Eh?"

"Right, Doc."

Ftaeml left. Kiku turned to Greenberg and said, "Get the Stuart boy here. Get him at once, yourself, personally. Umm . . . bring his mother, too. He's under age, isn't he?"

"Yes. Boss, what's the plan? You aren't going to turn him over to them? . . . after that wonderful kick in the teeth you handed them?"

"Of course I am. But on my own terms. I don't intend to let those animated pool tables think they can push us around. We'll use this to get what we want. Now get going!"

"I'm gone."

Mr. Kiku stayed at his desk, checking papers with part of his mind while letting his subconscious feel out the problem of Lummox. He had a strong hunch that tide was at flood . . . for humans. It was necessary to judge how to ride it. He was in this revery when the door opened and the Most Honorable Mr. Roy MacClure walked in. "There you are, Henry! Pull yourself together, man . . . Beulah Murgatroyd is coming to call."

"Beulah who?"

"Beaulah Murgatroyd. *The* Beulah Murgatroyd."

"Should I know?"

"What? Man, don't you ever watch stereovision?"

"Not if I can possibly avoid it."

MacClure shook his head indulgently. "Henry, you don't get around enough. You bury yourself in here and push your little buttons and don't even know what is going on in the world."

"Possibly."

"Positively. You're out of touch, man . . . it's a good thing you don't have to deal with people."

Mr. Kiku permitted himself a wintry smile. "I suppose so."

"I'll bet you three to one you don't know who is ahead in the World Series."

"The World Series? That's baseball, isn't it? I'm sorry but I haven't even had time to follow the cricket matches of late years."

"See what I mean? Though how you can mention cricket in the same breath with baseball . . . Never mind. Since you don't know who the famous Beulah Murgatroyd is, I'll tell you. She's Pidgie-Widgie's mother, so to speak."

" 'Pidgie-Widgie'?" Mr. Kiku echoed.

"You're pulling my leg. The creator of the Pidgie-Widgie stories for children. You know—*Pidgie-Widgie on the Moon, Pidgie-Widgie Goes to Mars, Pidgie-Widgie and the Space Pirates.*"

"I'm afraid I don't."

"That's hard to believe. But you don't have any kids, do you?"

"Three."

But Mr. MacClure was still talking. "Now she's taken Pidgie-Widgie on the air and it's really something. For the kids of course but so comical that the grown-ups follow it, too. You see, Pidgie-Widgie is a puppet about a foot high. He goes zooming through space, rescuing people and blasting pirates and having a grand ole time . . . the kids love him. And at the end of each installment Mrs. Murgatroyd comes on and they have a bowl of Hunkies together and talk. You like Hunkies?"

Mr. Kiku shuddered. "No."

"Well, you can just pretend to eat them, I suppose. But it is the biggest breakfast-food show on the air, reaches everybody."

"And this is important?"

"Important? Man, do you know how many people eat breakfast every morning?"

"No. Not too many, I hope. I wish I had not."

Mr. MacClure glanced at his watch. "We'll have to hurry. The technicians are setting up the gear now. She'll be here any moment."

"Technicians?"

"Didn't I say? Mrs. Murgatroyd will interview us, with Pidgie-Widgie in her lap and taking part. Then they'll patch it into the show. A wonderful boost for the department."

"*No!*"

"Eh? Mr. Kiku, did I understand you correctly?"

"Mr. Secretary," Mr. Kiku said tensely, "I couldn't possibly do that. I . . . I'm subject to stage fright."

"What? Why, that's absurd! You helped me open the Triangular Conference. You spoke without notes for thirty minutes."

"That's different. That's shop talk, with other professionals."

The Secretary frowned. "I hate to insist, if it really makes you nervous. But Mrs. Murgatroyd asked for you especially. You see . . ." MacClure looked mildly embarrassed. ". . . Pidgie-Widgie preaches racial tolerance and so forth. Brothers under the skin . . . the sort of thing we all want to encourage. So?"

Mr. Kiku said firmly, "I'm sorry."

"Come now! Surely you're not going to force me to insist?"

"Mr. Secretary," Kiku answered quietly, "you will find that my job description does not require me to be a stereovision actor. If you will give me a written order, I will submit it to our legal bureau for opinion, then answer you officially."

Mr. MacClure frowned. "Henry, you can be a stubborn little beast, can't you? I wonder how you got so high in the heap?"

Mr. Kiku did not answer; MacClure went on, "I won't let you pull the rule book on me; I'm too old a fox. Though I must say I didn't think you would do that to me."

"Sorry, sir. I really am."

"So am I. I'll try to convince you that it is important to the department, whether a civil servant can be ordered to do it or not. You see, Beulah Murgatroyd is the power behind 'The Friends of Lummox.' So . . ."

" 'The Friends of Lummox'?"

"I knew you would see it differently. After all, you've been handling that whoop-te-do. Therefore . . ."

"What in heaven's name are 'The Friends of Lummox'?"

"Why, you set up the original interview with them yourself. But if I hadn't happened to lunch with Wes Robbins, we might have missed the boat on it."

"I seem to recall a memorandum. A routine matter."

"Mrs. Murgatroyd is *not* routine, I've been trying to tell you. You precedent-and-protocol boys lose touch with the people. If you don't mind my saying so, that's why you never quite get to the top."

"I don't mind in the least," Mr. Kiku said gently.

"Eh?" The Secretary looked slightly embarrassed. "I mean, there's a place for a grass-roots politician, like me, with his finger on the pulse . . . though I admit I don't have your special training. You see?"

"There is work for both our talents, sir. But go on. Perhaps I did 'miss the boat' in this instance. The 'Friends of Lummox' memorandum must have come through before the name meant anything to me."

"Probably. I wasn't criticizing your attention to duty, Henry. Fact is, you work too hard . . . the universe won't run down if you don't wind it. But about this F. of L. deal—we intervened in some silly case out west; you know about it, you sent one of our people—the case turned out to be about his Hoorussian Lummox. The court's verdict . . . *our* verdict, you might say, was to destroy the beast. By the way, Henry, have you disciplined the man responsible?"

"No, sir."

"Why the delay?"

"He won't be disciplined, sir. He was perfectly right, on the evidence."

"I don't see it that way. Better send his file jacket to my office. I want to consider it myself."

"Sir," Mr. Kiku said softly, "were you thinking of reversing me on a matter of administrative discipline?"

"Eh? I intend to review the matter."

"Because if you are, sir, you can have my resignation now. My usefulness will be at an end."

"What? Henry, don't be nasty." The Secretary drummed on Mr. Kiku's desk. "Confound it, man, let's be frank with each other. I know that you career men can make it hard for an appointee if you try . . . I didn't get into politics yesterday. But as long as I am holding the sack, I intend to have discipline around here. My privilege?"

"Yes . . . your privilege."

"And my responsibility. Probably you are right about this man, whoever he is . . . you're usually right, or we couldn't keep things going. But it is my responsibility to review things whenever I think it necessary. However, there is no call for you to talk about resigning

until I actully do reverse you. Since you have forced
the issue, if I do find it necessary to reverse you on
this, I'll *ask* for your resignation. But until I do, keep
your shirt on. Fair enough?"

"Fair enough. I was hasty, Mr. Secretary. The file
jacket will be on your desk."

"On second thought, don't bother. If you are carrying one of your favorites . . ."

"I have no favorites, Mr. MacClure. I dislike them
all, impersonally."

"Sometimes I think you hate yourself. Now where
were we? Oh yes! Well, when we made that terrible
bust about the Hoorussian, Mrs. Murgatroyd saw a chance
to do a good deed. Oh, I suppose she was out to pep up
her program, but that's beside the point. Right away,
Pidgie-Widgie started telling all his little friends about
this terrible thing and asked them all to write in and
join the Friends of Lummox. She got over three million
replies in the first twenty-four hours. By now half the
kids on this continent and nobody knows how many
elsewhere are 'Friends of Lummox,' pledged to protect
him from persecution."

"Her," corrected Mr. Kiku.

"Eh?"

"I beg your pardon. I suppose neither term is correct.
The Hroshii come in six assorted sexes. You can call
Lummox either 'him' or 'her' . . . we really need new
words. But it doesn't matter."

"Well, it certainly doesn't to me," agreed MacClure.
"But if we had actually put the quietus on this Lummox, I believe the kids would have started a revolution.
I really do. Not to mention the adults who are Pidgie-
Widgie fans. Even so, the department got a black eye
out of it. But Beulah Murgatroyd is willing to go along
with a deal to help us out. She interviews us and I
answer the general questions and you back me up
on the details—all about how the department is care-

ful to protect the rights of our non-human friends and how everybody ought to be tolerant—the usual line. Then Pidgie-Widgie asks what happened to Lummox and you tell the kiddies how Lummox was really sort of a fairy prince in disguise . . . or princess . . . and how Lummox has gone away to his home in the sky. It will be terrific."

MacClure added, "That's all you have to do. They patch in a shot of Lummox getting into the Hoorussian ship and waving goodbye. Then we all eat a bowl of Hunkies—don't worry, I'll see that your bowl is empty! —and Pidgie-Widgie sings his 'Skylarker' song. End. It won't take twenty minutes and it will be a big thing for the department. Okay?"

"No."

"Now, Henry . . . All right, you won't even have to *pretend* to eat Hunkies."

"No."

"Henry, you're impossible. Don't you agree that it is our business to help train up the kids to understand their responsibilities and have right attitudes in this modern age—the age of the Community of Civilizations?"

"No, sir, I do not. That is the business of parents and educators, not of government. This department has more than it can do just to try to hold things together in the face of ever-increasing xenic problems." Mr. Kiku added to himself: even if I did agree, I wouldn't do it by eating Hunkies!

"Hmm . . . A narrow attitude, Henry. A bureaucratic one, if I may say so. You know perfectly well that we are in hot water about this Hoorussian thing from other directions, too, with The Society for the Preservation of the Status Quo screaming for isolation and the Keep Earth Human League jumping on us. It gets the Council uneasy. Along comes a chance to build up public opinion against such crackpots and you won't even help. You don't have the Status Quo people and the Human-Earth jokers bothering you—because *I* keep them off your neck."

"I'm sorry, sir. But you shouldn't waste time on them either. No doubt you know that there is a money motive back of every one of those apparently crackpot organizations. Let the people with opposing economic interests fight them—the shipping lines and the importers and the scientists. Our business is foreign relations. When we are bothered by pressure groups, we should let our public relations people handle them; that is what they are for."

"What am I but a glorified public relations man?" MacClure answered angrily. "I haven't any illusions about this confounded job."

"Not true, sir. You have the prime policy responsibility. I carry out policy—within the limits of my job."

"Hummph! You set policy. You drive me like a horse. I'm beginning to realize it."

"Sorry, sir. I suppose everyone makes policy . . . even the doorman . . . to some extent. It's unavoidable. But I try to do my job."

Mr. Kiku's private secretary called in by voice. "Mr. Kiku, is the Secretary with you? Mrs. Beulah Murgatroyd is waiting."

"Be right in," called out MacClure.

Kiku added quietly, "Mildred, see that she is entertained. There will be a slight delay."

"Yes, sir. The Secretary's aide is taking care of her."

"Good."

"There will be no delay," MacClure said to Mr. Kiku. "If you won't, you won't . . . though I'm disappointed in you. But I can't keep her waiting."

"Sit down, Mr. Secretary."

"Eh?"

"Sit down, sir. Even the mighty Mrs. Murgatroyd must wait on some things. A major emergency has come up; you will certainly have to face the Council about it . . . possibly a special session this evening."

"What? Why didn't you say so?"

"I was organizing my thoughts preparatory to briefing you, sir, when you came in. For the past several minutes I have been trying to tell you that this department has really important things to do—besides selling Hunkies."

The Secretary stared at him, then reached across Kiku's desk. "Uh, Mildred? This is the Secretary. Tell Commodore Murthi that I am unavoidably detained and that he is to do his best to keep Mrs. Murgatroyd happy."

"Yes. Mr. Secretary."

MacClure turned back. "Now, Henry, quit lecturing me and spill it."

Mr. Kiku began a full report of the new Hroshii crisis. Mr. MacClure listened without comment. Just as Mr. Kiku concluded his account of the rejection of the ultimatum the sound communicator again came to life. "Chief? Murthi here. Mrs. Murgatroyd has another appointment."

Mr. MacClure turned toward the voice. "Hush circuit?"

"Of course, sir."

"Listen, Jack, I'll be a few minutes yet. Keep her happy."

"But—"

"Make love to her, if necessary. Now switch off. I'm busy!" He turned back to Mr. Kiku and scowled. "Henry, you've shoved me out on a limb again. You've left me nothing to do but back your play."

"May I ask what the Secretary would have done?"

"Huh?" MacClure frowned. "Why, I would have said exactly what you said, I suppose . . . but in nastier language. I admit that I probably wouldn't have thought of cutting inside them through this Lummox creature. That was cute."

"I see, sir. It being a rejection of a formal ultimatum, what precautionary action would the Secretary have taken? I should add that I wanted to avoid having the department advise the Council to order battle stations for the entire planet."

"What are you saying? Nothing like that would have been necessary. I would have ordered the Inner Guard to close and blast them out of the sky, on my own responsibility. After all, they are at our inner defense zone and breathing threats . . . a simple emergency police action."

Mr. Kiku thought, that is what I guessed you would do . . . but what he said was, "Suppose it turned out that their ship failed to blast out of the sky . . . and blasted back?"

"What? Preposterous!"

"Mr. Secretary, the only thing I have learned in forty years at this trade is that when you are dealing with 'Out There' nothing is preposterous."

"Well, I'll be . . . Henry, you actually believed they could hurt us. You were frightened." He searched Mr. Kiku's face. "Are you holding something back? Do you have evidence that they might be able to carry out this preposterous threat?"

"No, sir."

"Well?"

"Mr. MacClure, in my country hardly more than three hundred years ago there lived a very valiant tribe. A small force of Europeans made certain demands on them . . . taxes, they called it. The chief was a brave man and his warriors were numerous and well trained. They knew the strangers had guns, but they even had some guns of their own. But mostly they relied on numbers and courage. They planned cleverly and caught the enemy in a box canyon. So they thought."

"Yes?"

"They had never heard of machine guns. They learned about them in a very final way—for they were very brave and kept coming on. That tribe is no more, no survivors."

"If you are trying to scare me, well . . . never mind. But you still haven't given me evidence. After all, we are not an ignorant tribe of savages. No parallel."

"Perhaps. Yet, after all, the machine gun of that era was only a minor improvement over the ordinary gun of the time. We have weapons which make a machine gun seem like a boy's knife. And yet . . ."

"You are suggesting that these Hoorussians have weapons that would make our latest developments as useless as clubs. Frankly, I don't want to believe it and I don't. The power in the nucleus of the atom is the ultimate possible power in the universe. You know that, I know that. We've got it. No doubt they've got it, too, but we outnumber them millions to one and we are on our home grounds."

"So the tribal chief reasoned."

"Eh? Not the same thing."

"Nothing ever is," Mr. Kiku answered wearily. "I was not speculating about magic weapons beyond the concepts of our physicists; I was merely wondering what some refinement might do to a known weapon . . . some piece of tinkering already implicit in the theories. I don't know, of course. I know nothing of such things."

"Well, neither do I but I've been assured that . . . See here, Henry; I'm going to order that police action, right away."

"Yes, sir."

"Well? Don't sit there frozen-faced saying 'Yes, sir.' You don't *know*, do you? So why shouldn't I do it?"

"I did not object, sir. Do you want a sealed circuit? Or do you want the base commander to report here?"

"Henry, you are without question the most irritating

man in seventeen planets. I asked you why I should *not* do it?"

"I know of no reason, sir. I can only tell you why I did not recommend it to you."

"Well?"

"Because I did *not* know. Because I had only the fears of a non-human who might be even more timid than myself, or badly misled by what appears to be almost superstitious awe. Since I did not know, I did not choose to play Russian roulette with our planet at stake. I chose to fight with words as long as possible. Do you want to give the order, sir? Or shall I take care of the details?"

"Quit badgering me." He glared at his Under Secretary, his face red. "I suppose your next move is to threaten to resign."

Mr. Kiku grudged a small smile. "Mr. MacClure, I never offer to resign twice in the same day." He added, "No, I will wait until after the police action. Then, if we are both alive, I will have been proved wrong on a major matter; my resignation will be necessary. May I add, sir, that I hope you are right? I would much rather enjoy a quiet old age than to have my judgment vindicated posthumously."

MacClure worked his mouth but did not speak. Mr. Kiku went on quetly, "May I offer a suggestion to the Secretary in my official capacity?"

"What? Of course. You are required to by law. Speak up."

"May I urge that the attack commence in the next few minutes? We may achieve by haste what might fail by delay. BuAstro can supply us with the orbit elements of the enemy ship." Kiku leaned toward his communicator.

It came to life before he could touch it. "Chief? Murthi here. I've done my best, but she . . ."

"Tell her I can't see her!"

"Sir?"

"Uh . . . butter it on. You know how. Now shut up and don't call me again."

"Aye aye, sir."

Mr. Kiku called BuAstro. "The chief ballistician, please . . . at once. Ah, Cartier . . . seal your end; this end is sealed. And put a hush on it. All right, I want the tactical elements of the . . ."

MacClure reached out and broke the connection. "All right," he said savagely, "you've outbluffed me."

"I was not bluffing, sir."

"All right, all right, you've convinced me that you have a wise head on you. I can't take a blind chance with the lives of five billion people any more than you can. Want me to crawl?"

"No, sir. But I am much relieved. Thank you."

"*You're* relieved? How about *me*? Now tell me how you intend to play this. I'm still in the dark."

"Very well, Mr. Secretary. In the first place I have sent for the Stuart boy . . ."

"The Stuart boy? Why?"

"To persuade him to go. I want his consent."

The Secretary looked as if he could not believe his ears. "Do I understand, Mr. Kiku, that after rejecting their ultimatum your only plan is to capitulate?"

"That is not how I would describe it."

"I don't care what diplomatese you phrase it in. We will not surrender the boy. I was not willing to take a risk blindly, but this is another matter. I will not surrender one human being no matter what the pressure is . . . and I can assure you that the Council will agree. There is such a thing as human dignity. I must add that I am astonished . . . and disgusted."

"May I continue, sir?"

"Well . . . go ahead. Speak your piece."

"No thought of surrendering the boy was ever in my mind. In the science of diplomacy appeasement has long been an exploded theory. Had I even considered sacrificing the boy, I would applaud your disgust. As it is, it missed me."

"But you said . . ."

"Please, sir. I know what I said. I sent for the boy to explore his own wishes. From what I know of him it is possible that he will be willing, even eager."

MacClure shook his head. "It's not something we could permit, even if the lad were crazy enough to do it. Nine hundred light-years from other human beings? I would as soon offer poison to a baby."

"That's not the picture at all, sir. If I have his consent, I can keep the fact to myself during negotiations . . . play from a concealed ace. There is much to negotiate."

"Such as?"

"Their science. Their trade. A whole new volume of space. The possibilities can be only dimly seen."

MacClure stirred restlessly. "I'm not sure but what that attack is still the thing to do. If men are men, some risks must be taken. Snuggling up to vermin who threaten us . . . I don't like it."

"Mr. Secretary, if my plans do not work . . . or fail to meet your approval, then I will join you in shouting defiance at the sky. We should bargain . . . but bargain as men."

"Well . . . go on. Tell me the rest."

XIII

"No, Mr. Secretary"

MR. KIKU's wife let him sleep late the next morning. She did this occasionally, reasoning that no crisis was important enough to wake him when he needed rest. When he got to his office he found Wesley Robbins, Special Assistant Secretary for public relations, asleep in his chair. Robbins was not a diplomat, did not want to be one, and made a point of showing it.

"Good morning, Wes," Mr. Kiku said mildly.

"What's good about it?" Robbins chucked a copy of the *CAPITAL TIMES* at the Under Secretary. "Seen this?"

"No." Mr. Kiku unfolded it.

"Twenty-three years in the newspaper business . . . to be scooped on my own beat."

Mr. Kiku read:

> ### ALIEN INVADERS
> ### THREATEN WAR ! !
> #### Demand Hostages
>
> Capital Enclave, Sep. 12 (GP) . . . Space Secretary MacClure revealed today that the xenic visitors dubbed "Hroshii" now landed at Capital port have demanded, under threats of war, that the Federation . . .

Kiku scanned down, saw that a distortion of his answer to the Hroshii had been credited to Secretary MacClure, with no mention of the possibility of peaceful settlement. A trailer story reported the Chief of the General Staff as assuring Earth and all the federated planets that there was nothing to fear from the insolent aliens. A South Asian senator demanded to know what steps were being taken . . . Kiku glanced at it all but discarded the meaningless 90%, including a blast from the Keep Earth Human League and a "We Stand at the Crossroads" editorial. There was an interview with Mrs. Murgatroyd but he did not take time to find out which side Pidgie-Widgie was on.

"Ain't that a mess?" Robbins demanded. "Where do you hide your cigarettes?"

"It does seem a rather lavish waste of paper," Kiku agreed. "In the arm of the visitor's chair."

"Well, how do we handle it? I was caught flat-footed. Why doesn't somebody tell me these things?"

"Just a moment." Mr. Kiku leaned to his desk. "Security? Ah, O'Neill . . . place more special police around the Hroshii landing craft . . ."

"You've got 'em, boss. But why doesn't somebody tell us these things?"

"A fair question. Whatever guard you are using, use more. There must not only be no riot; there must be no incidents. Station as many trained tension-dispersal technicians in the crowd as you can scrape up, then borrow more from other agencies. Then give special attention to lunatic-fringe organizations . . . xenophobic ones, I mean. Any trouble yet?"

"Nothing we couldn't snuff out. But I'm making no promises. I still think somebody ought to tell . . ."

"No doubt. Keep in touch with me." Kiku turned to Robbins. "Do you know how the interview happened to be granted?"

"Do I act like it? He was going to the 'Tri Con' citation dinner, safe as houses. I got his approval on his speech, gave him his copy and passed the others around to the boys, with suggestions on how to play it. Everybody happy. I get up this morning feeling ninety and before I've had my coffee I feel a hundred and fifty. Know anybody wants my job? I'm going to study how to be a beachcomber."

"A reasonable thought. Wes, let me bring you up to date. Nothing was to be released about this matter until it was concluded, but now . . . ." He quickly outlined the latest Hroshij crisis.

Robbins nodded, "I see. And Number One jerked the rug out from under you. A fine playmate."

"Well, we had better see him. Is he here?"

"Yes. I was waiting for you, pal. Will you hold him while I hit him? Or the other way around?"

"Whichever you wish. Shall we get it over with?"

The Secretary was in; they were admitted and Mac-Clure got up to seat them. After which they just sat. Robbins waited for Mr. Kiku to speak, but Kiku held still, face expressionless, a statue carved of ebony.

MacClure began to fidget. "Well, Henry? This is a busy morning . . . I've already been tied up with the S. G."

"I had thought that you would want to instruct us, Mr. Secretary."

"What for?"

"Have you seen the morning papers, sir?"

"Well . . . yes."

"There has been a change in policy. Assistant Secretary Robbins and I would like to be briefed on the new policy."

"What new policy?"

"Your new policy concering the Hroshii, Mr. Secretary. Or are the newspapers in error?"

"Eh? Well, no, not precisely. Exaggerated of course. But no change in policy. I simply told the people what they were entitled to know."

"The people are entitled to know." Mr. Kiku fitted his fingers together. "Ah, yes. In a government based on free consent of free men the people are always entitled to know. An old bureaucrat, such as myself, sometimes loses track of that fundamental. Thank you for reminding me." He seemed lost in cosmic thought for a moment, then added, "I suppose the thing now is to repair my failure and tell the people everything."

"Eh? What do you mean?"

"Why, the whole story, Mr. Secretary. How through our own ignorance and disregard for the rights of others, both now and in the past, we kidnapped a member of a civilized race. How blind luck alone kept that xenian alive. How as a result of this we now find our own planet threatened with destruction—and how a highly intelligent citizen of a friendly power (I refer to Dr. Ftaeml) assures us that these Hroshii can indeed destroy us. It would be necessary to tell them also that yesterday we were within minutes of ordering an attack on these xenians—but that we lost our nerve and decided to negotiate, since we had no knowledge of our strength relative to theirs, but only the very sobering opinion of Dr. Ftaeml to guide us. Yes, we must tell them that."

Secretary MacClure's mouth was as wide as his eyes. "Heavenly days, Henry! Are you trying to set off riots?"

"Sir? I have taken countermeasures to prevent riots . . . xenophobia is always ready to flare up and *that* . . ." He gestured at the newspaper. ". . . will have an inflammatory effect on some. But you must not be deterred. We bureaucrats become paternalistic; it is so much simpler to do what seems best and let the people know it afterwards . . . negotiate, or blast a ship out of the sky, or whatever. Mr. Secretary, you have kept in mind, of course, that this Secretariat of which you are a member is responsible not to the North American Union, nor even to the peoples of Earth, but to all sovereignties of the Federation, both on Terra and elsewhere?"

"What's that got to do with it? We're the leading power."

"Whom do you mean by 'we'? Not my little country certainly. No, I was thinking that this will now be settled by vote of the Council and I was wondering whether the Council might possibly vote to surrender one unimportant citizen of North America rather than risk an interstellar war? I wonder how Mars will vote?"

The Secretary got up and strode up and down his office. It was a large room, much larger than Mr. Kiku's. He stopped at the far end and stared out at the Tow-

er of Three Planets and the Hall of Civilizations, while
Kiku sat quietly. Wes Robbins slumped in a chair, his
bony legs stretched in front of him. He was trimming
his nails with a pocket knife; they were long and black
and needed the attention.

MacClure turned suddenly to Kiku. "See here, Henry, you confounded word splitter, I won't be bullied."

"Bullied, Mr. Secretary?"

"Yes, bullied. Oh, you dressed it up in your usual
double-talk, but I wasn't born yesterday. You know
perfectly well that if we give the press these unnecessary details . . . that nonsense this Dr. Fatima or
whatever his name is, this Rargyllian monster, filled
you with . . . yes, and you threatening to tell the press
that I got cold feet about an attack . . . that's a threat
if I ever heard one! . . . you give 'em all that junk
and we'd have a row in the Council that would be
heard from here to Pluto! With the home governments
sending special instructions to their delegates and maybe the Terran bloc getting outvoted. Right on top of
this ticklish Triangular Conference it could be disastrous. Yes, that's the word . . . *disastrous.*" MacClure
stopped and struggled for breath. "Well, you won't get
away with it. You're fired! . . . understand me? *Fired!*
I'll take care of having you removed for cause, or trans-
ferring you to the retired list, or whatever the red tape
calls for, but you are done, right now. I'm relieving
you. You can go home."

"Very well, Mr. Secretary," Mr. Kiku said evenly and
started for the door to his office.

In the silence Wes Robbins' knife clicked shut loudly. He stood up. "Hold it, Henry! Mac . . ."

Mr. MacClure looked around. "Huh? What's the matter with *you?* And don't call me 'Mac'; this is official
business. I'm still Secretary around here, as I just told
Kiku."

"Yes, you are still Secretary—for about two hours, maybe."

"What? Don't be ridiculous! Wes, you will force me to fire you too if you talk that way. Mr. Kiku, you are excused."

"Don't go away, Henry. And quit shoving that stuff, Mac. You can't fire me, I quit ten minutes ago. Mac, are you a complete stuffed shirt? Remember, I knew you when you were a shorthorned Senator, anxious to get a two-inch squib in a gossip column. I liked you then. You seemed to have horse sense, which is scarce in this business. Now you are ready to dump me and I don't like you either. But tell me, for old times' sake: why are you anxious to cut your own throat?"

"What? Not *my* throat. I'm not the Charlie to let a subordinate cut my throat. I've seen it done . . . but Kiku picked the wrong man."

Robbins shook his head slowly. "Mac, you are dead set on scuttling yourself. Hadn't you better cut Henry's tongue out before the newsboys reach him? Here, you can borrow my knife."

"What?" MacClure looked stunned. He swung around and snapped, "Mr. Kiku! You are not to speak to the press. That's an order."

Robbins bit off some cuticle, spat it out, and said, "Mac, for Pete's sake! You can't both fire him and keep him from talking."

"Departmental secrets . . ."

" 'Departmental secrets' my bald spot! Maybe you could fine him severance pay under the official-secrets rule but do you think that will stop him? Henry is a man with no fears, no hopes, and no illusions; you can't scare him. What he can tell the reporters will do you more harm if you classify it 'secret' than it would if you didn't try to gag him."

"May I say something?" asked the center of the storm.

"Eh? Go ahead, Mr. Kiku."

"Thank you, Mr. Secretary. I had no intention of telling the press about the messier aspects of this affair. I was simply trying to show, by reductio ad absurdum, that the rule of keeping the public informed can . . . like any rule . . . lead to disaster if applied blindly. I felt that you had been indiscreet, sir. I hoped to keep you from further indiscretions while we sought means to repair the damage."

MacClure studied him. "You mean that, Henry?"

"I always mean what I say, sir. It saves time."

MacClure turned to Robbins. "You see, Wes? You were barking up the wrong tree. Henry is an honorable man, even if we do have our differences. See here, Henry, I was too hasty. I honestly thought you were threatening me. Let's forget what I said about asking for your resignation and get on with our jobs. Eh?"

"No, sir."

"What? Come, man, don't be small. I was angry, I was hurt, I made a mistake. I apologize. After all, we have public welfare to consider."

Robbins made a rude noise; Mr. Kiku answered gently, "No, Mr. Secretary, it wouldn't work. Once having been fired by you, I would not again be able to act with confidence under your delegated authority. A diplomat must always act with confidence; it is often his only weapon."

"Um . . . Well, all I can say is I'm sorry. I really am."

"I believe you, sir. May I make a last and quite unofficial suggestion?"

"Why, certainly, Henry."

"Kampf would be a good man to keep routine moving until you work out your new team."

"Why, surely. If you say he is the man for it, I'm sure he must be. But Henry . . . we'll keep him there on a temporary basis and you think it over. We'll call it sick leave or something."

"No," Mr. Kiku answered coldly and turned again toward his own office.

Before he could reach it Robbins spoke up loudly. "Take it easy, you two. We aren't through." He spoke to MacClure: "You said that Henry was an honorable man. But you forgot something."

"Eh? What?"

"I ain't."

Robbins went on, "Henry wouldn't do anything that wasn't cricket. Me, I was raised in a river ward and I'm not bothered by niceties. I'm going to gather the boys together and give 'em the word. I'm going to tell them where the body is buried, how the apple cart was upset, and who put the overalls in the chowder."

MacClure said angrily, "You hand out an unauthorized interview and you'll never hold another job with the administration!"

"Don't threaten me, you over-ripe melon. I'm not a career man; I'm an appointee. After I sing my song I'll get a job on the *Capital Upside Down* column and let the public in on the facts about life among the supermen."

MacClure stared at him. "You don't have any sense of loyalty at all."

"From you, Mac, that sounds real sweet. What are you loyal to? Aside from your political skin?"

Mr. Kiku interposed mildly, "That's not exactly fair, Wes. The Secretary has been quite firm that the Stuart boy must not be sacrificed to expediency."

Robbins nodded. "Okay, Mac, we'll give you that. But you were willing to sacrifice Henry's forty years of service to save your own ugly face. Not to mention shooting off that face without checking with *me*, just to grab a front-page story. Mac, there is nothing a newspaper man despises more than headline hunger. There is something lascivious and disgusting about a man overanxious to see his name in headlines. I can't reform you and don't want to, but be sure that you are going to see your name in headlines, big ones . . . but for the last time. Unless . . ."

"What do you mean? . . . 'unless'?"

"Unless we put Humpty-Dumpty together again."

"Uh, how? Now look, Wes, I'll do anything within reason."

"You sure will." Robbins frowned. "There's the obvious way. We can serve Henry's head up on a platter. Blame that interview yesterday on him. He gave you bad advice. He's been fired and all is sweetness and light."

Mr. Kiku nodded. "That's how I had envisioned it. I'd be happy to cooperate . . . provided my advice is taken on how to conclude the Hroshij affair."

"Don't look relieved, Mac!" Robbins growled. "That's the obvious solution and it would work . . . because Henry is loyal to something bigger than he is. But that is not what we are going to do."

"But, if Henry is willing, then in the best interests—"

"Stow it. It won't be Henry's head on the platter; it will be yours."

Their eyes locked. At last MacClure said, "If that is your scheme, Robbins, forget it and get out. If you are looking for a fight, you'll get one. The first story to break will be about how I had to fire you two for disloyalty and incompetence."

Robbins grinned savagely. "I hope you play it that way. I'll have fun. But do you want to hear how it could be worked?"

"Well . . . go ahead."

"You can make it easy or hard. Either way, you are through. Now keep quiet and let me tell it! You're done, Mac. I don't claim to be a scholar of xenic affairs, but even I can see that civilization can't afford your county-courthouse approach to delicate relations with non-human races. So you're through. The question is: do you do it the hard way? Or do you go easy on yourself and get a nice puff in the history books?"

MacClure glowered but did not interrupt. "Force me to spill what I know, and one of two things happens. Either the Secretary General throws you to the wolves, or he decides to back you up and risk a vote of 'no confidence' from the Council. Which is what he would get. The Martian Commonwealth would gleefully lead the stampede, Venus would follow, the outer colonies and the associated xenic cultures would join in. At the end you would have most of the Terran nations demanding that the North American Union surrender this one individual to avert a bust-up of the Federation.

"All you have to do is to shove the first domino; all the others would fall . . . and you would be buried under the pile. You couldn't be elected dogcatcher. But the easy way runs like this. You resign . . . but we don't publish the fact, not for a couple of weeks . . . Henry, do you think two weeks will be long enough?"

"It should be ample," Mr. Kiku agreed gravely.

"During that time you don't wipe your nose without Henry's permission. You don't say a word unless I okay it. Then you resign in a blaze of glory, with the conclusion of the Hroshian Affair to crown your career. Possibly some way can be found to kick you upstairs to a gaudier job . . . if you are a good boy. Eh, Henry?"

Mr. Kiku nodded.

MacClure looked around from Kiku's expressionless face to Robbins' contemptuous one. "You two have it neatly plotted," he said bitterly. "Suppose I told you both to go to the devil?"

Robbins yawned. "It won't matter in the long run, believe me. After the administration falls, the new Secretary General will call Henry out of retirement, a safe man will be stuck in your place, and Henry will get on with outmaneuvering the Hroshii. Probably lose three days maybe less. Whitewashing you is harder, but we meant to give you a break. Right, Henry?"

"It would be better so. Dirty linen is best kept in a cupboard."

MacClure chewed his lip. "I'll think it over."

"Good! And I'll wait while you do. Henry, why don't you get back to work? I'll bet that trick desk is lighted up like a Christmas tree."

"Very well." Mr. Kiku left the room.

His desk did look like a fireworks celebration, with three blinking red lights and a dozen amber ones. He disposed of urgent matters, brushed off lesser ones, and began to reduce the stack in his basket, signing without bothering to consider whether his signature continued to carry authority.

He was just sustaining a veto on a passport for a very prominent lecturer—the last time the idiot had been off Earth, he had broken into a temple and taken pictures —when Robbins walked in and chucked a paper on his desk. "Here's his resignation. Better see the Secretary General at once."

Mr. Kiku took it. "I shall."

"I didn't want you there when I twisted his arm. It's harder for a man to say 'Uncle' with a witness. You understood?"

"Yes."

"I had to bring up the time we covered up for him about the convention with Kondor."

"Regrettable."

"Don't waste tears. Enough is enough. Now I am going to write the speech he will make before the Council. After that I'll look up the boys he talked to last night and beg them, for the sake of their dear old home planet, to take the proper line on the follow-up story. They won't like it."

"I suppose not."

"But they'll go along. Us humans have got to stick together; we are badly outnumbered."

"So I have always felt. Thanks, Wes."

"A pleasure. Just one thing I didn't mention to him . . ."

"So?"

"I didn't remind him that the boy's name was John Thomas Stuart. I'm not sure the Martian Commonwealth would have bolted, in view of that one fact. The Council might have sustained Mac, after all . . . and we might have found out whether the Hroshian laddies can do what they say they can."

Kiku nodded. "I thought of that, too. It didn't seem time to mention it."

"No. There are so many swell places for a man to keep his mouth shut. What are you smiling at?"

"I was thinking," Mr. Kiku explained, "that it is a good thing that the Hroshii do not read our newspapers."

XIV

"Destiny? Fiddlesticks!"

MRS. STUART did read newspapers. Greenberg had had great trouble persuading her to come to Capital and to bring her son, because he was not free to tell her why. But he did persuade her and she had agreed to go the following morning.

When Greenberg arrived the next morning to pick them up he found himself *persona non grata*. She was in a white fury and simply shoved the newspaper into his hand. He glanced at it. "Yes? I saw a copy at the hotel. Nonsense, of course."

"That's what I've been trying to tell mother," John Thomas said sullenly, "but she won't listen."

"John Thomas, you keep quiet. Well, Mr. Greenberg? What have you to say for yourself?"

Greenberg did not have a good answer. He had tried to call Mr. Kiku as soon as he saw the news story and had been told by Mildred that the boss and Mr. Robbins were with the Secretary and could not be disturbed. He told her that he would call later, realizing uneasily that trouble was not all at his end.

"Mrs. Stuart, surely you know that news reports are often distorted. There has been no talk of hostages and . . ."

"How can you say that when it says so right there! That's an interview with the Secretary of Space. Who knows more about it? You? Or the Secretary?"

Greenberg had his own opinion but did not dare express it. "Please, Mrs. Stuart. Newspaper stories should not be accepted at face value. This wild report has nothing to do with the case. I am simply asking you to come to Capital for a quiet talk with the Under Secretary."

"Not likely! If the Under Secretary wants to see me, let him come here."

"Madam, he will, if necessary. Mr. Kiku is an old-fashioned gentleman who would not ask a lady to come to him were it not for the press of public affairs. You know that there is an interplanetary conference in progress?"

She answered smugly, "I make it a rule never to pay attention to politics."

He sighed. "Some of us must. Mr. Kiku is unable to come here today because of that conference. We had hoped that you, as a private citizen, would come to him."

"Mr. Greenberg, I reluctantly consented. Now I find that you have deceived me. How do I know but what this is a trick? A plot to turn my son over to those *monsters?*"

"Ma'am, on my honor as an officer of the Federation I assure you . . ."

"Spare yourself, Mr. Greenberg. Now, if you will excuse me . . ."

"Mrs. Stuart, I beg you. If you will only . . ."

"Mr. Greenberg, do not force me to be rude to a guest. But I have nothing more to say."

Greenberg left. He looked around, intending to bring the boy into the argument, but John Thomas had quietly left. Greenberg went back to his hotel, with no intention of returning to Capital with mission incomplete but judging it useless to argue until she had time to simmer down.

He had his taxi driver drop him on the hotel roof in order to avoid reporters, but a man was waiting there, armed with an interview phone. "Half a mo', Mr. Commissioner. My name's Hovey. How about a few words on Secretary MacClure's announcement?"

"No comment."

"In other words you agree with it?"

"No comment."

"Then you disagree?"

"No comment. I'm in a hurry." This was true; he was anxious to call in and find out what in the name of blue blazing galaxies *had* happened.

"Just a second, please. Westville has a big local angle. I'd like to get a story before the main office sends heavyweights here to push me aside."

Greenberg relaxed a little . . . no sense in antagonizing the press and the fellow had a point; he knew how it felt to have someone senior sent to cope with a problem that had started as his. "Okay. But keep it brief; I really am in a hurry." He took out cigarettes. "Got a light on you?"

"Sure." They lighted up, Hovey continued, "People are saying that this blast of the Secretary's is just a smoke screen and that you have come here to get the

Stuart boy and turn him over to the Hroshii people. How about it?"

"No com . . . No, don't say that; say this and quote me. No citizen of the Federation ever has been or ever will be surrendered as a hostage to any power whatsoever."

"That's official?"

"That's official," Greenberg said firmly.

"Then what are you doing here? I understand you are trying to take the Stuart kid and his mother back to Capital. Capital Enclave isn't legally part of the North American Union, is it? If you got him there, our local and national officials couldn't protect him."

Greenberg shook his head angrily. "Any citizen of the Federation is on his home grounds in the Enclave. He has all rights there that he has at home."

"Why do you want him there?"

Greenberg lied fast and fluently. "John Thomas Stuart has knowledge of the psychology of the Hroshii held by no other human being. We want his help in dealing with them."

"That's more like it. 'Westville Boy Recruited as Diplomatic Aide.' How's that for a lead?"

"Sounds good," Greenberg agreed. "Got enough? I'm in a rush."

"Sure," agreed Hovey. "I can pad this to a couple of thousand words. Thanks, Commissioner. See you later."

Greenberg went down and locked himself in, then turned to the phone, intending to call the department, but it came to life first. Chief Dreiser looked out at him. "Mr. Commissioner Greenberg . . ."

"How do you do, Chief?"

"Well enough, thank you. But Mr. Greenberg—I've just had a call from Mrs. Stuart."

"Yes?" Greenberg had a sudden wish for one of those pills the boss ate.

"Mr. Greenberg, we always try to cooperate with you gentlemen."

Greenberg attempted a stop thrust. "So? Were you cooperating when you attempted to kill the Hroshia without waiting for authority?"

Dreiser turned red. "That was a mistake. It has nothing to do with what I must say now."

"Which is?"

"Mrs. Stuart's son is missing. She thinks he might be with you."

"So? She's mistaken. I don't know where he is."

"Is that true, Mr. Commissioner?"

"Chief, I do not tolerate being called a liar."

Dreiser went doggedly ahead. "Sorry. But I must add this. Mrs. Stuart does not want her son to leave town. The police department backs her up a hundred per cent." •

"Naturally."

"Don't mistake me, Mr. Commissioner. You are a very important official—but you are just another citizen if you get out of line. I read that news story and I didn't like it."

"Chief, if you find that I am doing anything illegal, I urge you to do your duty."

"I shall, sir. I certainly shall."

Greenberg switched off, started again to call in, and thought better of it. If the boss had new instructions, he would send them . . . and Kiku despied field agents who chased back to mama whenever there was a slight shift in the wind. He must change Mrs. Stuart's mind—or hole up here for the winter.

While he was thinking the phone again signaled; he answered and found himself looking at Betty Sorenson. She smiled and said, "This is Miss Smith speaking."

"Umm . . . how do you do, Miss Smith."

"Well, thank you. But busy. I have a client, a Mr. Brown. He is being urged to take a trip. What he wants to know is this: he has a friend at the city of his destination; if he makes this trip, will he be allowed to see his friend?"

Greenberg thought rapidly. The other Hroshii would be around Lummox as thick as flies; it might be dangerous to let the boy go where they were and he was sure Mr. Kiku had not so intended.

Oh, the police could throw a tanglefoot field over the whole space port if necessary! The Hroshii weren't superhuman. "Tell Mr. Brown that he will see his friend."

"Thank you. Uh, Mr. Jones, where could your pilot pick us up?"

Greenberg hesitated. "It would be better for Mr. Brown to make the trip by the commercial lines. Just a moment." He found the flight schedule folder provided in most hotel rooms. "There is a ship leaving Stateport in about an hour. Could he catch it?"

"Oh, yes. But . . . well, there is a matter of money."

"Oh. Suppose I make you a personal loan? You, not Mr. Brown."

She broke into a grin. "That would be lovely!"

"Have you any suggestion as to how to get it to you?"

Betty did have—a snack shop called *The Chocolate Bar* across from Central High School. A few minutes later he was waiting in it, sipping a chocolate-and-milk mess. Betty showed up, he passed her an envelope and she left. He stayed there until he could no longer face the contents of his glass, then went back to the hotel.

He waited two hours, then called Mrs. Stuart. "I have just heard that your son left for Capital on his own."

He waited for her to quiet down, then added, "Mrs. Stuart, I'm still in Westville but am about to fly back to Capital. Would you care to come with me? My ship is faster than the commercial liners."

Half an hour later they left for Capital.

Mr. Kiku saw John Thomas Stuart first. Old enough to be John Thomas's grandfather, he treated John Thomas as an equal, thanking him for coming, offering refreshment. He explained briefly that Lummox was unwilling to return home unless John Thomas went along. "It is extremely important to the Hroshii that Lummox return. To us it is important for other reasons."

"You mean," John Thomas said bluntly, "that they are going to fight us if I don't? That's what the papers say."

Mr. Kiku hesitated briefly. "They may. But that is not the reason I have consulted you. I doubt if the Hroshii would attempt anything if your friend Lummox opposed it—which I think Lummox would if it was something dangerous to you, such as an attack on this planet."

"Oh, I'm sure of that, if Lummie has anything to say about it. But why should they listen to him? Uh, is he royal, or something?"

"Perhaps 'royal' will do, since we don't understand their customs. But Lummox's wishes are important."

John Thomas shook his head in wonder. "Seems funny. The way I used to boss him around."

"In any case I am not asking you to save us from a possible war. I am thinking of positive benefits, not negative ones; we want to establish friendly relations with these people. I asked you here to find out your own wishes. If I make it possible for you to go with Lummox to their planet—Hroshijud it is called—what would your answer be? Think it over, you need not answer now."

John Thomas gulped. "I don't need to think it over. I'd go, of course."

"Don't be hasty."

"I'm not being hasty. Lummie will need me. He's never happy with strangers. Anyhow, he wants me to. You don't think I'd let him down, do you?"

"No. But this is a serious decision. You'll be going almost a thousand light-years from home."

John Thomas shrugged. "My great grandfather went there. Why shouldn't I?"

"Mmm . . . yes. I keep forgetting your ancestry. But aren't you interested in knowing what other human beings are going with you? Or even if there are to be any?"

"Huh?" John Thomas thought about it. "Oh, those details will work themselves out. It's not my business."

"They will be worked out," Mr. Kiku answered. He stood up. "Thank you for coming."

"Not at all, sir. Uh . . . when do I get to see Lummox?"

Mr. Kiku pursed his lips. "Not right away; I have matters to settle first. In the meantime, enjoy yourself. I'm assigning a man to guide you around and pay your expenses. He will act as bodyguard, too."

"A bodyguard? What for? I'm grown up."

"So you are. But, if for no other reason, I don't want you talking to reporters. Do you mind? I have no authority to tell you not to."

"Oh no, Mr. Kiku . . . if it will help."

"It will help."

Mr. Kiku had received John Thomas at his desk, Mrs. Stuart he received in a lavish room, one without a conference table and which had been designed by subtle psychologists to impress visitors. Mr. Kiku knew that he was in for a bad time.

He fended her off with tea and formality, forced the talk to trivia. "So good of you to come, madame. Sugar? Lemon?"

"Uh, neither, thank you. Mr. Kiku, I must make clear first off that . . ."

"Try these little puffs. Did Mr. Greenberg make you comfortable?"

"What? Oh, yes, a nice suite, overlooking the Gardens of Heaven. But Mr. Kiku . . ."

"I was sorry to ask you to come to me. But I am the

prisoner of my job. You understand?" He spread his hands helplessly. "I can't leave Capital at certain times."

"That's understandable, I suppose. Now . . ."

"Your kindness is appreciated. You must remain, as an official guest, as long as you see fit. Capital is worth seeing, even if one has seen it often . . . which no doubt you have. I understand that the shopping is excellent, too."

"Well, as a matter of fact I haven't seen it before. Some of the shops do look intriguing."

"Then enjoy it, dear lady. No reason not to mix pleasure with business. Which brings us to business, I suppose. I have been talking with your son."

"Mr. Kiku . . ."

"Indulge me, I will be brief. We are sending an extensive cultural and scientific mission to the home planet of the Hroshii. I want to send your son as a special aide. He has agreed to go." He waited for the explosion.

"Utterly unthinkable! Out of the question!"

"Why, Mrs. Stuart?"

"Mr. Kiku, what sort of inhuman beast are you? I know what you mean . . . you plan to turn my son, my only son, over to those monstrosities as a hostage. Unspeakable!"

He shook his head. "Ma'am, you have been misled by a wild newspaper story. Have you seen the later story? The Secretary's speech before the Council?"

"No, but . . ."

"I will supply a copy. It explains how that nonsense got into print. It also affirms the ancient policy of the Federation, 'All for One' . . . against the Galaxy if necessary. In this case your son is that 'one'; he has many planets behind him. But no such issues arises; your son will join a peaceful mission to a friendly people. He will help build a cultural bridge between two civilized but very different races."

"Hmmph! The paper said that these Hroshii demanded that you turn my son over to them. Explain *that* if you can!"

"Difficulties of translation. They asked for your son by name, but on behalf of that Hroshia which was for years part of your own household, Lummox. Because Lummox is deeply attached to your son. This friendship between these two, transcending form and kind and source and mind, is one of the greatest fortunes which has happened to our race since our people first discovered that we were not sole heirs of the Almighty. This unlikely circumstance will let us bridge in one leap a chasm of misunderstanding ordinarily spanned by years of trial and tragic error." He paused. "One is tempted to think of them as children of destiny."

Mrs. Stuart snorted. " 'Destiny'! Fiddlesticks!"

"Can you be sure, ma'am?"

"I can be sure of this: my son is *not* going to the other side of nowhere. In another week he is entering college, which is where he belongs."

"Is it his education which worries you, ma'am?"

"What? Why, of course. I want him to get a good education. His father set up a trust fund for it; I intend to carry out his wishes."

"I can put your mind at rest. In addition to an embassy, we will send a cultural mission, a scientific mission, an economics and trade mission, and many specialists, all topflight minds. No single college could hire such an aggregation of talent; even the largest institutions of learning would be hard put to match it. Your son will be taught, not casually but systematically. If he earns a degree, it will be awarded by, uh . . . by the Institute of Outer Sciences." He smiled. "Does that suit you?"

"Why, I never heard of such a silly arrangement. Anyway, the Institute isn't a college."

"It can bestow a degree. Or, if not, we will have its charter amended. But degrees are unimportant, ma'am, the point his that your son will have an unparalleled higher education. I understand that he wishes to study xenic science. Well, not only will his teachers be the finest possible, but also he will live in a new field laboratory of xenology and take part in the research. We know little of the Hroshii; he will labor on the frontiers of science."

"He's *not* going to study xenology."

"Eh? He told Mr. Greenberg that he meant to."

"Oh, he has that silly idea but I have no intention of indulging him. He will study some sound profession—the law, probably."

Mr. Kiku's brows went up. "Please, Mrs. Stuart," he said plaintively. "Not that. I am a lawyer—he might wind up where I am."

She looked at him sharply. He went on, "Will you tell me why you plan to thwart him?"

"But I won't be . . . No, I see no reason why I should. Mr. Kiku, this discussion is useless."

"I hope not, ma'am. May I tell a story?" He assumed consent and went on, "These Hroshii are most unlike us. What is commonplace to us is strange to them, and vice versa. All we seem to have in common is that both races are intelligent.

"To us they seem unfriendly, so remote that I would despair, were it not for one thing. Can you guess what that is?"

"What? No, I can't."

"Your son and Lummox. They prove that the potential is there if we will only dig for it. But I digress. More than a hundred years ago a young Hroshia encountered a friendly stranger, went off with him. You know our half of that story. Let me tell you their side, as I have learned it with the help of an interpreter and our xenologists. This little Hroshia was important to them; they wanted her back very badly. Their patterns are not ours; they interweave six distinct sorts of a genetic scheme we will be a long time understanding.

"This little Hroshia had a role to play, a part planned more than two thousand years ago, around the time of Christ. And her part was a necessary link in a larger planning, a shaping of the race that has been going on, I am told, for thirty-eight thousand of our years. Can you grasp that, Mrs. Stuart? I find it difficult. A plan running back to when Cro-Magnon man was disputing with Neanderthals for the prize of a planet . . . but perhaps my trouble lies in the fact that we are ourselves the shortest-lived intelligent race we have yet found.

"What would we do if a child was missing for more than a century? No need to discuss it; it in no way resembles what the Hroshii did. They were not too worried about her welfare; they did not think of her as dead . . . but merely misplaced. They do not die easily. They do not even starve to death. Uh, perhaps you have heard of flatworms? Euplanaria?"

"I have never taken any interest in xenobiology, Mr. Kiku."

"I made the same error, ma'am; I asked, 'What planet is it from?' Euplanaria are relatives of ours; there are many more flatworms on Earth than there are men. But they have a characteristic in common with Hroshii; both breeds grow when fed, shrink when starved . . . and seem to be immortal, barring accidents. I had wondered why Lummox was so much larger than the other Hroshii. No mystery . . . you fed Lummox too much."

"I *told* John Thomas that repeatedly!"

"No harm done. They are already shrinking her down. The Hroshii were not angry, it seems, over the theft or kidnapping or luring away of their youngster. They knew her—a lively, adventuresome disposition was part of what had been bred into her. But they did want her back and they searched for her year after year, following the single clue that she must have gone off with a certain group of visitors from space; they knew what those visitors looked like but not from what part of the sky they came.

"It would have discouraged us . . . but not them. I have a misty impression that the century they spent chasing rumors, asking questions, and checking strange planets was—*to them*—about what a few months would be to us. In time they found her. Again, they were neither grateful nor angry; we simply did not count.

"That might have been our only contact with the noble Hroshii had not a hitch developed; the Hroshia, now grown big but still young, refused to leave without her monstrous friend—I speak from the Hroshian viewpoint. This was terrible to them, but they had no way to force her. How bitter a disappointment it was I ask you to imagine . . . a mating planned when Caesar fought the Gauls all now in readiness, with the other strains matured and ready . . . and Lummox refuses to go home. She shows no interest in her destiny . . . remember, she is very young; our own children do not develop social responsibility very early. In any case she won't budge without John Thomas Stuart." He spread his hands. "You see the predicament they are in?"

Mrs. Stuart set her mouth. "I'm sorry but it is no business of mine."

"True. I suppose that the simplest thing to do is to let Lummox go home . . . to your home, I mean . . . and . . ."

"What? Oh, no!"

"Ma'am?"

"You can't send that beast back! I won't stand for it."

Mr. Kiku stroked his chin. "I don't understand you, ma'am. It's Lummox's home; it has been the Hroshia's home much longer than it has been yours, about five times as long I believe. If I remember correctly, it isn't your property, but your son's. Am I right?"

"That has nothing to do with it! You *can't* load me down with that beast."

"A court might decide that it was up to your son. But why cross that bridge? I am trying to find out why you oppose something so clearly to your son's advantage."

She sat silent, breathing hard, and Mr. Kiku let her sit. At last she said, "Mr. Kiku, I lost my husband to space; I won't let my son go the same way. I intend to see to it that he stays and lives on Earth."

He shook his head sadly. "Mrs. Stuart, sons are lost from the beginning."

She took out a handkerchief and dabbed at her eyes. "I can't let him go off into the sky . . . he's only a little boy!"

"He's a man, Mrs. Stuart. Younger men have died in battle."

"Is that what you think makes a man?"

"I know of no better gauge."

He went on, "I call my assistants 'boys' because I am an old man. You think of your son as a boy because you are, by comparison, an old woman. Forgive me. But the notion that a boy becomes a man only on a certain birthday is a mere legal fiction. Your son is a man; you have no moral right to keep him an infant."

"What a wicked thing to say! It's not true; I am merely trying to help him and guide him."

Mr. Kiku smiled grimly. "Madam, the commonest weakness of our race is our ability to rationalize our most selfish purposes. I repeat, you have no right to force him into your mold."

"I have more right than you have! I'm his mother."

"Is 'parent' the same as 'owner'? No matter, we are poles apart; you are trying to thwart him, I am helping him to do what he wants to do."

"From the basest motives!"

"My motives are not an issue and neither are yours." He stood up. "As you have already said, it seems fruitless to continue. I am sorry."

"I won't let him! He's still a minor . . . I have rights."

"Limited rights, ma'am. He could divorce you."

She gasped. "He wouldn't do that to me! His own mother!"

"Perhaps. Our children's courts have long taken a dim view of the arbitrary use of parental authority; coercion in choice of career is usually open-and-shut. Mrs. Stuart, it is best to give into the inevitable gracefully. Don't oppose him too far, or you will lose him completely. He is going."

XV

Undiplomatic Relations

MR. KIKU returned to his office with his stomach jumping but he did not stop to cater to it. Instead he leaned across his desk and said, "Sergei. Come in now."

Greenberg entered and laid down two spools of sound tape. "I'm glad to get rid of these. Whoo!"

"Wipe them, please. Then forget you ever heard them."

"Delighted." Greenberg dipped them in a cavity. "Cripes, boss, couldn't you have given him an anesthetic?"

"Unfortunately, no."

"Wes Robbins was pretty rough on him. I felt like a window peeper. Why did you want me to hear them? I don't have to deal with the mess. Or do I?"

"No. But someday you will need to know how it is done."

"Mmmm . . . Boss . . . did you have any intention of letting it stick when he fired you?"

"Don't ask silly questions."

"Sorry. How did you make out with the hard case?"

"She won't let him go."

"So?"

"So he is going."

"She'll scream her head off to the papers."

"So she will." Mr. Kiku leaned toward his desk. "Wes?"

"Mr. Robbins is at the funeral of the Venerian foreign minister," a female voice answered, "with the Secretary."

"Oh, yes. Ask him to see me when he returns, please."

"Yes, Mr. Kiku."

"Thank you, Shizuko." The Under Secretary turned to Greenberg. "Sergei, your acting appointment as diplomatic officer first class was made permanent when you were assigned to this affair."

"Was it?"

"Yes. The papers will no doubt reach you. You are now being promoted to chief diplomatic officer, acting. I will hold up the permanent appointment for ninety days to let some noses get back in joint."

Greenberg's face showed no expression. "Nice," he said. "But why? Because I brush my teeth regularly? Or the way I keep my brief case polished?"

"You are going to Hroshijud as deputy and chief of mission. Mr. MacClure will be ambassador, but I doubt that he will learn the tongue . . . which will of course place the burden of dealing with them on you. So you must acquire a working knowledge of their language at once. Follow me?"

Greenberg translated it to read: MacClure will have to talk to them through you, which keeps him in line.

"Yes," he answered thoughtfully, "but how about Dr. Ftaeml? The Ambassador will probably use him as interpreter rather than myself." To himself he added: boss, you can't do this to me. MacClure can short me out through Ftaeml . . . and there I am, nine hundred light-years from help.

"Sorry," Kiku answered, "but I can't spare Ftaeml. I shall retain him to interpret for the Hroshij mission they will leave behind. He accepted the job."

Greenberg frowned. "I'll start picking his brain in earnest, then, I've soaked up some Hroshija already . . . makes your throat raw. But when did they agree to all this? Have I slept through something? While I was in Westville?"

"They haven't agreed. They will."

"I admire your confidence, boss. They strike me as being as stubborn as Mrs. Stuart. Speaking of such, Ftaeml spoke to me while you were bickering with her. He says they are getting insistent about the Stuart kid. Now that you know he's going shouldn't we quiet them down? Ftaeml is jittery. He says the only thing that restrains them from giving us the works is that it would displease our old pal Lummox."

"No," answered Kiku, "we do not tell them. Nor do we tell Ftaeml. I want him to remain apprehensive."

Greenberg chewed a knuckle. "Boss," he said slowly, "isn't that asking for trouble? Or do you have a hunch that they aren't the heavyweights they claim to be? If it comes to a slugging match, can we outslug them?"

"I doubt it extremely. But the Stuart boy is my hole card."

"I suppose so. Far be it from me to quote you-know-who . . . but if the risk is that great, aren't the people entitled to know?"

"Yes. But we can't tell them."

"How's that again?"

Mr. Kiku frowned. "Sergei," he said slowly, "this society has been in crisis ever since the first rocket reached our Moon. For three centuries scientists and engineers and explorers have repeatedly broken through to new areas, new dangers, new situations; each time the political managers have had to scramble to hold things together, like a juggler with too much in the air. It's unavoidable.

"But we have managed to keep a jury-rigged republican form of government and to maintain democratic customs. We can be proud of that. But it is not now a real democracy and it can't be. I conceive it to be our duty to hold this society together while it adjusts to a strange and terrifying world. It would be pleasant to discuss each problem, take a vote, then repeal it later if the collective judgment proved faulty. But it's rarely that easy. We find ourselves oftener like pilots of a ship in a life-and-death emergency. Is it the pilot's duty to hold powwows with passengers? Or is it his job to use his skill and experience to try to bring them home safely?"

"You make it sound convincing, boss. I wonder if you are right?"

"I wonder also." Mr. Kiku went on, "I intended to hold the conference with the Hroshii tomorrow morning."

"Okay. I'll tell Ftaeml. They ought to stay quiet overnight."

"But, since they are anxious, we will postpone until the following day and let them grow still more anxious." Kiku thought. "Have Ftaeml tell them this. Our customs require that a party wishing to negotiate send presents ahead; therefore they must send us presents. Tell them that the lavishness of the gifts gauge the seriousness of the matter to be discussed; too poor a gift will prejudice their petition."

Greenberg frowned. "You have some swindle in mind, but I miss the point. Ftaeml knows that our customs don't call for it."

"Can you convince him that this is a custom which he has not encountered? Or can you take him into your confidence? I see conflict in him; his loyalty is to his clients but his sympathies appear to be with us."

"I had better not try to kid him. But getting a Rargyllian to lie when he is interpreting professionally . . . I doubt if he can."

"Then phrase it so that it is not a lie. Tell him that it is a very old custom . . . which is true . . . and that we resort to it only on sufficiently important occasions . . . which this is. Give him an out, let him see your purpose, gain a sympathetic translation."

"Can do. But why, boss? Just for bulge?"

"Precisely. We are negotiating from weakness; it is imperative that we start with the upper hand. I have hopes that the symbolism of the petitioner bearing presents is as universal as we have found it to be up to now."

"Suppose they won't kick through with the loot?"

"Then we sit tight until they change their minds." Kiku added, "Start selecting your team. Let me see a list tomorrow."

Greenberg groaned. "I was going to turn in early."

"Never count on it in this business. Oh yes . . . as soon as the conference is over, send a good man . . . Peters, perhaps . . . up to their ship to see what changes are needed for human passengers. Then we'll tell the Hroshii what we require."

"Wait a minute, boss. I prefer one of our own ships. How do you know they've got room for us?"

"Our ships will follow. But the Hroshia Lummox goes with them and young Stuart goes with Lummox, therefore our mission goes in their ship in order that the boy will be accompanied by humans."

"I see. Sorry."

"There will be room. They will leave their own mission behind at this same time . . . or no one will go.

One hundred Hroshii, to pluck a figure, will certainly vacate living space for one hundred of our sort."

"In other words, boss," Greenberg said softly, "you are insisting on hostages."

" 'Hostages,' " Mr. Kiku said primly, "is a word that no diplomat should ever use." He turned back to his desk.

The ground floor auditorium of the Spatial Affairs building was selected for the conference because its doors were large enough and its floors strong enough. It might have been safer to hold it at the space port, as Dr. Ftaeml urged, but Mr. Kiku insisted on the Hroshii coming to him for reasons of protocol.

Their presents preceded them.

The gifts were stacked on both sides of the great hall and were lavish in quantity; their values and qualities were still unknown. The departmental xenologists were as eager as a child faced with birthday presents, but Mr. Kiku had ordered them to hold off until the conference was over.

Sergei Greenberg joined Mr. Kiku in the retiring room behind the rostrum as the Hroshii delegation entered the hall. He looked worried. "I don't like this, boss."

Kiku looked up. "Why not?"

Greenberg glanced at the others present—Mr. MacClure and a double for the Secretary General. The double, a skilled actor, nodded and went back to studying the speech he was about to deliver, but MacClure said sharply, "What's the trouble, Greenberg? Those devils up to something?"

"I hope not." Greenberg addressed Kiku, "I checked arrangements from the air and they look good. We've got the Boulevard of the Suns barricaded from here to the port and enough reserves on each side for a small war. Then I picked up the head of their column as it left the port and flew above it. They dropped off reserves of their own about every quarter of a mile and set up gear of some sort at each strong point. It might just be communication links back to their ship. I doubt it. I think it must be weapons."

"So do I," agreed Kiku.

The Secretary said worriedly, "Now look here, Mr. Kiku . . ."

"If you please, Mr. MacClure. Sergei, the Chief of Staff reported this earlier. I advised the Secretary General that we should make no move unless they try to pass our barricades."

"We could lose a lot of men."

"So we could. But what will *you* do, Sergei, when you are required to enter a stranger's camp to palaver? Trust him completely? Or try to cover your retreat?"

"Mmm . . . yes."

"I consider this the most hopeful sign we have had yet. If those are weapons, as I hope they are, it means that they do not regard us as negligible opponents. One does not set up artillery against mice." He looked around. "Shall we go? I think we have let them stew long enough. Ready, Arthur?"

"Sure." The Secretary-General's double chucked his script aside. "That boy Robbins knows how to write a speech. He doesn't load up a sentence with sibilants and make me spray the first five rows."

"Good." They went in, the actor first, then the Secretary, then the Permanent Under Secretary followed by his assistant.

Of the long procession of Hroshii that had left the space port only a dozen had entered the auditorium, but even that number made the hall seem filled. Mr. Kiku looked down at them with interest, it being the first time that he had laid eyes on a Hroshiu. It was true, he saw, that these people did not present the golliwog friendliness shown in the pictures of the Hroshia Lummox. These were adults, even though smaller than Lummox. The one just in front of the platform and flanked by two others was staring back at him. The stare was cold and confident. Mr. Kiku found that the creature's gaze made him uneasy; he wanted to shift his eyes. Instead he stared back and reminded himself that his own hypnotherapist could do it as well or better than the Hroshiu.

Greenberg touched his elbow. "They've set up weapons in here, too," he whispered. "See that? In the back?"

Mr. Kiku answered, "We are not supposed to know that it is a weapon. Assume that it is apparatus for their own record of the conference." Dr. Ftaeml was standing beside the foremost Hroshiu; the Under Secretary said to him, "Tell them what our Secretary General is. Describe him as chief of seventeen powerful planets."

The Rargyllian hesitated. "What about the President of your Council?"

"The Secretary General embodies both of them for this occasion."

"Very well, my friend." The Rargyllian spoke in high-pitched speech which reminded Kiku of puppies whining. The Hroshiu answered him briefly in the same tongue, and suddenly Mr. Kiku no longer felt the dread that had been inspired by the creature's stare. It was not possible to feel awe for a person who sounded like a lonesome puppy. But he reminded himself that deadly orders could be given in any speech.

Ftaeml was speaking. "Here beside me is . . ." He broke into a multiple squeal of the strange tongue. ". . . who is commander of the ship and the expedition. She . . . no, perhaps 'he' would be better . . . he is hereditary marshal and . . ." The Rargyllian broke off and fretted. "You have no equivalent rank. Perhaps I should say 'mayor of the palace.'"

Greenberg suddenly said, "How about 'boss,' Doc?"

"A happy suggestion! Yes, this is the Boss. Her . . .

his social position is not highest but his practical authority is almost without limit."

Kiku asked, "Is his authority such that he may conduct plenipotentiary bargaining?"

"Ah, yes, certainly!"

"Then we will get on with it." He turned to the actor and nodded. Then he spoke to the desk in front of him, using a hush circuit: "Getting all this?"

A voice answered his ears alone. "Yes, sir. The picture pick-up faded once but it's all right now."

"Are the Secretary General and the Chief of Staff listening?"

"I believe so, sir. Their offices are monitoring."

"Very well." Mr. Kiku listened to the Secretary General's speech. It was short but delivered with great dignity and the actor paced it so that Ftaeml might translate. The Secretary General welcomed the Hroshii to Earth, assured them that the peoples of the Federation were happy that the Hroshii had at long last found their lost sibling, and added that this happy accident should be the occasion for the Hroshii to take their rightful place in the Community of Civilizations.

He sat down and promptly went to sleep for all practical purposes, eyes open and face fixed in kindly dignity. The double could hold this Roman-Emperor pose for hours without really noticing the review, or ceremony, or whatever he might be chaperoning.

Mr. MacClure spoke briefly, seconding the Secretary General and adding that the Federation was now prepared to discuss any matters of business between the Federation and the noble Hroshii.

Greenberg leaned to Kiku and whispered, "Should we clap, boss? Somebody ought to and I don't think they know how."

"Shut up," Kiku said amiably. "Dr. Ftaeml, does the commander have a speech of formality to deliver?"

"I think not." Ftaeml spoke to the leading Hroshiu,

then answered, "The reply is a serious comment on the two speeches made, rather than an answer of formality. He states that the Hroshii have no need of other . . . lesser . . . breeds and says we should not get to business without further, ah . . . trivia."

"If it is true that they have no need for other peoples, please ask him why they have come to us and why they have offered us presents?"

"But you insisted on it, my friend," Ftaeml answered in surprise.

"Thank you, Doctor, but I do not want your comment. Require him to answer. Please do not coach him."

"I will try." Ftaeml exchanged several sentences of the high whining with the Hroshij commander, then turned back to Kiku. "Forgive me. He says that he acceded to your childishness as the simplest means of accomplishing his purpose. He wishes to discuss now the surrender of John Thomas Stuart."

"Please tell him that the matter is not open to discussion. The agenda requires that we first settle the question of diplomatic relations."

"Pardon me, sir. 'Diplomatic relations' is a concept difficult to translate. I have been working on it for days."

"Tell him that what he sees now is an example of diplomatic relations. Free peoples, negotiating as equals, with peaceful intentions, to their mutual benefit."

The Ragyllian simulated a sigh. "Each of those concepts is almost equally difficult. I will try."

Presently he answered, "The hereditary marshal says that if what we are doing constitutes diplomatic relations you have them now. Where is the Stuart boy?"

"Not so fast. The agenda must be taken up point by point. They must accept an embassy and a mixed mission for cultural, scientific, and trade purposes. They must leave with us a similar embassy and mission. Regular travel between our two sovereignties must be planned.

Not until these are disposed of can there be any mention of the Stuart boy."

"I will try again." Ftaeml spoke to the "Boss" Hroshiu at length; the reply was short. "He tells me to tell you that all those points are rejected as not worthy of consideration. Where is the Stuart boy?"

"In that case," Mr. Kiku answered quietly, "tell them that we do not bargain with barbarians. Tell them to pick up the trash—be sure of forceful translation!—with which they have littered our home, and get quickly back to their ship. They are required to take off at once. They must bundle their precious Hroshia aboard, by force if need be, if they ever expect to see her again— they will never again be allowed to land."

Ftaeml looked as if he were about to burst into tears he was incapable of shedding. "Please! I beg you not to antagonize them. I tell tales out of school . . . I go beyond my professional duties . . . but they could now destroy this city without recourse to their ship."

"Deliver the message. The conference is ended." Mr. Kiku stood up, picked up the others with his eyes, and headed for the retiring room.

The double went ahead. MacClure caught Kiku by the arm and fell into step. "Henry . . . you're running this, granted. But shouldn't you talk it over? They're savage beasts. It could . . ."

"Mr. MacClure," Kiku said softly, "as a distinguished predecessor once said, in dealing with certain types you must step on their toes until *they* apologize." He urged the Secretary toward the door.

"But suppose they won't?"

"That is the hazard. Please . . . let us not argue in their presence." They went into the retiring room; the door closed behind them.

Greenberg turned to Kiku. "Nice try, boss . . . but what do we do now?"

"We wait."

"Okay." Greenberg went nervously to a wall relay, picked up the scene inside the auditorium. The Hroshii had not left. He could just make out Ftaeml, surrounded by creatures much larger than the medusoid.

The double said to Kiku, "Through with me, sir?"

"Yes, Arthur. A good job."

"Thanks. I've got time to get this make-up off and catch the second game of the doubleheader."

"Good. Perhaps you had better change your appearance here."

"Shucks, the photographers know. They play along."

He left, whistling. MacClure sat down, lit a cigar, took a puff, put it down. "Henry, you ought to notify the Chief of Staff."

"He knows. We wait."

They waited. Greenberg said suddenly, "Here comes Ftaeml." He hurried to the door and let the Rargyllian in.

Dr. Ftaeml seemed very tense. "My dear Mr. Kiku —the Hroshij commander states that they will agree to your strange wishes for sake of prompt settlement. He insists that you now deliver the Stuart boy."

"Please tell him that he misunderstands entirely the nature of friendly relations between civilized people. We do not barter the freedom of one of our citizens against their worthless favors, even as they would not barter the freedom of their Hroshia Lummox. Then tell him that I order them to leave at once."

Ftaeml said earnestly, "I reluctantly deliver your message."

He was back quickly. "They agree to your terms."

"Good. Come, Sergei. Mr. MacClure, there is no need for you to appear unless it suits you." He went out into the hall, followed by Greenberg and Ftaeml.

The Hroshij "boss," it seemed to Kiku was more baleful than ever. But the details went promptly forward —an equal number of Hroshii and of humans to con-stitute the missions, passage to be provided in the Hroshij ship, one of the Hroshii there present to be ambassador to the Federation. Ftaeml assured them that this Hroshiu was of practical rank second only to the expedition commander.

And now, said the Hroshij commander, it is time to turn over to us John Thomas Stuart. Ftaeml added anxiously, "I trust you have made arrangements, my friend? I dislike the tenor of this. It has been too easy."

With a feeling of satisfaction soothing his troubled stomach Mr. Kiku answered, "I see no difficulty. The Stuart boy is willing to go, now that we are assured of civilized relations. Please make sure that they understand that he goes as a free being, not a slave, not a pet. The Hroshii must guarantee his status and his return passage, in one of their own ships, whenever he so wishes."

Ftaeml translated. Presently he answered. "All of that is satisfactory except for something which I will translate as a 'minor detail.' The Stuart boy will be a member of the household of the Hroshia Lummox. Naturally—I translate here most carefully—naturally the question of the boy returning, if ever, is a personal prerogative of the Hroshia Lummox. Should she grow tired of him and wish to return him, a ship would be made available."

"No."

"No what, sir?"

"A simple negative. The subject of the Stuart boy is finished."

Ftaeml turned back to his clients.

"They say," he answered presently, "that there is no treaty."

"I know that. Treaties are not signed with . . . they have a word meaning 'servant'?"

"They have servants of several sorts, some higher, some lower."

"Use the word for the lowest sort. Tell them that there is no treaty because servants have no power to treat. Tell them to go and be quick about it."

Ftaeml looked at Kiku saidly. "I admire you, my friend, but I do not envy you." He turned to the expedition commander and whined for several moments.

The Hroshiu opened his mouth wide, looked at Kiku, and squealed like a kicked puppy. Ftaeml gave a start and moved away. "Very bad profanity, untranslatable . . ." The monster continued to make noises; Ftaeml tried frantically to translate: "Contempt . . . lower animal . . . eat you with relish . . . follow back your ancestors and eat them as well . . . your despicable race must be taught manners . . . kidnappers . . . child stealers . . ." He stopped in great agitation.

The Hroshiu lumbered toward the platform, reared up until he was eye to eye with Mr. Kiku. Greenberg slid a hand under his desk and located a control that would throw a tanglefoot field over the lower floor . . . a permanent installation; the hall had seen other disturbances.

But Mr. Kiku sat like stone. They eyed each other, the massive thing from "Out There" and the little elderly human. Nothing moved in the great hall, nothing was said.

Then from the back of the hall broke out a whining as if a whole basket of puppies had been disturbed at once. The Hroshij commander whirled around, making the floor shake, and shrilled to his retainers. He was answered and he whined back sharp command. All twelve Hroshii swarmed out the door moving with speed incredible for beings so ungainly.

Kiku stood up and watched them. Greenberg grabbed his arm. "Boss! The Chief of Staff is trying to reach you."

Kiku shook him off. "Tell him not to be hasty. It is most important that he not be hasty. Is our car waiting?"

XVI

"Sorry We Messed Things Up"

JOHN THOMAS STUART XI had wanted to attend the conference; it required a flat refusal to keep him away. He was in the Hotel Universal in the suite provided for him and his mother, playing checkers with his bodyguard, when Betty Sorenson showed up with Miss Holtz. Myra Holtz was an operative for BuSec of Dep-Space, and concealed her policewoman profession under a pleasant façade. Mr. Kiku's instructions to her concerning Betty had been: "Keep a sharp eye on her. She has a taste for excitement."

The two guards greeted each other; Betty said, "Hi, Johnnie. Why aren't you over at the heap big smoke?"

"They wouldn't let me."

"Me, too." She glanced around. "Where's the Duchess?"

"Gone shopping. I'm still getting the silent treatment. Seventeen hats she's bought. What have you done to your face?"

Betty turned to a mirror. "Like it? It's called 'Cosmic Contouring' and it's the latest thing."

"Makes you look like a zebra with the pip."

"Why, you country oaf. Ed, you like it. Don't you?"

Ed Cowen looked up from the checker board and said hastily, "I wouldn't know. My wife says I have no taste."

"Most men haven't. Johnnie, Myra and I have come to invite you two to go out on the town. How about it?"

Cowen answered, "I don't favor that, Myra."

"It was her idea," Miss Holz answered.

John Thomas said to Cowen, "Why not? I'm sick of checkers."

"Well . . . I'm supposed to keep in touch with the office. They might want you any time now."

"Pooh!" put in Betty. "You carry a bodyphone. Anyhow Myra does."

Cowen shook his head. "Let's play it safe."

"Am I under arrest?" Betty persisted. "Is Johnnie?"

"Mmm . . . no. It's more protective custody."

"Then you can protectively cuss him wherever he is. Or stay here and play checkers with yourself. Come on, Johnnie."

Cowen looked at Miss Holtz; she answered slowly, "I suppose it's all right, Ed. We'll be with them."

Cowen shrugged and stood up. Johnnie said to Betty, "I'm not going out in public with you looking like that. Wash your face."

"But Johnnie! It took two hours to put it on."

"The taxpayers paid for it, didn't they?"

"Well, yes, but . . ."

"Wash your face. Or we go nowhere. Don't you agree, Miss Holtz?"

Special Operative Holtz had only a flower pattern adorning her left cheek, aside from the usual tinting. She said thoughtfully, "Betty doesn't need it. Not at her age."

"Oh, you're a couple of Puritans!" Betty said bitterly, stuck her tongue at Johnnie and slouched into the bath. She came out with her face glowing pink from scrubbing. "Now I'm stark naked. Let's go."

There was another tussle at the lift, which Ed Cowen won. They went to the roof to take an air taxi for sightseeing, instead of going down to the streets. "Both you kids have had your faces spread around the papers the past few days. And this town has more crackpots than a second-hand shop. I don't want any incidents."

"If you hadn't let them bully me, my face wouldn't be recognizable."

"But his would."

"We could paint him, too. Any male face would be improved with make-up." But she entered the lift and they took an air taxi.

"Where to, Chief?"

"Oh," said Cowen, "cruise around and show us sights. Put it on the hourly rate."

"You're the doctor. I can't fly across the Boulevard of Suns. Some parade, or something."

"I know."

"Look," put in Johnnie, "take us to the space port."

"No," Cowen corrected. "Not out there."

"Why not, Ed? I haven't seen Lummox yet. I want to look at him. He may not be well."

"That's one thing you can't do," Cowen told him. "The Hroshii ship is out of bounds."

"Well, I can see him from the air, can't I?"

"No!"

"But . . ."

"Never mind him," Betty advised. "We'll get another taxi. I've got money, Johnnie. So long, Ed."

"Look," complained the driver. "I'll take you to Timbuctu. But I can't hang around over a landing flat. The cops get rude about it."

"Head for the space port," Cowen said resignedly.

There was a barricade around the many acres assigned to the Hroshii except where it had been broken to let their delegation enter the Boulevard of Suns, and even then the barricade joined others carrying on down the avenue toward the administrative group. Inside the enclosure the landing craft of the Hroshii sat squat and ugly, almost as large as a terrestrial star ship. Johnnie looked at it and wondered what it was going to be like to be on Hroshijud. He was uncomfortable at the thought, not because he was fearful but because he had not yet told Betty that he was going. He had started a couple of times but it had not worked out right.

Since she had not raised the subject he assumed that she did not know.

There were other sightseers in the air, and a crowd, not very thick, outside the barricade. No single wonder lasted long in Capital; its residents prided themselves on being blasé and in fact, the Hroshii were not fantastic compared with a dozen other friendly races, some of them members of the Federation.

The Hroshii swarmed around the base of their ship, doing unexplained things with artifacts they had erected. Johnnie tried to estimate their number, found it like guessing beans in a bottle. Dozens, surely . . . how many more?

The taxi cruised just outside the point patrol of police air cars. Johnnie suddenly called out, "Hey! There's Lummie!"

Betty craned her neck. "Where, Johnnie?"

"Coming into sight on the far side of their ship. There!" He turned to the driver. "Say, mister, could you put us around on the far side as close in as they'll let you?"

The driver glanced at Cowen, who nodded. They swung around the police sentries and came in toward the Hroshij craft from the far side. The driver picked a point between two police cars and back a little. Lummox could be seen clearly now, closely attended by a group of Hroshii and towering over them.

"I wish I had binox," Johnnie complained. "I can't really *see*."

"Pair in the glove compartment," offered the driver.

Johnnie got them out. They were a simple optical type, without electronic magnification, but they brought Lummox up much closer. He stared into his friend's face.

"How does Lummie look, Johnnie?"

"Okay. Kind of skinny, though. I wonder if they are feeding him right?"

"Mr. Greenberg tells me they aren't feeding Lummie at all. I thought you knew?"

"What? They can't do that to Lummie!"

"I don't see what we can do about it."

"Well . . ." John Thomas lowered the window and tried to get a better look. "Say, can't you take it in closer? And lower maybe? I want to give him a good checking over."

Cowen shook his head. The driver grumbled, "I don't want no words with the cops." But he did move in a little closer until he was lined up with the police cars.

Almost at once the speaker in the car's overhead blared, "Hey, you! Number four eighty-four! Where do you think you're going with that can? Drag it out of there!"

The driver muttered and started to obey. John Thomas, still with the glasses to his eyes, said, "Aw!" . . . then added, "I wonder if he can hear me? Lummie!" he shouted into the wind. "Oh Lummox!"

The Hroshia raised her head and looked wildly around.

Cowen grabbed John Thomas and reached for the window closure. But Johnnie shook free. "Oh, you go fry eggs!" he said angrily. "I've been pushed around long enough. *Lummox!* It's Johnnie, boy! Over here! Come over this way . . ."

Cowen dragged him inside and slammed the window shut. "I knew we shouldn't have come out. Driver, let's get out of here."

"Only too happy!"

"But hold it just back of the police lines. I want to check on this."

"Make up your mind."

It needed no binoculars to see what was happening. Lummox headed straight for the barrier, on a bee line with the taxi, scattering other Hroshii right and left. On reaching the barrier no attempt was made to flow over it; Lummox went through it.

"Jumping jeepers!" Cowen said softly. "But the tanglefoot will stop her."

It did not. Lummox slowed down, but one mighty foot followed another, as if the charged air had been deep mud. With the persistence of a glacier the Hroshia was seeking the point most closely under the taxi.

And more Hroshii were pouring out the gap. They made still heavier weather of the immobilizing field, but still they came. As Cowen watched, Lummox broke free of the zone and came on at a gallop, with people scattering ahead of her.

Cowen snapped, "Myra, get through on another circuit to the military! I'll call the office."

Betty grabbed his sleeve. "No!"

"Huh? You again! Shut up or you'll get the back of my hand."

"Mr. Cowen, will you *listen*." She went on hastily, "Its no good calling for help. There isn't anybody who can make Lummox listen but Johnnie—and *they* won't listen to anybody but Lummox. You *know* that. So put him down where he can talk to Lummie—or you're going to have a lot of people hurt and it will be all your fault."

Security Operative First Class Edwin Cowen stared at her and reviewed in his mind his past career and future hopes. Then he made a brave decision almost instantly. "Take her down," he snapped. "Land her and let the kid and me out."

The driver groaned. "I'm charging extra for this." But he landed the car so fast that it jarred them. Cowen snatched the door open and he and John Thomas burst out; Myra Holtz tried to grab Betty, was unsuccessful. She herself jumped out as the driver was already raising.

"Johnnie!" squealed Lummox and held out mighty arms in a universal gesture of welcome.

John Thomas ran to the star beast. "Lummie! Are you all right?"

"Sure," agreed Lummox. "Why not? Hi, Betty."

"Hi, Lummie."

"Hungry, though," Lummox added thoughtfully.

"We'll change that."

"It's all right. I'm not supposed to eat now."

John Thomas started to answer this amazing statement when he noticed Miss Holtz ducking away from one of the Hroshii. Others were milling around as if uncertain how to treat this development. When Johnnie saw Ed Cowen draw his gun and place himself between the Hroshiu and Myra he said suddenly, "Lummox! These are my friends. Tell your friends to leave them alone and get back inside. Quickly!"

"Whatever you say, Johnnie." The Hroshia spoke in the whining speech to her kin; at once she was obeyed.

"And make us a saddle. We'll go with you and have a long talk."

"Sure, Johnnie."

They got aboard, Johnnie giving Betty a hand up, and started in through the break in the barrier. When Lummox struck the tanglefoot field again they stopped and Lummox spoke sharply to one of the others.

That Hroshiu called out to one inside; the tanglefoot field disappeared. They moved on in without difficulty.

When Mr. Kiku, Sergei Greenberg, and Dr. Ftaeml arrived they found an armed truce, tense on both sides. All the Hroshii were back inside the broken barrier; military craft in quantity had replaced the police patrol and far overhead, out of sight, bombers were ready in final extremity to turn the area into a radioactive desert.

The Secretary General and the Chief of Staff met

them at the barricade. The Secretary General looked grave. "Ah, Henry. It seems we have failed. Not your fault."

Mr. Kiku looked out at the massed Hroshii. "Perhaps."

The Chief of Staff added, "We are evacuating the blast radius as rapidly as possible. But if we have to do it, I don't know what we can do for those two youngsters in there."

"Then let's not do anything, shall we? Not yet."

"I don't think you understand the seriousness of the situation, Mr. Under Secreaty. For example, we placed an immobilizing locus entirely around this area. It's gone. They cancelled it out. Not just here. Everywhere."

"So. Perhaps *you* do not understand the seriousness of the situation, General. In any case, a few words can do no harm. Come, Sergei. Coming, Doctor?" Mr. Kiku left the group around the Secretary General and headed for the break in the barricade. Wind sweeping across the miles-wide field forced him to clutch his hat. "I do not like wind," he complained to Dr. Ftaeml. "It is disorderly."

"There is a stronger wind ahead," the Rargyllian answered soberly. "My friend, is this wise? They will not hurt me; I am their employee. But you . . ."

"What else can I do?"

"I do not know. But there are situations in which courage is useless."

"Possibly. I've never found one yet."

"One finds such a situation but once."

They were approaching the solid mass of Hroshii around Lummox. They could make out the two humans on the back of the Hroshia a good hundred yards beyond. Kiku stopped. "Tell them to get out of my way. I wish to approach the Hroshia Lummox."

Ftaeml translated. Nothing happened, though the Hroshii stirred uneasily. Greenberg said, "Boss, how

241

about asking Lummox and the kids to come out here? That crowd doesn't smell friendly."

"No. I dislike shouting into this wind. Please call out to the Stuart lad and tell him to have them make way."

"Okay, boss. It will be fun to tell my grandchildren —if I have grandchildren." He cupped his mouth and shouted, "Johnnie! John Stuart! Tell Lummox to have them clear a path."

"Sure!"

A path wide enough for a column of troops opened as if swept with a broom. The little procession moved down the ranks of Hroshii. Greenberg felt goose flesh crawl up and down his back.

Mr. Kiku's only worry seemed to be keeping his hat on in the wind. He swore primly while clutching at his head. They stopped in front of Lummox. "Howdy, Mr. Kiku," John Thomas called out. "Shall we come down?"

"Perhaps it would be best."

Johnnie slid off, then caught Betty. "Sorry we messed things up."

"So am I. If you did. Will you introduce me to your friend, please?"

"Oh, sure. Lummox, this is Mr. Kiku. He's a nice fellow, a friend of mine."

"How do you do, Mr. Kiku."

"How do you do, Lummox." Mr. Kiku looked thoughtful. "Doctor, is not that the commander, there by the Hroshia? The one with the ugly glint in his eye?"

The Rargyllian looked. "Yes, it is he."

"Um. Ask him if he has reported the conference to his mistress."

"Very well." The medusoid spoke to the Hroshij commander, was answered. "He says not."

"Um. John Thomas, we concluded a treaty with the Hroshii to permit all that I discussed with you. Suddenly they repudiated the agreement when they discovered that we would not surrender your person without guarantees. Will you help me find out if such were the wishes of your friend?"

"You mean Lummox? Sure."

"Very well. Wait a moment. Dr. Ftaeml, will you report the essentials of our agreement to the Hroshia Lummox—in the presence of the commander? Or are the concepts beyond her?"

"Eh? Why should they be? She was perhaps two hundred of your years old when she was brought here."

"So much? Well, speak ahead."

The Rargyllian commenced the curious whines of the Hroshij tongue, addressing Lummox. Once or twice Lummox interrupted, then allowed him to continue. When Dr. Ftaeml had finished she spoke to the expedition commander. Ftaeml said to the humans, "She asks, 'Can this be true?'"

The commander made as wide a circle as space permitted, crept up in front of her, with the little group representing the Federation giving way. His legs were retracted so that he crawled like a caterpillar. Without lifting his head from the ground he whined his answer.

"He is admitting the truth but pleading necessity."

"I wish he would hurry with it," Kiku fretted. "I'm getting chilly." His thin knees trembled.

"She is not accepting the explanation. I will spare you the exact tenor of her language—but her rhetoric is superb."

Suddenly Lummox spat out one squeal, then reared up with four legs clear of the ground. With arms retracted the great beast swung down her head and struck the unfortunate commander a smashing sidewise blow.

It lifted him off the ground, bowled him into the crowd. Slowly he regained his feet, slunk back to the spot in front of Lummox.

Lummox began to speak. "She is saying . . . I wish

you could hear this in *her* language! . . . that so long as the Galaxy shall last the friends of Johnnie are her friends. She adds that those who are not friends of her friends are nothing, less than nothing, never to be suffered in her sight. She commands this in the names of . . . it is a recitation of her ancestry with all its complicated branches and is somewhat tedious. Shall I attempt to translate?"

"Don't bother," Mr. Kiku told him. " 'Yes' is 'yes' in any language."

"But she tells it with great beauty," Ftaeml said. "She is recalling to them things dreadful and wonderful, reaching far into the past."

"I am interested only in how it affects the future . . . and in getting out of this pesky wind." Mr. Kiku sneezed. "Oh dear!"

Dr. Ftaeml took his cape off and hung it around Mr. Kiku's narrow shoulders. "My friend . . . my brother. I am sorry."

"No, no, you will be cold."

"Not I."

"Let us share it, then."

"I am honored," the medusoid answered softly, his tendrils twitching with emotion. He spread it around them and they huddled together while Lummox finished her peroration. Betty turned to Johnnie.

"That's more than you ever did for me."

"Now, Slugger, you know you're never cold."

"Well, put your arm around me at least."

"Huh? In front of everybody? Go snuggle up to Lummox."

While speaking Lummox had stayed reared up. As the oration progressed the assembled Hroshii sank down, retracting their legs until they were all in the humble position of the commander. At last it was over and Lummox added one sharp remark. The Hroshii stirred and began to move. "She says," translated Ftaeml, "that she now wishes to be alone with her friends."

"Ask her," directed Kiku, "please to assure her friend John Thomas that all she has said is true and binding."

"Very well." As the other Hroshii hurried away Ftaeml spoke briefly to Lummox.

Lummox listened, then turned to John Thomas. Out of the great mouth came the piping, little-girl voice. "That's right, Johnnie. Cross my heart."

John Thomas nodded solemn agreement. "Don't worry, Mr. Kiku. You can depend on it."

XVII

Ninety-Seven Pickle Dishes

"SEND her in."

Mr. Kiku composed himself nervously, giving the tea tray one last glance, making sure that the intimate little conference room was all that he wished of it. While he was thus fussing a door dilated and Betty Sorenson walked in, said sweetly, "Hello, Mr. Kiku," and seated herself with composure.

He said, "How do you do, Miss Sorenson?"

"Call me Betty. My friends all do."

"Thank you. I would wish to be one." He looked her over and shuddered. Betty had been experimenting with a new design of bars; it made her face somewhat like a checker board. Besides that she had evidently been shopping and was dressed in styles far too old for her. Mr. Kiku was forced to remind himself that customs varied. "Um . . . my dear young lady, the purpose of this consultation is somewhat difficult to explain."

"Make it easy on yourself. I'm in no hurry."

"Will you have tea?"

"Let me pour for us. It's chummier." He allowed her to, then sat back with his cup in a relaxed attitude he did not feel.

"I trust you have been enjoying your stay?"

"Oh my, yes! I've never been able to shop before without counting pennies. Everybody should have an expense account."

"Enjoy it. I assure you it will never show in the annual budget . . . literally. Our discretionary fund. Uh, you are an orphan, are you not?"

"A legal orphan. I'm a Free Child. My guardian is the Westville Home for Free Children. Why?"

"Then you are not of age?"

"Depends on how you look at it. I think I am, the court says I'm not. But it won't be long now, thank goodness."

"Um, yes. Perhaps I should say that I knew all this."

"I figured you did. What's it all about?"

"Um. Perhaps I should tell a little story. Did you ever raise rabbits? Or cats?"

"I've had cats."

"We have run into a difficulty with the Hroshia we know as Lummox. Nothing disastrous; our treaty with them is not affected, since she has given her word. But, uh, shall we say that if we could oblige Lummox in a certain matter, it would make for better feelings, better future relations?"

"I suppose we shall say so, if you say so. What is it, Mr. Kiku?"

"Um. We are both aware that this Hroshia Lummox has long been a pet of John Thomas Stuart."

"Why, certainly. It worked out funny, didn't it?"

"Um, yes. And that Lummox was the pet of John

Thomas's father before him, and so on for four generations."

"Yes, of course. Nobody could want a sweeter pet."

"Now, that is just the point, Miss Sorenson . . . Betty. That is the point of view of John Thomas and his forebears. But there are always at least two points of view. From the viewpoint of Lummox she . . . he . . . was not a pet. Quite the contrary. John Thomas was *his* pet. Lummox was engaged in raising John Thomases."

Betty's eyes widened, then she started to laugh and choked. "Mr. Kiku! Oh *no!*"

"I am quite serious. It is a matter of viewpoint and made more reasonable by considering relative lifetimes. Lummox had raised several generations of John Thomases. It was Lummox's only hobby and principal interest. Childish, but Lummox was, and still is, a child."

Betty got herself under control to the point where she could talk through giggles. " 'Raising John Thomases.' Does Johnnie know about this?"

"Well, yes, but I explained it to him somewhat differently."

"Does Mrs. Stuart know about this?"

"Ah . . . I haven't found it necessary to tell her."

"May I tell her? I want to see her face. 'John Thomases' . . . oh my!"

"I think that would be cruel," Mr. Kiku answered stiffly.

"I suppose so. All right, I won't do it. But I can dream about it, can't I?"

"We all can dream. But to continue: Lummox appears to have been perfectly happy with this innocent hobby. It was the Hroshia's intention to continue it indefinitely. That was the reason that we found ourselves faced with this curious dilemma of being unable to get the Hroshii to leave after their sibling had been restored. Lummox wished to continue, uh, raising John Thomases." He hesitated.

Finally Betty said, "Well, Mr. Kiku? Go on."

"Uh, what are your own plans, Betty . . . Miss Sorenson?"

"Mine? I haven't discussed them with anyone."

"Um. Pardon me if I was unduly personal. You see, there are requirements in any endeavor and Lummox, it appears, is aware of one of the requirements . . . uh, let's put it this way. If we have here a rabbit . . . or a cat . . ." He stopped dead, unable to go on.

She searched his unhappy face. "Mr. Kiku, are you trying to say that it takes two rabbits to have more rabbits?"

"Well, yes. That was part of it."

"Now, really! Why make such a fuss about it? Everybody knows it. I suppose the rest is that Lummox knows that the same rule applies to John Thomases?"

He could only nod dumbly.

"You poor dear, you should have written me a note about it. It would have been less of a strain on you. I suppose I'll have to help you with the rest, too. You thought I might figure in this plan?"

"I had no wish to intrude . . . but I did want to sound out your intentions."

"Am I going to marry John Thomas? I've never had any other intention. Of course."

Mr. Kiku sighed. "Thank you."

"Oh, I won't be doing it to please you."

"Oh no! I was thanking you for assisting me."

"Thank Lummie. Good old Lummie! You can't fool Lummox."

"I take it that this is all settled?"

"Huh? I haven't proposed to him yet. But I will . . . I was waiting until it was a little nearer time for the ship to leave. You know how men are—nervous and skittery. I didn't want to leave him time to worry. Did your wife propose to you right off? Or did she wait until you were ripe for the kill?"

"Uh, well, the customs of my people are somewhat different. Her father arranged it with my father."

Betty looked shocked. "Slavery," she stated baldly.

"No doubt. However I have not been unhappy under it." He stood up. "I'm glad that we have concluded our talk so amiably."

"Just a moment, Mr. Kiku. There are one or two other matter. Just what are you doing for John Thomas?"

"Eh?"

"What's the contract?"

"Oh. Financially we mean to be liberal. He will devote most of his time to his education, but I had thought of giving him a nominal title in the embassy—special attaché, or assistant secretary, or some such."

Betty remained silent. "Of course, since you are going along, it might be well to give you a semi-official status, too. Say special aide, with the same salary? It would give you two a nice nest egg if you return . . when you return."

She shook her head. "Johnnie isn't ambitious. I am."

"Yes?"

"Johnnie is to be ambassador to the Hroshii."

Mr. Kiku had grave trouble talking. At last he managed to say, "My dear young lady! Quite impossible."

"That's what you think. Look, Mr. MacClure got cold feet and welched on you, didn't he? Don't beat around the bush; by now I have my connections inside your department. He did. Therefore the job is open. It's for Johnnie."

"But, my dear," he said weakly, "it is not a job for an untrained boy . . . much as I think of Mr. Stuart."

"MacClure was going to be dead wood, wasn't he? Everybody knows that. Johnnie would not be dead wood. Who knows the most about Hroshii? Johnnie."

"My dear, I admit his special knowledge; I grant that we will make use of it. But ambassador? No."

"Yes."

"Chargé d'Affaires? That's an awfully high rank, but I'm willing to stretch a point. But Mr. Greenberg must be the ambassador. We require a diplomat."

"What's so hard about being a diplomat? Or to put it another way, what could Mr. MacClure do that my Johnnie can't do better?"

He sighed deeply. "You have me there. All I can say is that there are situations which I am forced to accept, knowing them to be wrong, and others that I need not accept. If you were my own daughter I would paddle you. No."

She grinned at him. "I'll bet I outweigh you. But that's not the point. I don't think you understand the situation."

"No?"

"No. Johnnie and I are important to you in this dicker, aren't we? Especially Johnnie."

"Yes. Especially Johnnie. You are not essential . . . even in the, uh, raising of John Thomases."

"Want to put it to a test? Do you think you can get John Thomas Stuart one half inch off this planet if I set myself against it?"

"Hmm . . . I wonder."

"So do I. But I've got nerve enough to put it to a trial. If I win, where are you? Out on a windy field, trying to talk your way out of a mess again . . . without Johnnie to help you."

Mr. Kiku went over to a window and looked out. Presently he turned. "More tea?" Betty asked politely.

"Thank you, no. Miss, do you have any idea what an ambassador extraordinary and minister plenipotentiary is?"

"I've heard the term."

"It is the same rank and pay as an ambassador, except that it is a special case. This is a special case. Mr. Greenberg will be the ambassador and carry the authority; the special, and purely nominal, rank will be created for John Thomas."

"Rank *and* pay," she answered. "I'm acquiring a taste for shopping."

"And pay," he agreed. "Young lady, you have the morals of a snapping turtle and the crust of a bakery pie. Very well, it's a deal . . . if you can get your young man to agree to it."

She giggled. "I won't have any trouble."

"I didn't mean that. I'm betting on his horse sense and natural modesty against your avarice. I think he'll settle for assistant embassy secretary. We'll see."

"Oh. Yes, we'll see. By the way, where is he?"

"Eh?"

"He's not at the hotel. You have him here, don't you?"

"He is here, as a matter of fact."

"Good." She walked up and patted him on the cheek. "I like you, Mr. Kiku. Now trot Johnnie in here and leave us alone. It will take me about twenty minutes. You don't have a thing to worry about."

"Miss Sorenson," Mr. Kiku asked wonderingly, "how does it happen that you do not ask to be ambassador yourself?"

Lummox was the only non-human to attend the wedding. Mr. Kiku stood up for the bride. He noticed that she was wearing no make-up, which made him wonder if possibly the embassy's junior secretary might not be master in his own home after all.

They received the usual ninety-seven pickle dishes, mostly from strangers, and other assorted costly junk that they would not take with them, including an all-expense trip to Hawaii for which they had no possible use. Mrs. Stuart wept and had her picture taken and greatly enjoyed herself; all in all it was a very successful wedding. Mr. Kiku leaked a few tears during the responses, but Mr. Kiku was a very sentimental man.

He was sitting at his desk the next morning, ignoring lights, with his Kenya-farm brochures spread out before him, but he was not looking at them. Dr. Ftaeml and he had gone out together and done the town after they got the kids safely married—and Mr. Kiku was feeling it somewhat, in a pleasant, relaxed manner. Even though his head buzzed and his coordination was poor, his stomach was not troubling him. He felt fine.

He was trying fuzzily to sum up the affair in his mind. All this fuss, all this grief, because some fool spaceman more than a century ago didn't have sense enough not to tamper with native life until protocol had been worked out. Oh my people, my people!

On second thought, he told himself not to point the finger of scorn; he might be looking in a mirror.

There was something that good old Ftaeml had said last night . . . something . . . now what was it he had said? Something which, at the time, convinced Kiku that the Hroshii never had had any weapons capable of seriously damaging Earth. Of course a Rargyllian would not lie, not professionally . . . but would one skate around the truth in order to conclude successfully a negotiation which seemed about to fail?

Well, since it had all been settled without violence he could only wonder. Just as well, perhaps.

Besides, the next heathens to show up might *not* be bluffing. That would not be good:

Mildred's voice came to him. "Mr. Kiku, the Randavian delegation is waiting."

"Tell them I'm molting!"

"Sir?"

"Never mind. Tell them I'll be right in. East conference room."

He sighed, decided to treat himself to just one pill, then got up and headed for the door, ready to stick his finger in another hole in the dike. Chinese obligation, he thought; once you take it on you can't drop it.

But he still felt cheerful and sang a snatch of the only song he knew all the way through: "*. . . this story has no moral, this story has no end. This story only goes to show that there ain't no good in men.*"

In the meantime, out at the space port, the new Secretary for Spatial Affairs was seeing off the noble Hroshii. Her Imperial Highness, the Infanta of that race, 213th of her line, heiress to the matriarchy of the Seven Suns, future ruler over nine billion of her own kind, and lately nicknamed "The Lummox" contentedly took her pair of pets aboard the imperial yacht.

Available at your bookstore or use this coupon.